BOUND WITH LOVE

A Priceless Treasure
Changes the Lives of Four Couples

JOAN CROSTON
CATHY MARIE HAKE
KELLY EILEEN HAKE
JOYCE LIVINGSTON

BARBOUR
PUBLISHING

Right from the Start © 2004 by Cathy Marie Hake
A Treasure Worth Keeping © 2004 by Kelly Eileen Hake
Of Immeasurable Worth © 2004 by Joan Croston
The Long Road Home © 2004 by Joyce Livingston

ISBN 1-59310-141-4

Cover image © Corbis, Inc.

Illustrations by Mari Goering.

All Scripture quotations are taken from the King James Version of the Bible.

Published by Barbour Publishing, Inc., P.O. Box 719, Uhrichsville, Ohio 44683, www.barbourbooks.com

Our mission is to publish and distribute inspirational products offering exceptional value and biblical encouragement to the masses.

 Member of the
Evangelical Christian
Publishers Association

Printed in the United States of America.
5 4 3 2 1

BOUND

WITH LOVE

Right from the Start

by Cathy Marie Hake

Chapter 1

Germany, 1715

I t's so ugly, only Satan could covet such a place." Lorice of Saltzfeld stared at the granite castle atop the craggy cliffs ahead.

"You're not in league with the devil, so don't assume you know his preferences." Father Dominicus sat in the cart next to her and gave her arm a reassuring pat. "The outside may well look somewhat. . .intimidating, but you haven't seen the inside yet."

"I don't care what's inside; it's *who's* inside that has me knotted worse than the back of my first stitchery." For the past week, she'd had to face the dreadful revelation that she'd been betrothed from the cradle—promised in marriage to the son of a man who had become her father's worst enemy.

"A man's word is his bond," the priest said. He nodded his head to emphasize the importance of those words. "You read the contract yourself. You're legally Gareth of Ravenhurst's bride."

"Duty and honor," she recited under her breath.

"Duty and honor," the priest said, warming to his topic. "Our Lord demonstrated both qualities as He walked the earth. As His followers, we are to behave in the same manner. Your parents—God bless their dearly departed souls— conducted themselves in accordance with the laws of God and the land. Devotion to their memory and obedience to the Almighty demand that you fulfill the betrothal contract."

"Devotion to their memory is at odds with pledging her hand to the son of her father's enemy." Oswald von Still-hoven gave that pronouncement in a strong, sure voice.

The baron had been a stalwart neighbor and friend these last days. Upon hearing the sorrowful news of her parents' deaths, he'd come at once to offer his help. She'd been in sore need of his assistance, too. Bertolf the Wolf had come, certain his might and adjoining lands gave him the right to claim her as his bride. He rode in with a fair-sized army of his brawny warriors. Oswald commanded his own men to create a buffer, and he propped up Lorice in her deep grief by suggesting cunning ways to check Bertolf and his men from taking over her keep.

Even now, the complement of her own knights escorting her to Ravenhurst weakened the defenses of Saltzfeld. Oswald put his own lands in danger by stretching his men to cover her lands as well as his own. He'd also come with her, fostering her hope that he might free her from this betrothal contract if it still existed. A mature and powerful baron, he'd find a way to sway the negotiations in her favor.

"Your father said he was breaking the betrothal a handful of years ago, my lady. He was always quite diligent in such affairs. I know had I been blessed with a daughter, I would have seen to the matter." He gave her a broad smile. "It took my son's marriage to give me a daughter, and I was never granted a greater blessing. When I departed, she was well past the point of being sick of a morning. I'm hoping it means I can expect a second grandson when I return home."

"That would be a blessing, indeed." The cart hit a rut and jostled the smile right off her face. A lady would never complain of her hips being black and blue from the harsh ride, but Lorice didn't feel very much like a lady just now. After five days, she wore as much of the road as she'd traveled. Dust clung to every last inch of her. *My appearance should scare off my groom. Perhaps all this dirt is a mantle of protection, draped over me by God.*

As they turned a bend in the road and spied their first glimpse of the drawbridge through a momentary break in the trees, Lorice called the entourage to a halt. "Peter, you'll ride at the fore to announce our arrival." The young warrior nodded grimly and kneed his mount.

"Haug and Steffan have been in your father's service longer," Oswald said in a confidential tone. "They would have been wiser choices."

"My choice was based on the Holy Scriptures. I'll not change it."

Oswald's brow furrowed. He was unaccustomed to having his recommendations ignored. Pride obviously dented, he kicked his mount to go on ahead of the cart. Lorice still held with her decision, but she regretted her choice of words. Nonetheless, it was too late to undo the damage. In a matter of seconds, Oswald rode right alongside Peter.

"I spoke without thinking." She sighed. "He deserved better from me."

"You need to mind your tongue. I hope your husband will be as mild-mannered when you speak out of turn." Father Dominicus gave her a wry look. "What did the Scriptures have to do with your choice of warriors to send on this assignment?"

The priest had known her all her life, and Lorice knew he'd learned to be wary of her logic. This time, though, she felt certain he'd be pleased.

"Christ said the gates of hell wouldn't prevail against Peter." Lorice tried to give him a serene smile, but she could feel the corners of her lips wobble as she confessed, "The walls and drawbridge here have me sure this is the entrance to Hades."

"Since you commented earlier on the appearance of Ravenhurst Castle, I've pondered on it. I've decided you ought to take comfort in how hideous it is."

"Comfort?" Lorice gave the priest a flummoxed look.

His head bobbed affirmatively. "Lucifer was God's most beautiful angel. He was selfish, vain, and grasping. It would make sense that he's not changed. That would mean he'd want to inhabit a magnificent-looking citadel, not a functional granite stronghold like this."

"Because the devil is grasping, he'd take all he could get. He might not live in this place himself, but I wouldn't be surprised in the least if the inhabitants were counted among his wicked minions."

"Your parents shouldn't have let you talk them into having me teach you all of those lessons. You're a drain on my patience."

"You love to have me discuss and debate with you. I keep you young."

"You keep me bald. I pull my hair out by the handfuls over your escapades."

Lorice looked at the tonsure he kept so carefully groomed and laughed.

"Now that's better. You want to meet Gareth of Ravenhurst with a bright countenance."

"Don't play matchmaker at this late date. I'm not about to try to put on a maidenly show. You promised to help me see if there was a betrothal severance document. I know Father wouldn't want me dishonored by marrying the son of his sole enemy."

"In the meantime, your mother wouldn't want you dishonored by being seen in this state. See to your modesty and station."

Both heavy and hot, the customary coif gave her miserable headaches. An ages-old circlet worked no better. The weight of the scarves it held invariably tilted it until the golden piece dug into the forehead and tipped her into a wretched headache as well. Mercy caused her parents to allow her the freedom to cover her hair with nothing more than a wispy length of fine silk. 'Twas said that in England and France, fine ladies wore elegant wigs instead of the headcloths, but the practicality of Germans held out over the pretensions of the more frivolous countries—especially in the countryside.

Lorice didn't protest about donning the coif. She silently pulled a small sack from beneath her seat and set it on her lap. She removed her scarf and tucked it inside that sack and relished the utter freedom for a few seconds ere she drew all of her hair over her right shoulder. Finger-combing the snarls out of her hip-length tresses took some time. The winds must have sneaked under the scarf and played mischief.

Silver and gold, silver and gold. . . She bit back a cry at the memory of her mother chanting those words so lovingly when she'd taught Lorice how to braid. They'd been Mama's way of establishing a rhythm and weave in a loving description of Lorice's pale blond hair.

Soon, the white whimple banded all of her hair close to her head, and a mud-colored cloth formed a coif. The whole creation left her top heavy, and the only way it stayed in place was with a chin strap. Lorice stuck a finger underneath the thin fabric strip and tried to ease it a pinch.

"Don't be messing with that. How many times did your mother tell you a lady who fusses and scratches looks like she has fleas?"

Lorice gave the priest a disgruntled look.

He winked back. "If I had my way, you'd tighten it. Then you might not be able to open your mouth and horrify them with one of your odd opinions."

◆　◆　◆

"Baron, the entourage is almost to the drawbridge."

Gareth parted his templed fingers, leaned forward, and moved a chess piece. "Checkmate."

"How?" his reeve moaned. "Six moves. It only took you six moves."

Having already abandoned the game mentally, Gareth rose and folded his arms akimbo. He concentrated on his knight. "Is there any evidence of warriors following them or flanking my land?"

"None whatsoever," Christoff assured him.

"Keep the guard doubled, nonetheless."

The warrior nodded curtly. "It's the oddest thing, Sire— there's a woman in the midst of them."

"A woman." Gareth repeated the words without showing any emotion. He turned back toward the chessboard and paused to feed a snippet of raw meat to his raven, which perched on a small stand on the table. The raven gargled his thanks, and Gareth stroked his knuckles down the bird's breast once, then focused on the chessboard and started to right the pieces. "When they arrive, check to be sure they carry no disease. Allow the woman and three men to enter. Bring them here."

"I'll strip them of their weapons first."

"Only if you deem it necessary." Gareth replaced the last piece and motioned to the reeve to begin another game.

"An enemy within the gates ought never be armed." Christoff let out a rusty chuckle. "Then again, three men armed to the teeth wouldn't stand a chance against even one of your knights."

Gareth moved a black pawn. "Follow your training and instincts. You've proved your judgment is sound."

The warrior left, and the reeve frowned at the chessboard, then delayed making a move. "How did Christoff prove his judgment is sound?"

"By speaking a great truth."

"Ah." He moved a rook. "By saying your knights are mighty."

"No." Gareth crooked a slow grin, and he took that rook. "He recognized women are odd things."

Chapter 2

Transit epistola jucundus
nipretegora deumb

The lady and three men—no more."

Lorice stared at the knight who stood on the lowered drawbridge and gave that vile pronouncement. Several of her soldiers moved to close ranks about her cart. To their credit, they didn't mumble or dissemble. They took protective action and left it to their leader to act as spokesman.

A score of brawny soldiers came out of the castle and prowled about her retinue, prodding at sacks, digging through the carts, and making her men shed their shirts to prove they carried no disease. Lorice expected this poor welcome. Saltzfeld would have done the same if Ravenhurst came calling. It showed common sense, even if it lacked the merest scrap of hospitality.

Oswald separated from Peter and allowed his destrier to swing to the side in an impressive move of horsemanship. "I accompanied Lady Lorice, but I'm not part of the entourage. No doubt, Ravenhurst will welcome me as a neighbor."

The knight on the bridge folded his arms across his chest.

Stubbornness barked from every harsh line in his face and posture. "A neighbor has no need of the arsenal you're wearing."

"I wore it for safety during travel and for the sake of protecting the lady."

"Then you won't mind shedding all of that metal and leaving it outside the gates."

Lorice murmured to the priest, "If Baron Ravenhurst is half as contumacious as his man, you'd best sever the betrothal."

Peter turned. He needed not call out names. Haug and Steffan nudged their mounts forward to flank him. He stared at the knight. "Our lives and weapons are sworn to the safety of our lady. We'll not chance her welfare to calm your fears. Make way for the Lady of Saltzfeld."

The knight didn't budge. He lifted his chin a notch. "Three men. There's a man in the cart with your lady."

"Sir, you must be beggared for wits if you think a priest counts as a man." Lorice gave him her haughtiest look.

Father Dominicus choked momentarily, then cleared his throat. "I'm a man of God, not a man of war. As such, I'm sure Ravenhurst would wish me to enter for the sake of propriety."

"And I will, of course, require my maids."

"One maid. Three men."

"Sir, you are more tiresome than the entire trip here." Lorice turned. "Ilse, come climb up on this cart. You'll accompany me. Let's be done with this."

Ilse grabbed a bundle and joined her mistress. Lorice readjusted her headpiece and winced at the fact that a headache was already brewing.

The Ravenhurst warriors returned to the drawbridge. They stood across it, sentinels who looked far too ready to pick a fight. Lorice sighed. "Father, this has all of the makings of a miserable day. I'm counting on you to have a word with the Almighty to be sure I get to return home and never see this dreadful place again."

"If I were in your slippers," Ilse whispered, "I wouldn't be fretting about the place. I'd be terrified of the man inside of it!"

Father Dominicus muttered, "If anyone should be terrified, it ought to be the bridegroom."

◆ ◆ ◆

Gareth could see over the reeve's shoulder. Had there just been men entering, he'd have stayed seated and made another move on the chessboard. Since a lady accompanied the men, he rose.

"Ravenhurst, your men are antagonistic as starving dogs," Oswald von Stillhoven complained as he elbowed past Christoff and strode across the main room. "They stripped me of my weapons, as if I'd ever pose you any danger. My mission is one of peace."

"Then you have no need of the weapons." Gareth shook Oswald's hand and grinned. He cast a glance at the other men in the party. "I can see they clung to their swords."

None of the three warriors spoke, and a plump, wide-eyed serving woman tried unsuccessfully to hide behind the priest. The priest cleared his throat.

"They're minding their lady. Let me present Lady Lorice of Saltzfeld. The priest is Father Dominicus."

Gareth saw the priest dip his head in humble greeting, but he kept his eyes focused on the lady. Medium in height but willowy in build, she'd likely reach his chin if she took off that ridiculous head covering. She wore it wrapped so tightly, it pulled her green eyes back and upward in a catlike slant. Her gown, the color of a season's first plums, bore generous embroidery of gold at the neck, sleeve, and hem. The stomacher showed her waist to be tiny, and the full skirts blessedly lacked the ridiculous farthingale or padding he'd seen glimpses of on women of fashion over the last few years. All in all, Lorice of Saltzfeld looked every bit a woman of consequence even though dust covered every last inch. That being said, she'd probably be quite comely if she'd but smile instead of pinch her lips tightly together.

"Father. Lady Saltzfeld." Gareth nodded urbanely and gestured toward the hearth. He could see the travelers had just spied his raven, and their reactions amused him. As he had in the past, Oswald shifted uncomfortably, and the maid let out a small squawk of alarm and made the sign of the cross for protection.

" 'Tis naught to worry over," the lady murmured.

"Crows and ravens in a home mean death," the maid trembled.

"The Lord protects His own." The priest seemed untroubled by the superstitious nonsense, and Gareth hoped his common sense and unruffled attitude indicated the meeting would be tempered by wisdom.

"Come. Be seated." Gareth directed his words to the lady in particular. "Refreshments will be here shortly."

"Though your knight didn't allow entry to my men," she said in a carefully modulated tone, "I'd ask you extend them your hospitality. Travel leaves men thirsty."

Ah, so the Lady of Saltzfeld didn't accept for herself what was denied those who served her. 'Twas either a very calculated move or an indication of laudable character. After years of distrust between their families, she wouldn't come unless she wanted something of him. Odd that she had come. . . unless her parents—or at least her father—had died. He needed to take this woman's measure quickly and accurately.

Without looking away from her, Gareth made a single gesture. "Your men and horses will be seen to."

"Thank you." She dipped her head regally, but winced as if showing gratitude to him cost her dearly.

"Would you care for a moment to refresh yourself, Lady?"

"I'd rather we tend to the matter and be done with it."

"The trip here was long and hard," Oswald said in a kindly tone. He took the lady's arm and escorted her over to the hearth. "Please don't mistake Lady Lorice's weariness for impatience."

Lorice took a stool by the hearth and flashed a smile at Gareth. A more engaging smile, he'd never seen. It carried with it an impish sparkle. "Honesty demands I confess impatience is among my less desirable traits."

"Only Christ is perfect." The priest's knees creaked as he

sat on a handy bench. "We all have our flaws."

Gareth watched how Lorice's knights stayed close. From the moment they'd entered, the warriors hadn't shown a moment of ease. They'd continued to scan the room, scan him, and keep close to their lady. Disciplined. Vigilant. Loyal. The conduct of one's warriors reflected on the master. Lady Lorice's father still was—or must have been—a worthy adversary.

Closer inspection revealed a sad cast to her eyes and dark circles beneath them. From this distance, he saw a pallor the dust no longer concealed. A vain woman would have insisted upon washing her hands and face as well as changing her garments before facing her foe. Delightful as it had been, her smile didn't last. She sat with great composure and poise, but strain shouted from the tightening corners of her mouth. Her knuckles whitened as she knotted her hands in her lap.

Gareth chose not to tower over the girl. He sat and accepted a goblet as a maid served his guests. No one made a toast or said a word. The silence was notable, but he chose not to break it.

Oswald cleared his throat. "You've been baron now for two years."

Gareth gave no response to what was obvious.

The priest slid his hand onto the lady's arm and down to curl around her fingers. "The young lady's parents went to be with our Lord last month."

"My condolences." Despite the enmity between their families, Gareth felt compassion for the loss the girl had suffered.

She blinked away her tears, yet she clung tightly to the priest's hand. The maid she'd brought sniffled.

"As is fitting, we opened the coffer in which Lord Saltzfeld kept his papers." The priest's voice grew even more somber. "A betrothal agreement lay at the bottom of his documents."

Oswald made a brusque sound. "Your fathers hadn't spoken in a decade and a half. Surely, the betrothal was broken. I assured the lady—"

Gareth stood. "Are you implying I am betrothed to this woman?"

"You didn't know about it, either." She let out a relieved sigh. "The severance document must be in your keeping."

Gareth glowered at her. He knew his father had arranged a marriage, but neither parent wanted him to know the bride's identity. Indeed, he'd been instructed not to open the compartment in his mother's jewel case until the bride arrived or until he reached his twenty-first natal day. Surely, his father wouldn't betray him by agreeing to such a disastrous alliance. "What game do you play?"

"There, then." Oswald tugged at her arm. "We can take you back home now. See? I told you it must have been—"

"Halt." The priest's voice took on an air of authority. "The betrothal contract in our custody is valid. Whether Baron Ravenhurst possesses a copy or not is inconsequential. Such things are misplaced at times, which is why both parties keep a copy. The signatures and seals are unmistakable."

"I'll see that document." Gareth didn't want to call a man

of God a liar, and he'd spoken the truth—such items occasionally disappeared. This situation called for every shred of diplomacy he possessed.

Moments later, he stood at the table and weighted the top of the curled vellum as he unrolled the scrolled piece. The first things he'd seen were his name and hers. As soon as he had the whole page flat, he immediately identified his father's signature and seal.

Details. He needed to take a moment to read the whole agreement and determine the specifics of the arrangement.

"Shall I read it to you?" the priest asked in a low tone.

"I'm able to read." Gareth read the contents twice, then forcefully wrenched the scroll, turn by turn, until it resumed its coiled form. He turned and bowed stiffly. "Welcome to your new home, my bride."

Chapter 3

I'm not your bride." Lorice hoped the wimple she wore muffled sound and she didn't seem half that vague or helpless. She refused to wilt in front of this black-haired baron. The golden shards in his pale brown eyes gave him a predatory look, and if she cowered at all, he had the ability to tear her to shreds. "I came to assure myself that your father severed the arrangement."

"Lady, you proved a betrothal betwixt us of which I knew nothing. If either of us were to have knowledge of an annulment, I'd logically expect it to be you."

She snatched the scroll from the table and waved it up and down in a scolding motion. "Don't tell me you can read but don't bother to maintain records." The raven flapped in agitation, and the lady immediately ceased the action and tossed a tiny piece of meat to it.

Not in the least bit distracted from her intent, she continued. "The wedding was to have been on my eighteenth natal day, and the date is specified right there. Surely you refrained from coming to claim me as your bride last week because your father obtained some form of a divorcement."

"My father was a man of honor. He signed this betrothal; he'd not break it. Any severance would come from your family."

Lorice sucked in a sharp breath. "You vile man. How dare you speak poorly of my papa! He'd never do such a thing." *If only Ravenhurst were right. Why couldn't Papa just once have broken honor in order to rescue me from this dreadful fate?* Stricken again by the fact that he'd let years pass and never done a thing to dissolve this union, Lorice blurted out, "We both know this is a travesty—it must be broken!"

Ravenhurst studied her in complete silence. He took his sweet time, and she fought the way his scrutiny made her shiver.

"Stay here." He turned to go.

Lorice grabbed the deeply cuffed sleeve of his elegant black coat. "What are you doing?"

He looked at her hand until she turned loose of him, then gave her a glare that chilled her to the marrow of her bones. "At least once before, your father sent a secret communication to Ravenhurst." Without another word, he left.

She stared at the baron as he strode from the main room. As suited his name, he wore all black. *Black as his heart.* The width of his shoulders and the length of his stride bespoke power and confidence. She hastily patted Father Dominicus's arm. "Please go with him. I don't trust him."

"Now, Lorice—"

"Lady," Oswald murmured, "you cannot give orders here."

The impact of his words took her breath away. Here, she was powerless—a mere pawn to be moved at a strange man's whims. She couldn't bear to live like that. "He'd best return with a severance. He must!"

"Sit, Lorice," the priest said in a placating tone.

He was trying his hardest to calm her. Lorice didn't want to be disrespectful or disobedient, but she couldn't sit still. "I'll join you in a moment."

Lorice paced back and forth across the main room. The place was built with magnificent proportions. It measured half again as wide and long as Saltzfeld's great room. The usual array of tables and benches occupied the floor, but the room boasted a hearth large enough to roast a full ox. The smallest sound echoed within the place. Many beautiful tapestries and banners hung from the walls, but they needed a good beating and the thrushes on the floor smelled stale.

Father Dominicus was right—the inside of the keep helped make up for the ugly exterior. Lorice immediately banished that praise. The appearance of the inside or outside of this place didn't matter a whit. As soon as she managed to accomplish a release from the barbarous baron, she'd go back home.

"You're plowing a path on the floor," Haug growled at her.

She glanced down. Indeed, she'd paced until her hem parted the rushes much as Moses must have parted the Red Sea. Dismayed at the evidence of her agitation, she shot the beloved old warrior a rueful grin, went to the far end of the path, and proceeded to drag a bench up toward her people.

Ilse scampered over. "Lady Lorice!"

"What are you up to now?" Steffan rumbled. He'd sound threatening to anyone else, but Lorice knew that particular tone was the hulking knight's way of showing affection.

By the time Gareth reappeared, Ilse and Steffan were setting down the bench. Lorice glanced at the floor and let out a sigh of relief. While bringing the bench to this spot, they'd obscured her path in the thrushes.

"Just what are you doing?" Gareth looked sour as pickle brine.

"Lady Lorice wanted a bench that didn't have splinters." Haug gave the baron a surly look. "She had to search your room for a decent one."

"She had a stool—a fine one."

"My maid didn't." Lorice cast a smile at Ilse. She'd always loved Ilse, and Mama often wondered who pampered whom more—Lorice or her maid.

"You and your maid will go rest in the women's solar. You'll want to be well rested for tomorrow."

Lorice felt all of her tension drain away. "So you found a bill of severance. It's for the best. In truth, I'm so relieved, we'll just take our leave now."

Gareth's stare nearly bore a hole through her. "You mistake me, Lady. Tomorrow you become my wife."

◆ ◆ ◆

"It's the best I could do," the priest said much later. "He knew the betrothal document had been stored in his mother's cask of jewels, and he'd been honorable enough to leave it undisturbed as was his parents' wish. Surely, you can take some small comfort in knowing he'd been a dutiful son."

"I find no comfort in any of this. We came here to squelch a small fire, not fan it into a conflagration."

"Lorice, regardless of your wishes, there's no official decree of dissolution. Since the betrothal specified the marriage date as your eighteenth natal day, you are in arrears. It is too late to undo the pledge."

"But five days 'til we wed? I'd rather walk barefoot through tares than sit beside him at supper. How am I to—"

"Five days. I managed to buy you that much, but he's a man of considerable intensity. Be satisfied that you're being granted time to get to know him. Many a bride never so much as sees her groom until they meet at the altar. Duty and honor—"

"Here's the last of it." Peter and another of her men staggered past with a large wooden chest. The set it down, and as they turned to leave, Ravenhurst stood in the doorway to the women's solar.

"Five carts of goods hardly give the impression you only planned to tend to business and return home."

"I made her bring her things," Father Dominicus stated.

Lorice gave her husband-to-be a chilling look. "I scarcely consider it cordial for you to bid your men search my possessions before allowing them into the keep. Now I wish I would have packed thrice as much."

Gareth tilted back his head and let out a booming laugh.

The sound filled the solar and washed over her. Hearty, warm, masculine—it carried with it a sense of joy and safety she'd not known since Papa died. Papa used to laugh at her outrageous comments, too.

Merriment brightened the gold in Gareth's eyes. "Which shall I pity more—the beasts that hauled the carts or your men who carried all of this up the stairs?"

"Is this your way of hinting that you have compassion?"

The rascal winked at her. "My lady, you can depend on me having every bit as much compassion as you have. . . ." He glanced meaningfully at the array of goods crammed into the solar. "Collection."

"If you truly had the merest scrap of mercy—"

The priest groaned loudly and interrupted, "The lady requires rest. She needs to settle in."

"Horses settle in. I'm not a horse!" The baron's sly smile made Lorice's blood run cold. In the short time she'd known him, Lorice discovered his tongue worked every bit as quickly as his mind.

"I can see you're not a horse. My horses are well disciplined and don't chomp at the bit."

Lorice could scarcely credit he'd been so crude. She stared at the baron for a few moments, then rasped, "My father was too kind to speak ill of another, so I know not what dreadful thing your father did to cause the rift between our families. One thing I do concede: Your father struck his worst blow when he doomed me to have you as my husband."

◆   ◆   ◆

Oswald prattled on about rainfall and the rye crop. Schwartzbein, a well-known peddler of fine jewels, had arrived and proceeded to give his opinion on just how fat the landowners' coffers would grow this season with such fine weather fostering a bountiful yield.

Normally, Gareth would attend to such topics, but his concentration strayed toward the baffling fact that his father had let the betrothal stand. Often, arranged marriages forged a so-called peace between warring families, but such was not the case here. The betrothal had been made when he and Lorice were no more than mere babes and relations between the two houses stood in good stead. *Not only did Father permit the arrangement to endure, he took measures to keep the bride's identity a secret while turning my heart against her family. Why?*

Time lagged, and Gareth began to wonder when his betrothed would arrive for the meal. He'd been informed the lady's maid assisted her with a bath, and he hoped the woman's temper cooled as fast as the water did.

Her men would now be his men, so he'd ordered their admittance. Then, too, Oswald's men came along. More tables crowded the main room to accommodate them, and the room swarmed with boisterous warriors. The moment the men fell silent, Gareth turned.

His bride looked like a nun. An unshaped and unadorned gown the color of mud billowed about her. She'd put on another head covering that drew her features back as if she'd been blasted by a mighty wind. White and brown, the coif might fool some into thinking the woman lived in a nunnery, but the flash in her eyes warned patience was not her virtue. *She told me that, herself.*

To her credit, she came to his side without him needing to beckon or call her. That bit of decorum pleased him. Whatever strain existed between them ought not be played out in the presence of all the castle inhabitants. Lorice accepted his arm, let him escort her to the high board, and took the stool to his right. Though she made little conversation through the meal, he didn't mind. No doubt, sorrow over the terrible loss of her parents and anxiety at facing a new life occupied her thoughts. Those, coupled with being exhausted from travel, showed her at her worst during their first meeting. Whether she appreciated the priest's words, they still held truth: She'd need a chance to settle in. Gareth determined to make the adjustment as easy on her as he could.

Dainty manners and a modest appetite carried her though the meal, but almost as soon as the maids cleared away the last course, the lady murmured, "I'd prefer to retire now."

Gareth took in her pallor and frowned.

"You have a habit of scowling." She winced as soon as the words left her mouth. "Please excuse me."

Gareth rose, and every last man in the hall immediately followed suit. Lorice took his hand and allowed him to assist her off her stool. He escorted her to the stairs and waited until they were halfway up the flight before he asked, "Are you unwell?"

"I'm in need of rest."

Her maids had been in the hall, and as soon as he'd led her across the room, they'd scurried ahead. Just as Gareth and Lorice arrived at the doorway to the women's solar, the maids had managed to light the oil lamps to illuminate the room. One of the maids let out a terrified shriek.

Gareth instinctively shoved Lorice behind himself, drew his sword, and scanned the room for danger. The other maids all clumped together and made panicked sounds, and he quickly saw the cause of their upset.

Someone had thrust a dirk into the pillow.

Chapter 4

Y ou're quite creative in attempting to break the betrothal."

Lorice stared at the baron and blinked. Surely she'd heard him wrong.

"What is your motive?" His voice remained bland, but the set of his jaw and the heat in his eyes underscored his demand.

This man was her enemy, yet he would become her husband in a matter of days. The thought of living in such a state of danger and strife made her feel even sicker.

"I posed you a question."

Nettled by his persistence when he'd probably arranged this himself, she snapped. "I confess I'm not pleased I must marry you, and with the passage of time, the notion becomes increasingly less appealing. But I had nothing to do with this." She gestured toward the bed. "If I were to use a knife, I'd use it on you instead of something of worth like that pillow."

His hand tilted her face up to his. Rough fingers held her chin, forcing her to face him fully. Furrows plowed his brow, then he cast a glance at her maids, who fluttered and whimpered over by the bed. "So you had nothing to do with this?"

"Of course not. You'll be a widower in a matter of days if this is the best protection you offer. Is that *your* motive?"

"I'm no more deserving of your accusation than you were of mine."

Reacting to the maid's scream, several warriors crowded around. Lorice felt a few men behind her and heard Haug's rough voice, "Your men will guard your door, Lady."

Gareth nodded. "As will mine. Two-hour shifts. A guard from each house at the lady's chamber door." He strode to the bedside, pulled the dirk from the pillow, and inspected it closely. "If anyone recognizes this, you're to let me know."

The headache that had been building steadily all afternoon grew worse by the moment. Lorice fought the throbbing pain and swallowed the surge of bile in her throat at the sight of her groom holding the weapon. He drew closer, and it took every scrap of her courage not to cower away.

Gareth passed the dirk to a soldier. "Find the owner." He then wrapped his arm around her. "The wedding will be on the morrow."

◆　◆　◆

Gareth felt the shudder go through her. She didn't say a word. His men went down the stairs at Christoff's orders, and Adelman remained behind as the first guard. Lorice's men argued over the privilege of guarding her door. One finally glared at Gareth. "Two of us at each shift. We won't risk our lady."

"And you think I'd put *my* lady at risk?"

"You're not wed yet. She's not yours." The man who spoke cast a frown at Lorice. "Be sure one of your maids tests your potion before you take it."

"What potion?" Gareth demanded.

"It's nothing." She said the words in a vague tone and didn't meet his eyes.

"For her head," one of the maids said. "She's wearing that covering for your sake, but it costs her dearly."

Gareth made an impatient sound and tucked Lorice closer still. He reached over, tugged the chinstrap loose, and hastily robbed her of the yards of cloth. A braid thick as his wrist finally snaked free. He unraveled the pale golden tresses and ignored Lorice's weak protest. He'd never seen a more stunning sight.

"You'll not wear that again. 'Tis too heavy. Ugly, too."

She lifted her hand and rubbed her temple as she asked in a muted tone, "Are you always this imperious?"

"I'm no more imperious than you are impractical." He lifted her into his arms and carried her to the bed. Earlier in the day, she'd blazed like a fire; now she reminded him of no more than a wisp of smoke. One of the maids swiped away the destroyed pillow, and Gareth gave Lorice a small squeeze before he bent to lay her down. "You'll be safe. I vow it."

He'd barely settled her on the bed, when she started to rise. "My lady—"

"I end my days with prayer."

He sat on the edge of her bed and pressed her slender hands between his own. "Almighty Father, grant us a home filled with peace and faith. Bless my bride and ease her pain. Gift her with a sound night's sleep, I pray. Amen."

Without the coif framing her face and pulling, her features looked far softer. Her eyes still carried a slight tilt he found beguiling. Gareth wasn't prepared for the tears that glossed them. "What is it?" he asked softly. "Are you afraid?"

"Papa often started his prayers with the very same words."

"Then we have common ground on which to build our marriage. Faith can light the path for us. 'Tis time to set aside whatever discord existed." Only after having prayed with her did he feel able to speak those words. He lifted her hand, pressed a kiss to the back of her fingers, then left her to her maids.

As soon as he shut the door, he turned to the guards. "Protect her at all costs."

One of her guards dared ask, "What are you going to do?"

"Catch the vermin who dared threaten my bride."

◆　◆　◆

"Men." Gareth stood in the center of the stairs. The Saltzfeld warriors all stood to his left, distrust plain as could be on their faces. Ravenhurst warriors filled the room to the center and right. They looked every bit as suspicious.

He didn't blame them. His own father fostered such animosity for Saltzfeld; the malice undoubtedly ran true from Lorice's house. Years of training made a man hold allegiance

37

and carry enmity. Gareth felt the dark pull of those ugly emotions himself. He dared not allow them to triumph. If this marriage were to succeed, he'd have to take the first step. Truthfully, it would take a miracle for the marriage to work and the men to blend.

"I demand respect and loyalty from all of my people. I am certain Lady Lorice does as well."

"And she has it!" one of the older men shouted. All of her men nodded and rumbled agreement.

"Tomorrow's marriage will meld the two houses into one. We cannot afford to wait to unify until then. Someone has threatened my bride. She is to be protected at all times, at all costs."

"We'll protect our lady," another of her knights growled.

Oswald elbowed his way between the two groups of warriors.

"A half dozen of my finest warriors accompanied me. Instead of each faction spending a sleepless night distrusting the other, let my men guard the lady. Surely, once you are married, whoever wished to keep your powerful houses from combining will be thwarted. The danger will pass."

Schwartzbein nodded. "A fair plan. I'm adept with a sword myself. I'll keep watch, too."

"Generous offers, but ones I'll not accept." Gareth stared at his men. "Years ago, the two families lived in harmony. A rift formed, but it will be sealed with this union. The discord between two men who are now dead ought not be carried on. Wisdom dictates we use our strength to forge an alliance that keeps our people safe and content."

"The lady was not content to come here," one of Oswald's men said.

"But women change their minds, as we all know." Gareth paused for the inevitable laughter. He jutted his chin toward one of the foremost Saltzfeld men. "Hang the Saltzfeld banner alongside Ravenhurst's. The time has come for the silver to shimmer alongside the black."

◆　◆　◆

"It is unlucky. You can't!"

Lorice curled her toes on the cold wooden floor and clutched her robe more closely about herself. Morning's first rays no more than sneaked past the window covering, and she'd crawled out of the enormous bed just before someone tapped on the door. All four of her maids crowded around the chamber door, fighting to keep it shut. "It's unlucky, I tell you!"

"Luck is for pagans," Gareth explained in a voice Lorice assumed was supposed to sound patient. It came across more as disgruntled.

"So says the man who keeps a black bird of death in his home," Ilse squawked breathlessly. "The lady is in no condition to see you."

"She's still ailing?" The bass rumble should have given warning, but it didn't. He thrust the door open and plowed inside.

Myla dashed across the solar and planted herself in front of Lorice. Ilse trundled at her greatest speed and did likewise.

Together, they formed a formidable hedge. By standing on her toes and tilting her head, Lorice could barely see him discover the empty bed and turn toward her.

"Lady Lorice," he spoke as if no barrier stood between them, "I'm pleased to see you've recovered. You end each day with prayer. I came to invite you to join me in the chapel to start our day with a moment of devotion."

"The sacrament of marriage is devotion enough," old Agathe muttered. She waggled her gnarled finger at the baron. "You'll spoil the future by grabbing for the present. Everyone knows a groom isn't to see his bride until they're at the altar."

"This matters to you?"

To Lorice's surprise, he hadn't asked her—he'd asked her old nursemaid! She watched as Agathe nodded. "Give me time, and I'll make her pretty for you."

"God already made her beautiful."

"Then she'll be worth waiting for."

Gareth chuckled. "How old are you, ancient one?"

"Too old to put up with this nonsense. I'll have my little Lorice at your altar at sunset and not a minute earlier."

"You do that." He headed for the door. He turned back around. "Don't claim to be so aged, Grandmother. I want you lively enough to serve as nursemaid to the next generation."

Once the door closed, Lorice moaned. His flattery toward her might be relegated to a glib tongue, but his kindness to an old woman surely counted in his favor—and by winning Agathe's devotion with such a pledge, he'd just turned Lorice's greatest ally into his own.

Agathe wheeled around and started right in. "Now don't you start off on the wrong foot. You're a lady, and it's past time you stopped charming everyone into giving you your way. That's a fine man. A godly man. Wise enough to retreat so he could win a war."

"So you admit this union is a war, and I'm losing?" Lorice stepped into the middle of the room. Agathe never gave an inch. Lorice loved her for it, but there were times her nursemaid's wisdom grew maddening.

An impish smile lit Agathe's face. "Indeed. To the victor go the spoils, and we all know you're spoiled rotten."

Chapter 5

Gareth stood at the wall and squinted at the column of soldiers in the distance. "Bertolf of Nordwald."

Lorice's warrior spat. "Baron Saltzfeld's body was barely shriven when the Wolf appeared. He expected to be the bridegroom."

"Wolf?" Gareth hadn't had any dealings with Bertolf, but his reputation didn't recommend him as a friend.

"Aye. He howled like a rabid wolf when the priest showed the betrothal parchment. He's not a man to give up a prize."

"The contingent is small," Christoff mused. "What does he hope to gain?"

"The logical answer is, he's come in hopes the betrothal has been severed. You're right; he's not a man to give up easily."

Steffan, Lorice's man, placed his hands on the parapet and leaned forward. Gareth watched as he assessed the castle's architecture and defenses from this vantage. The slow smile easing the warrior's rugged features counted as praise enough for the well-fortified place. The fact that he'd volunteered information about a possible enemy and demonstrated defensive planning proved he'd already expanded his allegiance. 'Twas a good sign.

By noon, Gareth sat beneath the black and silver banners. He cast about a satisfied look. All morning, Lorice's maids came in and out of the solar bearing tapestries, banners, and flags. His chatelaine and maids eagerly joined in, and in no time at all, the flock of women had the great hall embellished worthy of a king's visit. Fresh rushes covered the floor, and the aroma of rich meat filled the air.

The far doors parted, and Bertolf swaggered in. Just four paces into the hall, that swagger lost its arrogance and changed into a purposeful step. Oswald lifted his goblet and muttered from behind the rim, "Watch your back."

Gareth waited until Bertolf drew nigh. "So you come to celebrate my marriage."

The baron from Nordwald grimaced. "I expected you'd let the woman recover from her journey before you dragged her to the altar. I can see from the fripperies she's already settling in."

Settling in. Lorice would seethe over that characterization. Cheered by the thought, Gareth called out, "Give our wedding guests refreshment."

Hope flashed in Bertolf's eyes—or was it greed? "You've not yet wed her?"

"At sunset." Precisely as he'd ordered, two warriors—one

from Saltzfeld, the other of Ravenhurst—tromped down the stairs, carrying the altar between them. "As you can see, we're making the final preparations."

Bertolf's expression shifted. He accepted the tankard given him and took a large quaff. "There are plenty of hours 'til sunset. We should discuss trade."

"Until I review the books my lady brought, I'd be a fool to discuss business."

"Just summon her," Bertolf grumbled. "The woman kept the books herself. She can tell you down to the last calf and goat what she brings to the marriage."

Gareth disciplined his features so he'd not divulge his utter amazement at what he'd just been told. His bride could read? Not only read, but cipher? No wonder Bertolf looked like he'd been forced to eat a bushel of bitter apples.

"You and your men ate plenty of her calves when you paid your sympathy call." Oswald couldn't stay silent any longer. "The valuable salt she gave you as a parting gift was far above generous. What more would you want of the girl?"

"He's not dealing with the lady; he's dealing with me." Gareth rose and added, "In a few days. For now, I'll permit you to use the bath prepared for me. There is enough time for me to have a fresh one drawn before the ceremony."

"My back could use a good scrubbing." Bertolf scanned the hall. "I see you have many a comely wench."

Though familiar with the custom, Gareth was disgusted and took no pains to hide it. "The offer was for a bath, not a bedding. The women in my service are virtuous."

Bertolf finished his drink. "For all of the tales of the strife between your families, you and your bride seem to share many of the same practices."

"It will make for a sound union."

◆ ◆ ◆

"There's no helping it. Besides, it's not what you wear that counts—it's the vows you speak."

Lorice stared at the wedding gown the women of Saltzfeld had hurriedly stitched for her before her hasty departure. They'd stayed up all night to create the wondrous sea green silk gown. It drooped over Ilse's arms like seaweed. It was twice as wet as seaweed, too.

"I didn't think that slight shower would soak through the sack." The maid sniffled. "I should have checked earlier. We could have put it in the sun to dry."

Myla mourned, "It's a travesty. The hall is beautiful, and the bride will—"

"Be lovely as ever," Agathe cut in. "She can wear the same gown she wore last eve."

"Nonsense." Lorice headed for one last chest and rummaged through it. She pulled out a gown and shook it.

"Black!" All of the women in the solar shrieked the word in outrage.

Deep in her heart, Lorice felt every bit as horrified as they sounded. If she gave in to the storm of emotions she felt, her wedding day would be an event to remember—but not in the way she'd always hoped. *Lord, why do these blunders always happen to me?*

A Ravenhurst maid timidly touched the cloth. "Black is the baron's color."

"Indeed. Wearing it will honor him." Lorice bobbed her head as much to convince herself as to persuade the other women. "It's fitting for a bride to meet her groom with respect. I'll wear my cloth-of-silver stomacher and the silver-and-white lace on the sleeves."

Agathe patted her cheek. "There's my lamb. Ravenhurst will be pleased."

Lorice desperately wanted to grouse about not caring what Gareth thought or felt, but she couldn't. Years of her mother's counsel echoed in her mind. *A lady cannot run her household if she proves herself unworthy of the servants' respect.* The time had come for her to shut the door on her childhood. No more outspokenness—except in the privacy of the master's chamber. There, diplomacy would yield to honesty. This would be the first of many times to come when she would hold her tongue. *Besides*, an inner voice niggled, *I do care what he thinks—but only a little.*

❖   ❖   ❖

Gareth evaluated his bride as he met her at the base of the stairs. He'd put a fistful of grain in his pocket to represent wealth and good fortune. Had she followed tradition and carried bread and salt for plenty? A quick glance downward allowed him to spy the small black velvet pouch connected to her girdle. A few salt crystals sparkled from it. Warmth filled his chest. Mayhap this marriage would, with care and attention, be a sound one. His bride gave every appearance of having put aside the obstinance she displayed on the first day and seemed set upon making the best of a difficult match.

As befitted the solemn occasion, Lorice neither smiled nor spoke, but nodded her gratitude as she accepted his arm. Her hand was steady, her bearing queenly. The black and silver gown showed great diplomacy, an indication that his bride meant to cooperate fully as a helpmeet. A man could ask no more than that—especially under the strained circumstances of their union.

He'd sent word he didn't want her veiled—mostly because he didn't wish her to suffer a headache but also because beauty like hers ought to be appreciated, not hidden. He'd ordered a wreath be made for his bride to reflect her purity and his regard, and the flowers that came from the Mary's garden now adorned her hip-length golden waves.

"My lady." He accepted a fine beeswax candle, decorated with silver ribbons and edelweiss, from a maid and handed it to Lorice. The reeve brought a blazing reed from the hearth to Gareth, who then illuminated the candle with it.

The glow lit Lorice's features, bringing out the deepening green of her eyes and highlighting the soft blush in her cheeks. For a moment, tears filled her remarkable eyes, but she blinked them away and took the first step.

'Twas not well done for a bride to weep at her wedding, and it also made for a bad start when the woman led the man. Gareth had hoped to keep matters pleasant, but commanding the respect of the men of both houses was vital—more vital than humoring a woman's snippy mood. He resolved at that point to abide by the custom of kneeling on the hem of her dress at the altar to show he'd keep control of his woman.

He also determined not to allow her the opportunity to step on his foot as they rose so she couldn't take advantage of the bride's traditional signal that he'd not keep her in line. A woman with her fire would undoubtedly display that sign of protest.

A walk toward the altar, a prayer. Holy Communion and vows. All went as it should. He took the elegant ring he'd just bought from Schwartzbein last night and placed it on her forefinger. "In the name of the Father. . ." He removed it and slipped it onto her middle finger. "And the Son. . ." He then slid it completely onto her fourth finger, where it would stay forever, "And the Holy Ghost."

"Amen," she whispered amidst the robust voices of their men.

Indeed, Gareth knelt on her hem, but as they rose, much to his surprise, Lorice made no attempt to step on his toes. The ceremony ended with the priest's blessing and invitation to greet one another with a kiss. Gareth felt a bolt of surprise when Lorice slipped her arms about his neck and cuddled close. He wrapped his arms about her tiny frame, dipped his head, and gladly sealed their union with a kiss. It wasn't until he lifted his head that he realized she was standing on not one, but both of his feet.

Chapter 6

Lorice eased away from Gareth's hold and silently slipped from her side of their wedding bed. She took care to barely part the deep slate-and-black brocaded bed curtains so her husband could slumber on and she could dress in private. They were one in body and in name, but could they become one in spirit?

She tiptoed to the table and dipped the edge of a fine linen towel into the water pitcher. The icy wetness woke her more fully. After washing herself with uncustomary swiftness, she slipped into her smock and wiggled into the now-dry, sea green silk that should have been her wedding gown.

The ring on her left hand felt substantial. She'd have to become accustomed to it. Mama wore a simple band of gold; this ring measured twice as wide and held a large, rectangular emerald.

Last night, Gareth had looked into her eyes and kissed the backs of her fingers, then kissed the ring. Shivers ran through her. *"I hope you're pleased with my choice, Lorice. My father appreciated fine jewels and taught me some of the lore. Shall I tell you about the emerald?*

"*Twelve stones on Aaron's breastplate in the Bible. . .twelve months. . .Emerald for May, and you just celebrated your natal day this month. . .Early Christians thought the emerald represented Christ's resurrection. . .said to symbolize faith, hope, and fertility.*"

His words echoed in her mind, and she whispered a quick prayer that the thoughtful reasons behind the choice were an indication of what kind of husband Gareth would be.

Arms wrapped around her, and she let out a gasp. Gareth's deep voice rumbled next to her ear, "Good morning, Wife."

"You. . .I. . .good morning," she stammered. He nuzzled a kiss on her cheek, and she turned around. He'd already donned his clothing. "How did you sneak up on me?"

"I'm a warrior, Woman. Stealth is my ally." He reached down and gently tugged on the laces of her gown, causing it to conform to her shape, then tied them. His mouth crooked upward as he studied the big, clumsy bow he'd made. "I'm not much of a lady's maid."

"Ilsa and Myla will be glad to hear that." Lorice kept her head dipped as she retied the bow in an attempt to hide her blush from her groom. "Though you told Agathe you'd welcome her to be nursemaid to our children, Ilsa and Myla worried there might not be a place for them here."

Gareth wouldn't allow her any privacy. He cupped her chin and tilted her warm face to his. "In God's kingdom, there is a place for everyone. I want our home to be like that, too." He gave her a lingering kiss, then rubbed noses with her. "I start my mornings with a trip to the chapel. In the future, you'll join me, then your maids can fulfill their usual duties. Henceforth, you'll not try to sneak from my arms to dress, but you'll wake me with a kiss and simply slip into a robe de chambre for our private devotions."

Lorice presumed a husband instructed a wife in such matters. Papa always planned the day with Mama. There was a bittersweetness in knowing her own husband planned to carry that practice into their marriage.

A frown furrowed his brow. "Are you unhappy about starting the day with the Lord?"

Lorice shook her head. "No. No, of course not. I was just remembering my parents." Her voice caught and dropped. "Some things just—"

"Ahh, my sweetling." Gareth drew her close and held her.

"Right before we went to the altar yesterday, I worried about whether we could have a marriage half so dear as theirs was."

"It'll take work." He smoothed his hand down the length of her hair in a calming, repetitious stroke. "We must not allow circumstances and others to rule our marriage. Our allegiance is to God and one another."

Lorice nodded.

He kissed her brow. "Come to the chapel with me."

Hands clasped, fingers entwined, they left the master's chamber and went to the small chapel directly across from the women's solar. The walnut doors baffled Lorice. Sizable raised squares ran down the length of both doors. Four of the uppermost squares on the left and three on the right bore beautiful carvings; the remainder of the squares remained unadorned.

Gareth ran his blunt fingers over them. "Family tradition is for each couple to commission their square's carving. My grandparents chose the shepherd and sheep. My parents wanted the Alpha and Omega."

"Have you decided what our square is to be?"

"The decision is ours to make, not mine to order." He pushed open the door and led her inside. Lorice inhaled sharply. She'd never seen anything this wondrous. Shafts of golden morning light flooded through a pair of long, narrow, arch-shaped windows. Between those arches was a much larger window that took her breath away.

The intricate stained glass contained multiple designs done in a combination of colored and painted glass. She recognized one section at once: Ravenhurst Castle, itself. Elsewhere in the window, saints, warriors, flowers, and angels abounded. The edges of the entire window carried a green glass border of an ivy pattern that held an occasional heraldic shield. At the very center of the bottom was one holding a raven with his wings widespread. Lorice wanted to stand there and bask in its beauty.

"Come." Gareth placed his hand at the small of her back and led her forward.

It wasn't until they reached the altar that Lorice took her attention off the remarkable window and looked down.

Before them, on a cloth-covered stand, were two large, thick books! Gareth traced the leather-covered brads on the first brown leather tome. They'd been placed to form a cross.

She slowly reached over and barely circled her fingertip around one of the four brads that also framed the beautiful book's cover. The other book drew her attention. Just as her groom had, she gently traced the cross on it. Why did he have two of the same book?

"I cannot tell you how much delight I took in hearing that you can read, because you, too, can share in this treasure." He opened the cover and turned a few of the vellum pages. Awe-inspiring rubrication of ornate vines, flowers, and golden bars embellished the pages.

Lorice leaned a bit closer and started to read the Latin. She clutched his hand and whispered in awe, "This is part of the Bible!"

"Better yet, Sweetling. More than two hundred years ago, one of my ancestors purchased this from a man named Gutenberg as a gift for her husband. Between these two books, we own an entire copy of the Word of God."

◆ ◆ ◆

Gareth hoped if they both relied on God, the wide river of distrust between them might narrow. Lorice's eagerness to share time in devotion, her response to the chapel, and her immediate love of the Bible boded well. Best of all, during the time they read the Holy Scripture and prayed together, God formed a bridge over that seemingly impassible river. Gareth didn't deceive himself into believing that one crossing of that fragile bridge would solve all of their problems, but with each of them willing to take steps and with God's wisdom and love, they could conquer the past and forge a future.

After their devotions, Gareth accompanied his bride down the steps and into the main room. Whoever left the dirk in her pillow two nights ago was still around. He refused to leave his wife in danger, so he led her toward the high board.

"Baron—"

"Gareth," he corrected.

"Gareth." She smiled at him. "I ought to confer with the cook and housekeeper."

"You will. . .in time. A bride deserves a little while to—"

Her green eyes sparked. "Settle in?"

"Become accustomed to her new home and staff." He seated her and took his place, then leaned closer and whispered with barely restrained laughter in his voice, "You'll find I rarely repeat a mistake, Lady."

"Lorice." An impish smile lit her face.

He chuckled. "I suspect that the same can be said of you."

"True." Her smile took on a wry twist. "But that can only be said because I'm adept at finding some other type of trouble."

A servant brought cider, hot barley cereal, and thick, black bread to the table. Another servant followed close behind with a small pitcher of cream, butter, a bowl with honey, and another with currants.

When Lorice didn't make any move, Gareth cast her a curious glance. She'd barely eaten at all since her arrival. Did she wait for him to taste each dish because she feared being poisoned?

She smiled. "I need to learn your preferences, Husband. Do you take butter or cream, honey, or currants in your morning gruel?"

She's unafraid. That fact and her attendance to such wifely concerns warmed his heart. Gareth grinned. "Butter and honey in my cereal and on my bread. What of you?"

"I'm spoiled. Saltzfeld has a vast orchard. I prefer cream with fruit. I'll see to it fresh and dried pears and apples are brought to your kitchen."

"Our kitchen."

She nodded acknowledgment of his correction, then her features tightened. "My apologies, Sire. It seems trouble has already followed me here."

Gareth turned his attention to the doorway where she focused. Bertolf stood there, yawning. Oswald shifted to the side and gave him a disgruntled look.

"Bertolf came in hopes of learning our betrothal had been severed. I credit him for having enough sense to recognize a prize and the courage to reach for it."

"I might well have been a ferret-faced hunchback, yet he'd still have wed me for my land." She grabbed the butter and honey and fixed his barley cereal. The effort she put into the act tattled on her anger. That task done, Lorice attacked the second bowl with a generous slosh of cream and a fistful of currants. "I hoped I'd gotten rid of him with the gift of some salt."

"Had I been offered salt instead of your hand, I'd have yet pursued you." Gareth surprised himself with that comment. Indeed, Lorice was a treasure worth pursuing; he'd just have to determine how far he could trust her, though. All good things, he'd learned, came at some cost.

Gareth noticed her violent stirring of the cereal slowed a bit. His bride didn't hide her emotions well—a fact he found rather endearing. "Henceforth, Bertolf will have to deal with me."

"His lands are especially rich with game. Father bartered Saltzfeld's salt for sizable stores of meat thrice a year." Her shoulders relaxed, and she moved the butter closer still and took up a slice of bread. "Oswald's household boasts particularly fine weavers. Mother sent a portion of wool there each year."

Oswald came to the high board and slapped Gareth on the shoulder before sitting on a stool. "I didn't expect to see you up this morning."

Bertolf made for the seat next to Lorice, but Christoff caught Gareth's subtle signal and took that place himself. Bertolf inclined his head toward his host and hostess, then took the next stool. "We should talk today, Baron."

Schwartzbein, who sat at a nearby table, called out, "I've fine things yet to show you. That wedding ring was but a sample of what I carry. Mayhap your bride and honored guests should join us as I display them."

Gareth swallowed a bite of his barley cereal. "I plan to show my bride our home. I'm sure you men will understand your business will have to wait."

Father Dominicus waddled in and amused Gareth by coming up to the high board, standing opposite Lorice, and swiping the slice of bread she'd just buttered. He folded it in half, took a big bite out of the center, and smacked his lips. "If my flock back at Saltzfeld didn't need me so badly, I'd stay here with you, my little lamb."

Lorice gave the priest a startled look, then turned to Gareth. Betrayal painted her features.

Chapter 7

Gareth refused to explain the priest's impending departure. His wife needed to learn to trust him.

"Gareth invited me to stay, Lorice, but I spent the night in prayer. My place is back home. Few are left who can scribe. I'll be sure to send you a message each season." He gulped another big bite and waggled his brows. "I might even be tempted to be here each year to break my Lenten fast."

Oswald leaned forward. "He'll come to bless my new grandchild. You could travel to my castle and be our guest."

"Hold there." Gareth cast a dark look at him. "No groom wishes his bride to leave his side. Mayhap, if the Lord blesses us, you men will all return here in a year to celebrate the birth of the next generation of Ravenhurst."

"You've embarrassed the girl," Oswald growled.

Gareth turned to his bride and witnessed the flush on her cheeks. Before he could speak, she straightened her shoulders. "It is a wife's duty and blessing to bear children."

Gareth stroked the back of his fingers down her cheek in a slow caress. "May the Lord bless us with several."

Father Dominicus popped currants into his mouth. "The Holy Scripture says, 'Happy is the man that hath his quiver full.'"

"Speaking of quivers. . ." Gareth gave Christoff a telling look. His foremost knight rose and bowed. "No change in my orders."

Christoff gave him a curt nod and briskly marched out of the main room.

"Hulking man, that Christoff." Oswald patted the table. "Good to know little Lorice will have brawny men to see to her safety here in her new home."

"Any and all of my men would gladly lay down their lives for my wife." Gareth lifted his goblet of cider and stared into its depths. "But make no mistake. *I* see to my bride's welfare and happiness."

Bertolf's smile was grudging, but Gareth judged it to be genuine. "You wed a prize. 'Tis good to see you treasure her."

Lorice tugged on Gareth's sleeve. "Your prize seems impatient."

Father Dominicus cackled. "No matter where she is, a goose will still honk."

Try as she might to keep composure, Lorice's voice still held merriment. "A goose ought be in the yard or the kitchen."

"Well then." Gareth stood and helped her to rise. Her hand felt small and steady in his. He gave it a squeeze. "Permit me to take my goose about the keep and show her such places. We'll start in the mews so I can fetch the raven I'm training."

◆　◆　◆

The next morning, Lorice felt more than a little abashed at the thought of boldly kissing her husband awake. She lay in the bed and tried to build up her courage or concoct an excuse.

"The day will be half over ere you begin it, Wife."

She startled at the husky sound of Gareth's deep voice. "I'll meet you halfway." He pulled her into his arms. The security and warmth that enveloped her made kissing him easy. After the kiss, he tucked her head in the crook of his neck and continued to hold her. "We must talk, Wife."

"You sound serious."

"Indeed I am. I put Bertolf off yesterday when it came to business. Oswald's hints about wishing to deal have been as subtle as a boar. I need time to familiarize myself with the books from Saltzfeld this morning."

"I brought them along, but my father had me keep the records so I can give you whatever information you require." She lifted her head and added, "If you feel you can trust me."

"In speaking the wedding vows, you entrusted yourself and all you own into my hands. Your allegiance belongs to me."

She entrusted him; *her* allegiance belonged to him. The man took far too much for granted by expecting such faith from her. What of the reverse? That path ought to lead both directions. Gareth acted as if it were his right to be granted her trust rather than earn it. *Impossible man!* He asked for something he'd not give himself. How deeply could she rely on him?

He jostled her lightly. "Are you falling back to sleep?"

"No." She sat up. Starting the day off with an argument would be a mistake. He sought information he could easily obtain. This was a time she could prove herself at no true personal cost. "So what would you like to know?"

"Speak to me of what Saltzfeld lacks and trades for." He sat up and crossed his long legs. "Tell me what she has in surplus and trades or sells. Who comes to trade, what do they want, and did your father strike bargains or send them away?"

"Could we talk as we dress? I don't want to miss our time in the chapel."

"Yes, Wife." He tugged on her hair. "But dress more quickly than you did yestermorn, and speak twice as fast."

Lorice told him of Saltzfeld's riches: salt, goats and sheep, apples and pears. Peas and barley were sufficient, but her father traded for wheat each year. "Bertolf trades cured meats and fresh venison for salt. He wanted peas this past year, but father had none to spare. Oswald, as I told you, takes a third of our wool and returns a portion of it as woven cloth. He trades wheat for apples and iron."

He slanted her a sharp look. "You have iron?"

"Father trades for it. Herman, from across the river, takes salt in exchange for iron, wheat, and rye." She drew the brush through her hair once more and began to separate it so she could plait the length.

Gareth reached out and stopped her. "Leave it down for

now. Allow your maids to tend to it. During the day, modesty and practicality demand it be tamed; but for me, in our hours alone, I'd have it free."

Lorice felt flustered by his admission, but it also pleased her. A wife wanted to know her husband found her appealing, and Gareth was generous in his attention. Still, she didn't wish him to know he'd thrown her off balance. *If only I could remember what we were talking about. . . .*

"Did your father trade with others as well?"

His prompt saved her from making an utter fool of herself. Lorice shook her head. "Other than that, there are only occasional barters for silver or cheese—but those are quite minor and neither of great value nor consistently conducted with any one person."

"But I detected you knew Schwartzbein."

Lorice wrinkled her nose. "He came by a few times. Papa never bought anything from him. Mama always ordered the salt cellars be filled, and each time Schwartzbein left, they were empty. She told Papa the trader paid for the salt with the news he brought."

As Gareth buckled on his belt and slid a small dagger into the sheath, he commented, "The very salt that provides Saltzfeld's greatest wealth is also the reason crops are harder to grow. I have some sheep and goats, but cattle are my primary livestock. Crops grow well. Berries and grapes are also plentiful."

"And does Ravenhurst lack anything?" Before she'd come, Lorice had ascertained those facts. Would Gareth be as forthcoming about his weaknesses?

"Iron, copper, and brass. Salt and spices." He led her toward the chapel. "But as you've come, we no longer lack what is most precious of all: a lady."

◆ ◆ ◆

Gareth escorted Lorice toward their chamber. He'd ordered a private supper for them—not because he had intimacy on his mind, but because the set of her jaw let him know she'd held her tongue as long as he could expect. He no more than shut the door behind them, then she whirled around.

"Obedience doesn't come easily to me, Husband. I held my tongue when you offered Bertolf twice his yearly allotment of salt. I managed to smile when you pledged half of my wool to Oswald instead of the customary third. You didn't trust me to give you sound information!"

He refused to respond.

Her anger flared brighter. "You instructed me to answer only your questions and stay silent for the remainder of your dealings, and the inside of my cheek is raw from biting it. How could you refuse to buy wheat from Oswald? Didn't you listen to me this morning—my people will need it!"

"They're not your people any longer." He leveled a gaze at her. "They are our people." Her stunned expression let him know she'd not yet accepted that fact.

Lorice groaned. "You're right."

"Was it so hard to admit that?"

She gave him a wry look and shrugged. "I told you I'm stubborn."

Gareth nodded. "You've confirmed that fact." She no longer acted like an avenging angel, but worry still darkened her eyes.

"I warned you already. I'm impatient. Until I'm certain no one will go without daily bread, I'm going to fret."

"You would do well to listen and trust, Wife." Part of him wanted to explain to her why he'd kept her by his side and silent most of the day. She'd wanted to assume the mantle of lady of the manor—not for the sake of privilege, but because she'd already mentioned wanting to see to several details and wifely tasks. Instead, he'd anchored her to his side for the sake of her safety. For all of his inquiries and his men's searching, he had no clue as to who had left the knife in her pillow. Then, too, by keeping her virtually silent, he'd eliminated the possibility of her inadvertently saying something that would ruin his plan to shake up the carefully balanced economy of the region. Most murders of highborn women, he'd reasoned, revolved not around love, but money and land. By upsetting the usual equilibrium, he expected the culprit to become apparent.

But I vowed to protect her, and she is already grieving the loss of her parents and home. Better she is angry with me than living in fear every moment of the day and night.

"As for wheat, I refused Oswald's plan to sell grain to Saltzfeld for a logical reason. In the past, I've sold excess wheat to Oswald. It makes no sense for me to sell to him— which he'd asked—only to have him then barter it to Saltzfeld. We'll simply distribute it across the lands. All we have, we hold in common."

Lorice rubbed her forehead. "You allowed me to worry all day about this?"

"You were to have faith in me."

She popped a bilberry into her mouth and shuddered.

"Is it that difficult? Have I given you cause to doubt my integrity?"

After grabbing a goblet and taking a few deep gulps, she shook her head. "The tartness of the berry hurt my mouth."

"You really did chew the inside of your cheek?"

"How could you expect any less when you led me down a merry path this morning, seeking guidance, only to then ignore everything I told you?"

"You are mistaken. I asked for information, not guidance." While she spluttered, Gareth sat next to the hearth and lifted a wedge of yellow cheese. "This morning, did not the second Proverb you read speak of seeking wisdom, yet not being misled by a woman?" He took a huge bite.

"I'm not the kind of woman that Proverb meant! You're—"

She went silent for a second, then started giggling. "You're goading me, just as my father used to tease my mother."

"Sit and eat." He pointed at the stool on the other side of the small teak table. "We need to be of one accord, and 'tis best we work out our opinions and differences in private."

"Your face grew dark at the mention of my father." She folded her arms across her chest and frowned at him.

Gareth took time to slice the capon with his sharp eating

dagger. His moves remained deliberate, but it took no thought to carve the small bird.

"Have you no reply?"

He continued to watch the dirk slice between the joints and said in a bland tone, "I invited you to sit, Wife. Until you obey me, I'll not continue our conversation."

"There's a difference between an invitation and an order." She glowered. "Just as there was a difference between a quest for information instead of guidance this morning."

Gareth ignored her and ate a bite of the capon. 'Twas moist, succulent, and carried the tang of some herb he vaguely recollected from his childhood. The second bite tasted as delectable as the first. Lorice reached for the leg, barely curled her slender fingers about it, and he smacked the back of her hand.

"Ouch!" She dropped the leg and gave him an outraged look.

"That didn't even sting. You have a propensity for drama, Wife. Just as you seem to wish to test my resolve. Sit, and we will share the table. Stand, and go hungry." He watched her take stock of the spread before him and added, "The meal is well worth your cooperation."

"Very well." She let out a sigh and drew closer to the table. Before he could anticipate her move, she sat on the plush white fur beneath the small teak table and swiped the dirk from his hand. She speared capon, then cheese, then more capon, another piece of cheese, and as many grapes as would take up the remainder of the blade. She locked eyes with him as she took her sweet time to eat each bite in turn.

Gareth tipped back his head and roared. He might not be able to fully trust her yet, but he certainly could enjoy her. "Oh, Wife! You may not lead me astray, but you're surely leading me on a merry chase!"

Chapter 8

Gareth smacked his hand against the lintel of a new hut as was his custom before entering, only to hear a disturbing series of creaks. He jumped back and watched the door and roof tumble into a pile of timbers. The past two days counted as among the most trying of his life. A violent spring storm sent mud cascading across the road, meaning Oswald, Bertolf, and Schwartzbein would remain guests until men cleared the path. Lightning struck a barn and burned it and all of the hay it contained. Praise be to God, the fire hadn't spread.

The good news was, Lorice was a woman of duty; the irritating and vexing news was, Lorice was a woman of conscience and duty. As his wife, it was her position to oversee the running of the keep. The responsibilities required much time and attention, but that meant he needed to leave her side to tend to his own obligations. She'd been tolerant of his order to have two men shadow her wherever she went, and she'd even endured being restricted to the keep, gardens, and yard. Unusual dishes arrived at the table, and most of them pleased him, but at midday, she'd changed the recipe for his favorite dish and it tasted no better than the mud-spattered, moldy bread he'd eaten in his youth while out on the battlefield.

His favorite steed went lame, his raven pecked at him this morning, and now this—the first of several huts he'd ordered built for some of Lorice's favorite artisans who would move from Saltzfeld proved to be unstable. He scowled at the master builder, who looked poleaxed.

The master builder bent down, lifted a beam, and cast Gareth a worried look. "The men did everything right. We wanted to get this done as rapidly as possible, knowing how important it is to you. I drove the pegs into this very beam last evening, but they're missing now."

"You've kept your wife by your side every minute." Oswald wrung his hands. " 'Twas remarked on last night that you'd be inspecting this hut today. You don't imagine the same man who put the dirk in her pillow thought she'd be with you so he—"

"Speculation wastes time," Peter said as he squatted beside Gareth to study footsteps in the mud. "I prefer to gather facts rather than go on mere suspicion."

Gareth frowned at the trampled earth. "Too many have been here to determine who did the deed." He stood and ordered, "Reconstruct this. I'll not allow a vandal to keep Ravenhurst in check. We move forward with our plans."

As men jumped to do his bidding, he demanded, "My

ladywife is not to hear of this episode. I'll not have her troubled."

Bertolf shrugged. "She's your wife. It's your business."

Oswald shifted nervously. "I hate to be leaving her here under the circumstances. Mayhap she ought to accompany me back to my keep. Once you determine who is behind these threats, she can come back."

"Ravenhurst is more than capable of protecting his bride and tending his own business." Peter folded his arms across his chest.

Gareth said nothing. He strode back toward the keep. Schwartzbein hadn't accompanied the men out today, and Gareth had ordered men to shadow him. The jewel trader already stole salt from Lorice's home. He couldn't be trusted.

Gareth entered through the great oak doors and didn't need to speak a word. One of his men pointed toward the kitchen. Two dozen strides carried Gareth within earshot. Lorice's voice sounded slightly strained, so he made haste. The minute he reached the kitchen, Gareth scanned for his bride. Dressed in her ugly, mud-colored gown, she sat at the table and mixed some sort of potion.

Schwartzbein sat on a stool, rocking back and forth. Pain etched his features. The cook scolded a maid to keep her busy with the preparations for supper while the guards doggedly remained in the room.

"What's happening here?" Gareth glowered at everyone.

"The trader was clumsy with his sword." Adolph leaned against the table. "He cut himself."

"What were you doing with your sword?" Gareth directed his harsh words at Schwartzbein.

"Making a fool of myself."

Lorice shoved the mug across the table. "This will lessen the pain." She looked up at Gareth. "The stillroom was locked."

"She used silk thread from her embroidery bag to sew up his leg." Haug's voice held malicious pleasure.

"Your guest endured the pain because I couldn't gain access to the stillroom." Lorice kept on that paltry subject as if it carried any significance. Clearly, his dainty bride had grown rattled while seeing to the gory matter. The used needle with bloody floss lay on the table beside the graceful flow of a rainbow of prettily embellished ribbons that spilled from her stitching bag. The contrast underscored her youth and delicacy—such tasks had not yet fallen to her.

Gareth glanced at the bandage on Schwartzbein's left leg and decided to soothe his sweet bride's worries with a bit of praise. "You cared for him quite nicely, my lady." He watched the jewel trader gulp down the potion. "I commend you on your ability to substitute something from the kitchen herbs."

Her face went red as a sunset when Haug cleared his throat. She shot her seasoned warrior a silencing glare.

Gareth refused to allow any subterfuge. As his wife, she owed him full knowledge of everything that happened. This attempt to withhold something made him wonder how many secrets she kept. He'd also not countenance any warrior showing split allegiance. He locked eyes with one of Saltz-feld's most venerated knights.

"She didn't substitute anything, Baron." Haug stood straight as a lance, but something about the glimmer in his eyes set Gareth's nerves jangling. Granite-faced, Haug said without any inflection whatsoever, "Your ladywife picked the lock."

Chapter 9

Lorice pulled the brush through her hair with such force, it would be a wonder if she wasn't bald by bedtime. *And it would all be his fault, too.* She kept her eyes focused on her husband, who stood less than two paces away, slowly coiling her favorite blue ribbon with tulips on it around his fingers. *No one in their right mind locks a stillroom. By its very nature, it needs to be accessible for emergencies.*

She set aside the brush and separated her hair into three segments. *Silver and gold. Silver and gold. Mama, you taught me to braid. You taught me to stitch. You taught me all you knew about healing. You—*

"Did not your mother teach you to honor the presence of a lock?"

"My father never once locked Mama from anything." She twined the sections together with a rhythmic swish that punctuated her anger. "My father trusted his wife."

"Whatever trust I might hold for you is not the issue. Someone's threatened to kill you, and I'll not allow them access

73

to a roomful of elixirs, potions, and herbs to do the deed."

Her hands halted. Hair slipped from her fingers. "That dirk in my pillow didn't keep us from being wed."

Gareth cast aside the ribbon and closed the distance between them. He enveloped her in his arms and said nothing.

Lorice frowned and wiggled so she could look up at his stern face. "You think I'm still in danger."

He didn't respond.

She wrapped her arms around his waist and gave him a jubilant kiss. "I thought you had those men following me because you didn't trust me!"

"I told you, as soon as we wed, your allegiance belonged to me. You're daft to be so happy you're in danger."

She rested her cheek against his chest. "Oh, but I trust you to keep me safe, Husband."

He forked his fingers through her hair and unraveled her plait. "How am I to safeguard you when you pick at locks? How did you learn that despicable skill, anyway?"

"Father Dominicus taught me. He's a fine man of God, but he's a bit forgetful. Many a time, he'd lose track of where he kept the key to the sacramental wine. He's old, Gareth. I'm sure you didn't notice just how old he is because he's so jovial and energetic, but his hands shake. I learned to use the metal clasp on my brooch to open the lock for him. Surely, that's not a sinful thing."

"I'll give you keys so you don't have to display that dubious talent again."

"I don't understand why you leave the chapel unlocked if you fear someone here poses any threat. The Bible is a priceless treasure."

"Few who come are permitted abovestairs, and among them, hardly any trouble themselves to seek out the chapel. Of those, most cannot read, so they haven't realized what the books are. It pleases me no end that you are literate."

"It's turned into a source of vexation to Father Dominicus. On the road here, he declared my lessons in reading and logic equipped me to try his patience. More than once, he's faulted me for making him old before his time."

Gareth chuckled. "I'll take that as a warning."

"Where is worship held, if the chapel is only for the family?"

"Until last year, we had a wooden church at the edge of the bailey. I ordered it torn down because the wood was rotten. A stone church is to be erected in the same location. In the meantime, services are held in the main room of the keep. Our cleric fell ill and is at the abbey. I've prodded Father Dominicus into staying another week."

Lorice slipped away and untied the sash to her robe de chambre. "We'll have your guests at least that long, too."

"Nay. I have men working to clear the road. Two days more, and they'll leave."

"Except for the jewel peddler." She parted the brocade curtains and knelt by the bedstead. "His leg requires a full week ere the stitches are removed."

"He'll go with the others. Until I capture the man who

threatened you, I'll not rest easy." Gareth knelt and nestled her close to his side. "King of heaven, grant a host of Your guardian angels to watch over my wife and allow Your justice to shine on our lands and people. Bless us with restful sleep tonight so we can better serve Your kingdom here on the morrow. We give praise for Your grace and protection. Amen."

As they snuggled in the large bed, Lorice sleepily asked, "How would you feel about having a lion and a lamb carved on our square for the chapel door?"

"A lamb is weak and docile." He propped himself up on one arm and shook his head. "You'd have us lie?"

Lorice patted his chest and murmured, "It wouldn't be a lie. It'll take time, but I'll tame you."

◆　◆　◆

Gareth smiled as he descended the stairs the next morning. The devotional time they spent together in the chapel, reading the Holy Scripture, discussing the passage, and praying, had become a time of union and comfort. God had blessed him with an exceptional wife—firm of faith, intelligent, and lively. The feisty streak she exhibited from the start hadn't changed, but she seemed intent on steering her energies toward worthy pursuits.

Haug met him at the foot of the stairs, covered from head to toe in dried mud. "The road is cleared, Baron."

Gareth gave the warrior a curt nod of approval. The task had been nearly backbreaking, yet the warrior from Saltzfeld muttered not a word of complaint. Under his leadership, the contingent of workers accomplished the goal a full day sooner than Gareth projected. "Join me to break our fast."

The warrior's eyes widened. The honor of the invitation to sit at the high table surprised him.

Gareth slapped him on the shoulder. "I'd rather dine with a hard-working knight whose hands are dirty than an immaculate nobleman with an unclean heart."

Lorice, encircled by her maids and followed by Steffan and Christoff, descended the stairs. Steffan didn't bother to hide his grin. "Lady Lorice, it would appear that Haug's been back home in the pigpen."

"Haug held my father's respect, and Gareth has remarked on Haug's fine service. I'm sure whatever he's done to come out in such a state would be a mark in his favor." Lorice came to a stop beside Gareth and whispered an order to Ilse and Myla, who both scurried off in opposite directions.

"Our guests will be leaving today," Gareth said as she scanned the main room. The tilt to her lips let him know she was as eager as he to be free of their meddling.

"I'll need to arrange for adequate provender for their journeys."

"Do so with my blessing as soon as we've broken our fast. I've sent word to the stables to prepare the wagons and horses."

"I'll be generous," she lowered her voice to a mere whisper as she completed the thought, "so they cannot speak ill of Ravenhurst's hospitality."

Ilse appeared with a ewer of water and a fresh towel. Myla emerged from the other direction with a clean shirt.

Gareth excused Haug, then gave his wife an approving look. Once again, she'd demonstrated the ability to tend to matters effectively, subtly, smoothly.

Perhaps she was right: She didn't need to settle in. She had a way of influencing the people and things about her instead of having to make the changes herself. Such was the mark of a skillful ladywife who could run a household well. The only ones to whom she ought submit were her husband and God.

Oswald chuckled loudly as he entered the room, slapped one of his warriors on the arm as if he'd been told a fine joke, then headed toward them. When Bertolf turned from warming his hands at the hearth, Oswald's visage grew dark. Clearly, the two harbored an odd animosity. Gareth hadn't yet determined the root cause, but such matters had a way of surfacing, given time.

What will it do to my wife when she finally learns the reason why Ravenhurst and Saltzfeld were enemies? I cannot lie and say I don't know, but telling her will more likely shatter our marriage than spoil her memories of her father.

"Ouch!" Schwartzbein protested in a girlish yelp as a warrior brushed by him. His eyes narrowed and his lips thinned. "I should have ordered a tray."

Gareth wondered where the whining peddler procured the gnarled walking stick he now leaned upon. Lorice had warned him Schwartzbein wouldn't take kindly to being sent on his way. His wife was a shrewd judge of character. Her compassion would undoubtedly be a hurdle, though. Today, she'd need to set aside that sympathy because Gareth was determined to send packing every last person who belonged to neither Ravenhurst nor Saltzfeld.

"I'm hungry as a spring bear. Let me escort you to the table." Gareth threaded Lorice's hand through the crook of his elbow and made a point of directing his gaze at Haug. "Come join us. Schwartzbein, go ahead and sit at that table there. You'll want to reserve your strength for your travels today."

Judging from the peddler's dark expression, neither the demotion from a place of honor at the high board nor the order to leave settled well.

Oswald jockeyed to sit at what had become his customary place at Gareth's right side, but Gareth signaled Haug to that stool. The older baron made as if to move around to Lorice's other side, but Bertolf swiftly took that seat. Father Dominicus toddled in and scratched at his tonsured head. He glanced at the subtle scramble at the high board, unsuccessfully smothered a smile, and bumped a warrior over so he could join the knights of Ravenhurst. Though the tables yet lay barren, he remained standing and offered a blessing for the food.

"I don't want him to leave," Lorice whispered in a tight voice as she watched him lower himself onto the bench.

"He's prayed about it. He'll stay until after celebrating this week's services." Gareth gave her a tender look. Because she'd done such a remarkable job of fitting into life here, it would be easy to forget she'd just suffered the terrible loss of her parents. The handful of her men, her maids, and the priest were the remnants of her old life. "I'll arrange for him to visit often, and when he leaves, he'll be sending whomever you request to come live here."

"Haug would be the best to suggest which warriors ought remain home and who ought travel here."

"This is home now," he corrected softly.

She gave him a tremulous smile. "Indeed."

" 'Twill feel more like your home once you've—"

"Settled in?" The gloss of tears in her eyes disappeared and turned into a playful twinkle. Her humor lent a resilience he appreciated.

"That's not what I was going to say, but if the thought crossed your mind. . ."

"It didn't." The smile tugging at her lips dared him to call her a liar. "I'm learning how you think, Baron."

"Your lessons are scant, at best. I've told you I rarely repeat a mistake. I was prepared to think aloud that you'll feel more at peace when the artisans and servants you sent for from Saltzfeld arrive."

"Peace? I thought it might cause unrest if I bring many. I'd not want any of your loyal retainers to feel unappreciated or replaced." As everyone had been seated, Lorice gave a signal for the meal to be served.

"With the way you thank and praise them?"

"I suppose we'll have to discuss what plans you have for the Saltzfeld keep. That will influence what decisions I make."

"I believe in making decisions on a full stomach." Gareth nodded approvingly at the heaping trencher placed before him.

Well trained and devoted, the servants quickly saw to bringing out the food and beverages. As was customary, husband and wife shared a single goblet. It had become a bit of a game betwixt them. Gareth felt it chivalrous to see that his bride enjoyed the first sip; Lorice grew up with the custom that a woman always made sure the master of her home was served first. He slid the goblet toward her. She ignored it. He slid it closer still, and to his delight, she glanced at him and curled her slender fingers about the stem. Cupping her other hand beneath the bowl of the chalice, she lifted it and twisted toward him, intent on tilting it to his mouth.

"Little vixen," he murmured.

Suddenly, she placed the goblet back onto the table and slipped her hand beneath the table to squeeze his leg. Even so, she managed to face him and smile as if all were well.

"What is it?"

"Almonds. I caught the scent of almonds coming from the drink." She tilted her head in an utterly charming way, yet the lack of color in her cheeks bespoke great shock. "There is a poison that gives off such a scent. Someone is trying to kill you."

Chapter 10

S omeone is trying to kill *you*," Gareth rasped back.

"What is this?" Haug leaned inward.

Aware something was wrong, Bertolf did the same. "Baron? Lady Lorice?"

"My wife caught the scent of poison in our cup."

The words rippled across the room. Lorice scooted closer to Gareth. He rose, pulled her to her feet, and tucked her behind himself. Haug stepped back to protect her from the side, and she could feel Bertolf and someone else boxing her in.

"It's that raven he keeps," Oswald said. "Black birds invite death."

"Superstitions like that invite the devil to dance in weak minds," the priest fired back. "This is the work of a wicked man, not the fault of a winged pet."

Lorice tugged on Gareth's shirt. "The villain is after you, Husband."

When he didn't move, she elbowed Haug. "Protect your overlord."

"Take the trenchers out to the yard and burn them." Gareth directed his orders at the steward. "Do the same for all of the cooking utensils and dishes."

The cost of replacing metal items was horrendous. Lorice stood on her toes and whispered over her husband's shoulders. "Empty the pots, scrub and rinse them seven times, then boil water in them for an hour. The same can be done with all of the iron, brass, pewter, silver, and gold."

"I'll take no chances, Wife."

"The priest will pray over them as well."

"Christoff, take this woman to my chamber and guard her. Adolph, Conrad, Fritz—you are all to stand watch. Myla, shatter the pitcher and basin in that room."

Lorice could scarcely credit his orders. *Can't he see the truth? He's the intended victim!*

"Haug, Peter, Steffan—remain here."

She stiffened. He'd ordered Ravenhurst men to guard her and kept the Saltzfeld warriors with him. Why?

Rumbles and whispers filled the hall in a chaotic buzz. Here and there, words rose above the confusing drone— *poison, stillroom, cup, kitchen, marriage.* The words were dizzying enough, but the fierce and outraged expressions borne by the warriors chilled her to the depths of her marrow. *They think I did this!*

Bertolf grudgingly yielded his position as Peter demanded of Conrad, "Mind her gently."

Panic washed over her. Lorice grabbed at Gareth's jacket. "Husband—"

He didn't bother to turn as he rasped his curt order, "Go."

◆   ◆   ◆

Thud. The drawbridge opened with a solid sound. The mighty chains holding it taut didn't so much as dare rattle. Every last warrior of Ravenhurst and Saltzfeld lined the walls and filled the yard. Anger darkened their features.

Wrath boiled in Gareth's veins. The union of the two houses forged a power that changed the balance of the economy and command of the region. Once the marriage took place, the shift was complete. For anyone to murder Lorice made little sense. Either as her husband or her widower, Gareth held both lands and their riches.

He'd been mindful of the threats. Lorice couldn't draw a breath without anyone reporting it to him. He'd not confronted her about the fact that someone had slashed the tapestry of the Nativity she'd been working on. No less than six women whispered that dreadful news to him within the hour Lorice discovered the destroyed piece in the women's solar. Nonetheless, Gareth made a point of holding his wife extra tight that noon. She'd melted into his arms and clung fast, but since she didn't confide in him, he kept his silence. Her persistent doubts stung—would she not let go of her father's lies and come to see the truth? How long before she understood he'd never break honor, never allow harm to come to her? Until she felt she could come to him with everything, he didn't want to destroy the endearingly absurd faith she had that the women who tended her would keep such a secret from him.

By ordering her most seasoned and trusted knights to stand with him as he rid Ravenhurst of all visitors, he wanted to make clear to those who departed the fact that both houses had melded into one. He'd hoped, too, that one of the warriors might think of some minor fact that would allow him to solve the mystery.

Oswald took the sudden withdrawal of hospitality with a combination of mild offense and fatalistic acceptance. "Our houses have ever been allies. I pose you no threat." His wrinkled face relaxed into a smile. "I confess, though, I'm ready to return home. I couldn't turn my back on a woman in distress, but she's your wife and your responsibility now. I ought to be home in time to bring in the harvest and for the birth of my next grandson." He led his men out the gate, across the drawbridge, and toward home.

"Where is your mercy? I cannot travel." Schwartzbein balanced precariously with the walking stick and waved toward his bandaged leg.

"Anyone can slice out the stitches in just under a fortnight." Gareth didn't yield an inch. "You can still ride."

Schwartzbein watched as a stable boy approached with his small cart. Someone had gathered the peddler's few belongings, which now sat in the dust by his feet. He gave Gareth a resigned look. "You mentioned purchasing other jewels for your bride. . . ."

"I'm in no mood to conduct business."

"I'll go next toward the river crossing. Herman sells iron. He—"

"You will not visit Saltzfeld, nor will you cross that land." Gareth watched a flush fill the peddler's cheeks. He couldn't determine whether 'twas from guilt or anger. Neither reaction showed goodwill. He didn't soften his pronouncement or give explanation.

Bertolf and his men left last. His banner, bearing the wolf, went ahead, but the baron stayed back. He kneed his destrier beside Gareth, folded his wrists across his thigh, and leaned toward Ravenhurst. "You wed a fine bride. I pray you'll be able to keep her safe and happy."

"Lorice is no concern of yours."

"Admittedly, I came in hopes of having the woman as my own bride. She's a prize in her own right—aside from whatever holdings were her dowry. Lorice is an honorable woman, and I find you to be an honorable man. Regardless of the strife betwixt your families, it is a sound match." He looked up at the keep. "I counted Saltzfeld not just as a neighbor, but as a friend. Now that Ravenhurst and Saltzfeld have consolidated, I hope to expand the amity."

"I have more urgent matters to attend." Gareth stared at him.

"So you do." Bertolf rode across the drawbridge to his contingent.

Gareth didn't wait until they rode out of sight. He gave a signal. The portcullis dropped with a satisfying *thump,* and the chains on the drawbridge began to strain as they pulled it upward. Even if it meant Ravenhurst never again extended hospitality to a soul, Gareth vowed he would refuse admission to another guest until he eliminated whoever threatened his beloved bride.

♦ ♦ ♦

Lorice decided to sit with her back to the chamber door. She'd been sent here like a naughty child, and once her groom deigned to come up here, she was going to ignore him until he apologized for daring to think she would ever be behind such a vile plot.

Even then, that would be too little, too late. He'd proven he didn't hold the merest scrap of faith in her. Those mornings by the Bible when they'd read and prayed made her feel so close to him. She'd watched each day how he treated the lowliest servant. Gareth had earned not only her respect, but her trust as well. She choked back tears. He'd also sneaked into her heart.

That hurt the most. She'd come to love him, yet he still considered her his enemy—one who would stoop to any level to harm him. She'd overheard the servants whispering about how she could have "discovered" the poison she herself planted to foster false trust. Her husband obviously held that dark suspicion, too, since he'd locked her in here and separated her from Saltzfeld's men.

The leather hinges on the thick door creaked. Myla popped up like a brainless grouse and curtsied while Christoff's deep voice murmured, "Baron." A second later, both were gone.

I'm glad. I don't want an audience when I give him an earful for doubting my allegiance.

Odd, the enormous chamber seemed to shrink just from

Gareth's presence. *Why did my husband have to be such a giant?* He flooded Lorice's senses—the warmth of his being, the essence of his scent, the sound of the single step he took. Masculine. Commanding.

He's going to have to take more than that one step. She curled her hands around the arms of the chair to anchor herself. *He's going to cross this entire chamber, come to his right mind, and beg my forgiveness.* Her knuckles went white with the effort. *After I've been his wife completely and worshiped by his side, how could he doubt me?*

"Lorice." Her name whispered through the room in a rough, deep tone.

I'm not going to turn around.

She couldn't resist. She peeped. He stood just inside the bolted door. He leaned indolently against the wall, his shoulder braced against a corner beam. Missing was the deeply cuffed, black coat he often wore. A thick stream of sunlight slanted across him from the window, illuminating his sword and buckler. He looked like a fallen angel with nothing better to do than waste time.

Lorice couldn't help herself. She shot out of the chair, across the chamber, and crashed into his chest. "I've been scared half out of my wits. How could you?" Grabbing his shirt, she tried to shake him. "At least you finally came to your senses and realized you were the target, but how could you ever consider me a threat?"

He said nothing, and she barely drew a breath before continuing. "Then the hut fell yesterday. Yes, I knew about that.

Don't think I didn't. The goose girl saw it and reported that attempt on your life to me at once. How many other things have you hidden? I'll not let go of you until you tell me. No, I won't. And I'm going to prove to you I'm not responsible for any of those episodes."

"What are you talking about?"

"Oh, don't try to act as if nothing ever happened. I know better!"

"There's no denying things have happened." His brow furrowed, adding to his fierceness.

"But I'm not responsible." She poked him in the chest to emphasize her words. "I picked the lock to the stillroom. Of course I know which chalice is yours, but that doesn't mean anything. Any number of others could have done that horrible deed. And you told me that first night that you believed that I didn't put the dirk in my pillow. You should just make up your mind. You told me—"

He pressed his fingers to her mouth. "Hush. I know you're innocent of any evil intrigue. I sent you here to be safeguarded."

"You separated me from anyone from Saltzfeld. I thought—"

"I am the warrior; leave the strategizing to me."

Tears filled her eyes. "Even though our fathers were sworn enemies, you've abandoned all you were told and believe I've done the same? You didn't think I was behind that attempt on your life?"

Gareth made a derisive snort. She finally let herself go.

She burst into tears. "It crushed me to think you didn't trust me."

Gareth scooped her into his arms. He carried her over toward the hearth, sat on a bench, and cradled her to his chest. "I thought we settled that matter days ago, Lorice. Whatever happened betwixt our parents is over and done. We cannot be accountable for an incident we had no hand in. Wouldn't it be far wiser for us to take the opportunity to heal the breach rather than to constantly refer to it?"

"I'd like that."

"Then let's look toward what can be. With God leading us, we can do great things."

"As long I can keep you alive. You do know I didn't—"

"Of course you didn't." He caressed her cheek. "A marriage must be based on trust if it is to thrive. You showed yourself to be honorable in coming here, though doing so went against all you felt. When faced with the fact that our betrothal still stood, you became my wife. I judge you to be of fiery spirit, but not foolish. You may be hasty, but never hateful. I know you'd do no harm to anyone, but you also seem unable to comprehend someone means you harm. Until I capture that man, you're not safe."

She nestled her cheek into his chest and let out a choppy sigh. "The hut—"

"Is of no consequence. Speak to me about the tapestry."

Lorice closed her eyes and muffled a moan.

"Confess, Wife. You didn't fully trust me, so you kept your silence on that matter."

"I did wonder if you were behind that, but only fleetingly. Then I knew better and decided you were too busy to bother with anything so mundane."

He squeezed her. "It was not mundane, and well you know it. Half a dozen maids ran to me on your behalf."

"You're impossible. You've turned my people into yours. You've earned their trust and allegiance to the point that they won't even hold the smallest confidences for me."

"Since you're to hide nothing from me, that should pose no problem."

"What are we to do, Gareth? We must find whoever is trying to kill you."

"There's not a baron or knight in the kingdom who doesn't have enemies, Lorice. Wisdom demands I trust implicitly those who serve within the walls of the keep. Until I unravel the mystery of who is after you, no one will enter our home."

"I came here, not knowing what caused the schism between our parents. My father refused to speak of it other than to say he'd been betrayed."

"Trust was broken."

Something in his tone made her stare at him. "You know what happened!"

Chapter 11

Her accusation hung in the air. Slowly, Gareth nodded.

"So you've withheld this from me? Where is the trust of which you just spoke?"

Gareth looked grim. He traced her jaw with his hand. "My father told me, but the cause is past. It is of no consequence because the problem no longer exists."

"No consequence? It is a wall between us! You're refusing to extend the trust you value so highly by keeping a secret."

"Secrets, when revealed, can hurt."

"Hurts can heal." She looked at him steadily.

Gareth stared past her, into the fire, and thought at length. Lorice waited. His words finally shattered the tense silence. "A note was intercepted—a love note to my mother." He paused. "It bore your father's seal."

Lorice went breathless, then shook her head in disbelief.

"I'm sorry, Dearling. Telling you that, knowing the pain it would cause—"

She started laughing.

"Lorice—"

She crawled off his lap. "I'm not hysterical, Husband. I'm astonished your father would forsake a deep friendship and believe such stupidity. Papa adored Mama."

"I told you, the note bore your father's seal."

"Then someone forged a replica." She rubbed her forehead. "I cannot believe your father refused to see reason." She gave him an astonished look. "Papa said he'd been betrayed, but he never said your father betrayed him. I just assumed it to be so because they were known to be enemies."

"Yet there was never any blood shed in battle between our families," Gareth mused. "My father never ordered any attack, but he always made sure Ravenhurst stood ready."

"Oh, the irony to discover that they might well have been right from the start in linking our two families in a betrothal."

"You speak of the devotion your parents shared. My father loved my mother. I cannot blame him for safeguarding her, just as I'm safeguarding you."

She folded her arms across her chest. "Misguided obstinancy must run in your family."

Gareth chuckled. "Stubbornness and leaps of logic seem to be in yours."

Her eyes widened. "Lord have mercy! What kind of children will we have?"

◆ ◆ ◆

The next few days, Gareth allowed his bride the illusion of safety. She'd been badly rattled by the ugly events, and as long as he was by her side, he reasoned she'd be secure. On the occasions where he needed to speak to those whom he had collecting information, he made a point of having multiple warriors in the room with her, but gave excuses for their presence so she wouldn't fret. He suspected she saw straight through his flimsy pretexts, but she said nothing, so it became a bit of a game.

In truth, the playfulness between them caused joy to flourish within the marriage. What might have been a disastrous union was becoming affectionate and comfortable. She proved to be a worthy, though completely illogical, adversary at chess. Later, she sat beside him by the hearth and counted stitches on an ornate ribbon pattern as he played a game of Nine Man's Morris with the reeve. Just to confuse her, Gareth started randomly booming out, "Six. Twelve. Fourteen. Fifteen. Nine."

"You made me lose count!"

He winked. "Concentration, Wife. You must discipline yourself to apply your mind to a task regardless of whatever else might be occurring about you."

"Yes, Husband." She bowed her head over the fine threads and resumed her work. Shortly thereafter, when the reeve had taken his turn and Gareth studied the board to determine his next move, Lorice scooted closer. Her scent and softness enveloped him. Gareth steeled himself with a deep breath and lifted a piece. Lorice gave him a swift kiss on the cheek, and he hastily set down the game piece, only to have the reeve unsuccessfully muffle a gleeful laugh.

Gareth's poor move lost the game. He gave Lorice a dark look, and she studiously avoided his eyes as she grabbed her needle.

"Baron," Christoff said from the doorway, "a moment, if you please."

Gareth cast his most charming smile at Lorice. "Sweetling, why don't you and the maids go up and work on that tapestry? You've been doing an outstanding job of repairing it."

Lorice opened her mouth to protest, then must have thought better. She quietly placed her needlework aside and rose. "I'm sure the maids and I can find something to occupy ourselves so you can confer in private."

Gareth stood, gave her an approving nod, and watched her ascend the stairs.

"She's settling in well," the reeve said.

"Aye," Gareth grinned at him. "But don't let her hear you say so."

Much past midnight, after the spies and messengers he'd sent out all returned and shared their meager news, Gareth headed upstairs. He'd hoped the knights he'd assigned to follow his recent guests might hold valuable clues. Instead, they reported Oswald had made good time toward his land and a messenger had brought word that his daughter-in-law delivered a girl-child. Though he'd wanted a man-child, Oswald's first concern had been for the health of the mother and babe. There was much to be said of a man who treated women well. Oswald had protected Lorice and helped deliver her here. His interest in his daughter-in-law's well-being was to be commended.

According to Fritz, Bertolf invited Schwartzbein to his keep. The peddler had given serious consideration to the offer, then decided he'd rather cross the river from Ravenhurst land and deal with Herman first. He'd taken money from Bertolf and was to purchase iron and bring it along with him later in the month.

Was it possible Bertolf and Schwartzbein were in league with one another? Could they have joined to accomplish the mischief? What did either have to gain? If anything, Bertolf's willingness to honor the marriage and simply discuss making a mutually beneficial alliance showed common sense. Had he accepted things too easily? Could Lorice be right? Had he, Gareth, actually become the target? If he were killed, Lorice would own both lands and be free to wed again.

The meeting had lasted long, and the women's solar lay still. Gareth turned toward the master chamber. He opened the door to utter darkness and promptly stumbled over something.

"Lorice!"

"Yes?" Her much-too-sweet voice whispered from somewhere on the far side of the chamber.

"What—" He knocked into something and nearly broke a shin. "Ouch!"

"Oh, my."

"The staff was careless to set such a poor fire that it went out." He hobbled to the side, wondering what he'd struck and trying to avoid another such mishap.

"I thought it rather warm and didn't have the maids light it tonight."

"Well then, why didn't you—" *Thump.* "Argh! What is this?"

"Unless I miss my guess, that was your clothing coffer."

"What is my coffer doing over here?" He stood stock-still, suspicion starting to dawn.

"You wanted me to stay busy and leave you alone, did you not?"

"I didn't ask to be booby-trapped in my own bedchamber!"

"We merely rearranged the furniture."

Gareth extended his arms outward and felt his way in the dark. "You could have left the window covering off. There's a half moon tonight."

"Why, thank you for telling me. I'll have to be sure to plant more peas. They always grow best if planted on the increase of the moon."

"Lorice, light a lamp or a candle." He tamped back a grunt as he banged his knuckles against something metal.

Bedclothes rustled in the dark. She yawned loudly. "But I'm sleepy."

Her voice was closer. He inhaled and caught the scent of her perfume. A slight turn to the left, shuffling steps that ought to embarrass a warrior, then he took a chance and dove. Lorice squealed as the feather mattress whooshed under his impact. He grabbed her and rested his forehead against hers as he growled softly, "What was that all about?"

"Gareth, please don't complain. It was the only way I could get across to you that you've kept me in the dark too long."

◆　◆　◆

Early the next morning, Lorice gave Gareth a kiss as he stirred. Then she rose and shoved most of the bedchamber's furnishings back into their usual spots. She looked at the obstacle course of chests, ornate tables, an embroidery stand—even the fireplace screen—and marveled that Gareth had navigated through it as well as he did. He'd conceded her point quite graciously, and she wanted to set things to rights.

She'd even dressed and sewn a button on his shirt before he rose. Gareth thanked her with a kiss and led her to their chapel, where they spent their usual time of devotion. Lorice felt a special glow inside. This man—her husband—was all any woman might ever want. The distrust had given way to devotion.

Lorice treasured hearing Gareth read aloud from their precious Bible. Though one of them usually read and the other prayed, this morning, he'd done both. He'd clasped her hands in his and asked the Lord for special protection for them and thanked God for the blessing their marriage had become.

"Are you afraid?" she asked him softly afterward.

Gareth considered for a moment, then shook his head. " 'Perfect love casteth out fear.' I love our Holy Father, and know you love Him, too."

She drew in a deep breath and took the chance. "I love you, too, Gareth."

"A man could ask no more of life." He flashed a quick smile that faded just as rapidly. "I hold concerns for you, though. Pledge to me that you'll be diligent, cooperate with the guards, and that you'll always let me know where you are."

"You have my word." *If only he'd declared his love for me, too.* She tried to hide her hurt by reaching up and catching the ribbon as it slid from her hair.

He took it from her, ran his hand down the length of her hair, then tied her tresses at her nape. "Come."

"I'd like to forego breakfast and remain here this morning."

Gareth kissed her cheek and left her.

Lorice moved from the one volume of the Bible to the second. She opened the cover and carefully turned the pages until she reached the Book of Proverbs. Somewhere in this book there was a chapter about being a good wife. She'd study each word, take them to heart, and apply them. Hopefully, by living them, she would win Gareth's love.

The rubrication on the first page of the book caused her such joy. To think that someone had spent countless hours embellishing a single page to the glory of God—it deserved a moment of appreciation. She knelt there and read the verses, line after line, page after page.

The door opened behind her, and she didn't turn. "Gareth, listen to this verse."

"Gareth did not come for you. I did."

Chapter 12

A sense of foreboding hovered. Gareth sat alone through breakfast and tried to identify the cause. He ordered the guard doubled. His uneasiness grew, yet nothing occurred to warrant such wariness. Gareth determined to have Lorice by his side for the day. He thought to order a maid to fetch her, then decided he'd go up and gather the books from both holdings to see if he could stumble across a small fact that would shed light on who the enemy might be.

The women's solar lay empty, as did the master's chamber. Gareth figured Lorice might still be in the chapel. She'd become as delighted by and devoted to the wondrous Bible as he had. That Bible had been a blessing that forged their hearts together when family histories and allegiances might well have made them uneasy mates. He paused for a moment by the carved doors and whispered, "Lord, thank You for the blessings of Your Holy Word and for a wife who treasures it and You. Help us through the darkness and hold her safe to Your bosom, I pray."

He opened the doors and saw the sun streaming through the stained glass. One volume of the Bible was closed—the other lay open. Lorice's shawl formed a slash on the floor. Gareth scanned the small chapel as dread mounted. It was empty.

Gareth let out a bellow.

Maids and knights came at once. "My wife," he demanded. "Where is she?"

No one had seen Lorice. A quick search didn't reveal her whereabouts. "Get every last hunting dog from the kennels." He bent to grab Lorice's shawl from the floor so he could give the hounds her scent. As he straightened, the open half of the Bible captured his attention again. Her ribbon—the very ribbon he'd tied in her hair that morning—lay across the page. One end was deliberately tucked into the center of the fold, the ribbon stretched across the page, and the far end was beneath the cover. The arrangement looked deliberate.

Heart in his throat, Gareth stared at the page. Two columns of forty-two lines apiece marched down the page. What had his wife marked? The ribbon went across the Latin words, underlining the Gothic letters. Gareth read them aloud. " 'The righteous is delivered out of trouble, and the wicked cometh in his stead. An hypocrite with his mouth destroyeth his neighbour: but through knowledge shall the just be delivered.' "

"But which neighbor?" Christoff asked.

"Pledge to me. . .that you'll always let me know where you are."

His words echoed, as did her promise. Gareth jolted. "Her shawl—it was in a line pointing west. Oswald has her."

◆ ◆ ◆

"Let go of me."

"Your father should have beaten you until you learned silence and obedience." Oswald tightened his grip on Lorice.

"My father was a good man, a kind one. The only mistake he made was in counting you as a friend."

"The mistake he made," Oswald sneered, "was making that betrothal. My son was born a full year earlier, and by rights you should be his wife."

Lorice stared in astonishment at Oswald. From the moment he'd entered the chapel, dragged her through a hidden passageway, and held a dirk to her ribs to force her to mount the horse, this man had taken her by complete surprise. She'd never imagined beneath the kindly exterior lurked such evil. At the moment, she wondered about his sanity. She'd gotten a good look at the dirk and knew it matched the one that had been in her pillow. He'd likely used it to slash her beautiful tapestry, too.

Lord, please let Gareth find me. Keep him safe—don't let evil win, but bring victory to the righteous as Your Word promises.

"Yes, you and all of Saltzfeld should be my son's. I'll still see that it ends that way, only better. Gareth will look for you, and when he eventually approaches me for an ally's help, I'll kill him. It will be arranged to look like an accident."

"Gareth is keen of mind and surrounded by powerful knights." She struggled against his tight hold to distract him as she kicked off a slipper to mark a trail for her husband. "You'll not succeed. God will keep him safe."

"Not long ago, you thought Gareth to be one of Lucifer's minions. Had not your own warriors been so diligent, I'd have swept you to my land instead of delivering you to that braggart." His chest puffed with pride. "Everything has played to my advantage, though. As Gareth's widow, you'll bring Ravenhurst as well as Saltzfeld to my family."

"Your son is already wed."

"Aye, but to a woman who is stupid as a sheep. None will think things went awry when she dies from her childbearing." Oswald shrugged carelessly at her shocked gasp. " 'Tis common enough."

Lorice didn't want to hear his evil thoughts, but she tried to keep a conversation going for the sake of the noise. She needed to kick off her other shoe, drop the few ribbons from the purse tied to her waist—anything to signal her path. Then again, even if Gareth understood her message in the chapel, he might not take this road. He'd once told her he had several different routes about his land, but he'd suffered keeping Bertolf, Schwartzbein, and Oswald as guests for an extra day rather than make them aware of that fact. He might need that military advantage one day.

Lorice loathed riding before Oswald on the horse, but fighting him would be foolish at this point. She opened her mouth, but he gave her a blood-chilling look.

"Hold your tongue, else I'll gag you." Oswald dug his heels into the horse, and it picked up speed. Accustomed to carrying a man in full armor, the beast didn't seem to notice the addition of Lorice's slight weight to Oswald's.

She closed her eyes. *Lord, You granted me love. I don't believe You would snatch it away this quickly. Please help us. Be our stronghold and deliverer.*

"That's my wife."

Lorice's eyes popped open at her husband's roar. Gareth sat ahorse not ten yards away, smack in the middle of the road. The raven Oswald hated so much sat on Gareth's leather-gloved wrist. No less than fifty warriors emerged from both sides of the woods. All had their weapons aimed at Oswald.

Gareth's words echoed in her memory. *Stealth is a warrior's ally.*

Oswald yanked the dirk from his belt and held it to Lorice's neck. "Stay back. Back, I say." His mount took a skittish sidestep.

" 'The righteous is delivered out of trouble, and the wicked cometh in his stead. An hypocrite with his mouth destroyeth his neighbour: but through knowledge shall the just be delivered.' "

Gareth quoted the verses from the Bible that she'd marked. Lorice felt a sense of calm envelope her. As she slumped in relaxed assurance, Gareth subtly moved his arm, signaling his raven to take flight.

Oswald, bound by his superstitions and fears, let out a shout and shook his head. He tried to keep the dirk on Lorice, but his agitated moves loosened his hold. As the bird started to swoop, Lorice twisted to the side, slipped free, and slid to the ground. Her feet barely brushed the road when Gareth's mount sped past and Gareth swept her to safety. He clutched her to himself and held so tightly, she knew he'd never let her go. "You're safe, my love. I have you."

Oswald panicked as the raven screeched and battered him with its long, pointed black wings. Startled by the frenzy, the horse reared. Oswald fell, and when the horse ran, he trampled his fallen rider.

Gareth held Lorice's head to his shoulder so she couldn't see what happened next. She heard men moving. "Baron, his wounds are grave."

Lorice shuddered, then tried to push away from Gareth. He didn't ease his hold one bit. "Let me go to him. Mayhap I can help him somehow."

Gareth forced her to wait until he assured himself that Oswald could do her no harm. He knelt beside her over their enemy. One quick glance told Lorice that Oswald wouldn't survive, yet she tried to render comfort.

"Oswald, you'll not survive," Gareth rasped. "Repent now. Christ granted the thief on the cross pardon. It's not too late."

Oswald snarled and pushed Lorice's hands away. "Saltzfeld and Ravenhurst both wed the women I courted. They cheated me out of all I was due." His breaths were labored, yet he fought to speak. "When they left out my son and betrothed you, I knew all would be lost if I could not drive a wedge between them."

"You caused the rift?"

"One letter," he gloated even in his extreme condition. "All it took was. . .one forged letter."

Gareth wrapped his arm around Lorice and held her tight. "Your jealousy caused damage, but 'twas repaired. You can still repair your soul. Call upon God."

"I want. . . ," Oswald gasped, "no part of Him. . .or you." Moments later, he died.

Gareth scooped Lorice into his arms. Sadly, he said, "He made his choices."

" 'The wicked cometh in his stead,' " Lorice quoted into her husband's shirt in a tremulous voice.

"And the Lord spared you, my beloved." He clutched her tightly. "Praise be to Him."

Epilogue

S hall we proceed?" Gareth smiled at Lorice outside the chapel door.

She traced the carving of the vine and the branches on the door and smiled. "Yes. Shall I hold him?"

Gareth clutched their year-old son closer. "I think not."

They entered the chapel and awaited Bertolf and his wife. They'd come with their baby daughter, and 'twas time for the betrothal to take place.

"May this union of our families bring as much joy as mine has to my beloved wife," Gareth said.

Lorice smiled up at him. "I pray our children will be blessed by the Lord and discover this decision was right from the start because we sought His wisdom and consulted His Word."

Bertolf shuffled. "As for that Word. . .we would ask your vow that when our Greta comes here as a bride, you will still have the Bible here for her."

"Indeed. It, and love, are the legacy of Ravenhurst."

CATHY MARIE HAKE

Cathy Marie is a Southern California native who loves her work as a nurse and Lamaze teacher. She and her husband have a daughter, a son, and two dogs, so life is never dull or quiet. Cathy Marie considers herself a sentimental packrat, collecting antiques and Hummel figurines. She otherwise keeps busy with reading, writing, and bargain hunting. Cathy Marie's first book was published by **Heartsong Presents** in 2000 and earned her a spot as one of the readers' favorite new authors. Since then, she's written several other novels, novellas, and gift books. You can visit her online at www.CathyMarieHake.com.

A Treasure Worth Keeping

by Kelly Eileen Hake

Chapter 1

England, 1827

e had a deal!" Stephen Montebourn, Earl of Pemberton, turned from the window to glare at Emma. Grown military men blanched under the force of his gaze, but not his younger sister.

Far from cowering, she met his gaze steadily. Only the telltale red of a blush betrayed her guilt.

"How many are there?" No sense wasting time on anger. For now, he needed a plan to avoid the approaching danger.

"Nine."

"Specific threats?"

Her hesitant pause underscored the gravity of the situation. "Four," Emma confessed apologetically.

"Modus operandi?" Stephen regretted the curt way he ground out the words, but information was vital—the enemy was closing in. As well versed in military strategy as his captaincy had left him, he still found his mother, who'd waged many a campaign on the home front, a formidable opponent. The countess's current mission: to see her only son leg-shackled as quickly as possible. From the moment Stephen arrived home after his father's death, his mother had begun foisting "marriageable" females on him at every opportunity. It constantly ruined his plans.

"You know, the usual." Emma paced over to the window. "Although there are some unknown quantities—"

Their mother sailed into the room, effectively cutting Emma off.

"Stephen, it's time. We need to be ready for them!" His mother's expression could have been hewn from granite as she set herself for battle. She knew very well that the expert he'd hired to organize and restore the once-magnificent library of Pemberton Manor would be arriving tomorrow.

Stephen collected rare and valuable tomes during his travels and had anticipated the coming month. Finally, after a year of tending to the various properties his father had left him and evading simpering misses with frills and gew-gaws—not to mention their determined mamas—he would be able to devote time to his books.

He'd thought he'd survived the worst of her marital campaigns. Early on he'd enlisted his sister, Emma, as an ally and sort of spy in the feminine camp. Unfortunately, Mother had apparently discovered the arrangement and, in a brilliant last-ditch effort, sprung a house party full of eligible females upon them without either of her children knowing until it was too late.

"Mother, I would have been ready for them, had you informed me they were expected."

The countess skewered him with a steely gaze. "I know. That's precisely why I didn't. For this to be a success, you can't be miles away!"

Too true. The impossibility of a dignified retreat loomed before him. As the occupants of the first coach emerged, he eyed them with despair, then blinked. Twins? Did his mother really think that mirror images would increase the odds he would choose one as his wife? These young girls couldn't be his mother's candidates—surely there must be an older sister. . .but no. The carriage door shut behind a woman whom he assumed was their grandmother. He bristled. He wanted no schoolroom miss whose head was full of giggles and gowns. When he decided to marry, he would choose a woman to share his life—his heart, his home, his family.

Then again, he reconsidered as his mother glared determinedly at him, *we could take a continental tour. . . .* But all of that would be very far into the future. For now, he had to deal with the present ordeal of actually welcoming young women into his home with the pretense that they would be welcome company. In truth, he felt they were all assassins with one target: his bachelorhood.

◆ ◆ ◆

Paige Turner leaned back against the squabs of the well-sprung hired coach. Papa, despite his protests against the cost of such luxury, snored softly in the opposite seat. Usually,

Paige bowed to her father's wishes, but in this she'd stood firm. When they'd used a less expensive conveyance to visit Lord Linbrooke a scant two months ago, her father's rheumatism flared with a vengeance. He never complained, but she could always tell when the pain grew. This time, Papa himself decided it was *she* who needed the extra comfort. She didn't bother to disabuse him of the notion so long as it would spare his pride and his joints.

Standing five feet, seven inches tall, Paige knew no one else shared her doting papa's view that she embodied the phrase "delicate blossom of womanhood." At the advanced age of four-and-twenty, she accepted her status as a spinster, though her father seemed determined to ignore social convention in this regard.

Ever since Mama had died three years ago, Papa had immersed himself in the quest to find a suitable helpmate for his only daughter. Unfortunately, his requirements reflected an elevated estimation of her matrimonial worth. Her father's determination to see her espoused to one of the gentry sprang from the roots of his own marriage.

When Papa first met Mama, she'd come in to have an old copy of *Canterbury Tales* rebound. Four months later, their whirlwind, forbidden romance culminated in a quick trip to Gretna Green. Once Mama's family became aware she had eloped with a commoner, they relinquished her dowry and washed their hands of her forever.

Father determined Paige would receive all the luxury he hadn't quite been able to give his beloved wife. The only solution was for Paige to "take her place" in society, although she protested her place remained alongside him with the books and work she'd learned to love, not among the callous aristocracy whose cruelty to her mother cut deeply. He stubbornly closed their rare books and bookbinding shop to travel the country, renovating rundown manor libraries in hopes of finding Paige her husband.

"I know what you're thinking, Daughter." Her father lazily opened one eye to peer at her. "You place too low a value on yourself."

"Oh, Papa." She shook her head. "When will you believe me when I tell you that I'm happy? Besides, you're the only one who doesn't think I'm on the shelf!"

Her father gave a derogatory snort. "You're an intelligent young minx with a sense of humor, and I am not the only one to notice. What of Lord Linbrooke? You two got along rather well. It's a pity there was nothing more I could do. . . ."

Paige's eyes narrowed at the cryptic comment. "For his library, or to push us together?"

"Both." His wide grin faded somewhat as he looked at her speculatively. "It's a pity you won't wear something other than gray, Paige. . .blue or green does you much better."

"Gray doesn't show the dust, Papa. It's very serviceable."

"Makes you look like a maid."

She hadn't weathered this same conversation dozens of times only to lose now. She craved no wardrobe crammed with fashionable garments practically impossible to put on without assistance and just as difficult to move around in.

She didn't need to waste time carefully packing, washing, pressing, and repairing expensive, colorful fabrics.

"Look on the bright side, Papa. At least everything I own matches!" *Even my eyes.* Occasionally, she had to stifle a pang of remorse when she read a book where the heroine had eyes of gorgeous green, sparkling hazel, deep blue, or even intriguing brown. Still, it wasn't as though she'd never had an offer.

James Tuttle, the baker; Otis Boggs, the blacksmith; and even Lyle Jessup signaled interest at one time or another. Perhaps she was just too exacting. So what if the baker thought bringing a bag of flour every bit as romantic as a bouquet of flowers, or the blacksmith's idea of a bride price was his earnest offer to shoe her father's horse free of charge for life, or that the cobbler's apprentice insisted on taking her for long walks in the new shoes he'd made for her—two sizes too small. They'd all make fine husbands—for someone else.

Paige enjoyed the freedom she'd gained as a spinster, and besides, her father needed her. *If* she ever married, she wanted a man strong in the Lord, who would love his family and could carry on an intelligent conversation. Papa would also prefer him to be rich, titled, and handsome. Only a complete dunderhead could think matchmaking mamas any worse than a plotting papa!

◆　◆　◆

Matchmaking mamas are a blight. Stephen stepped into the library for a brief respite as the guests prepared for dinner. For the most part, their daughters were just pawns. And to think, he'd actually been looking forward to the next few weeks! Freddy Linbrooke spoke so highly of Samuel Turner and his assistant, Stephen couldn't wait until they arrived to begin the categorization and renovation of his library. During his military travels, Stephen had greatly enlarged his collection of rare and ancient manuscripts.

There was something about books, especially older books, that appealed to him. He could hardly explain it even to himself. All he knew was that each volume contained not only the knowledge of its author, but also the skill and love of those who translated, scribed, printed, and bound it. Every tome represented the transmission of thoughts, beliefs, and ideas that connected mankind from one end of the continent to the other.

If only men could live up to the ideals found on treasured pages, there would be no war or murder or any of the unspeakable things human beings do to one another. Stephen had long ago made peace with it all, giving his anger and disappointment to God, but he still found himself longing for a world where people weren't so self-involved. To his way of thinking, these books were tangible evidence that man could look at himself and society critically and attempt reformation.

But one couldn't live in books forever, and for now, he had a situation to deal with. How could he avoid the trap of marriage to a woman he didn't, and possibly couldn't, love?

He brightened as Emma strode into the room. She was already nearing nineteen, years past the age when most debutantes made their coming out. Stephen privately agreed with their mother that young girls fresh from the schoolroom were not ready for marriage, but his sister had long passed that stage. Perhaps this house party would provide her an opportunity to hobnob with some of the people she'd meet in London.

He and his sister had formed a sort of partnership since his return. She'd warn him when Mother planned to throw an eligible female in his path, and in return, he'd arrange for her season. He couldn't really blame her that Mama had figured out their partnership and made this last ploy to entangle him in matrimony. Father's death had made Mama aware of her own age, and she was very determined to see her grandchildren.

"You've already met most of the guests, so your first impressions are probably accurate." Emma got to the point.

"Still, I'd like your opinion. The twins?"

"The Misses Pertelote are seventeen years of age, accompanied by their grandmother, Lady Pertelote. To be honest, none of them seems overly heavy in the brainbox, Stephen. I don't think you have a lot to worry about there. They're not mean-spirited or fortune hunters, and they made their come-out a year ago. The only trouble will be telling who is who, since they dress identically, and you don't want to insult them."

Stephen took a moment to think it over. *Well, it could be worse. . . .*

"Miss Abercombe, accompanied by her cousins, Mr. Flitwit and Mr. Ruthbert, is nearing her majority and rather independent. Most think her past her prime, but I believe

Mother invited her because she has the reputation of a blue-stocking, so she might share your interest in books."

Why a woman in her early twenties merited the status of unmarriageable was beyond Stephen. Older women were more mature, confident, and interesting. He might enjoy the company of the bluestocking, but he'd take pains to make sure his attention wasn't misconstrued. He relaxed a bit. He could handle a pair of young twins and an intellectual.

"Why have only two parties arrived?"

"Mother arranged for a rather intimate party in the hopes that the fewer females, the more time you'd have to spend with each of them. She knew Lord Freddy would be coming a bit later after the Turner party arrived for the library, so she didn't invite many gentlemen."

"So she only invited three girls and their entourages?" Emma wasn't meeting his gaze any longer, and Stephen sensed she was avoiding something. "That's a bit odd."

"Well. . ." Emma faltered, cleared her throat, and pushed on. "There is another party."

Something clunked into place in the back of Stephen's mind. "She didn't. She *wouldn't*. Not. . ." His heart plummeted at the misery etched on Emma's face.

"Arabella Poffington." His sister spoke the foul name in a single breath, as though getting it over with quickly would diminish the horror of it.

Arabella Poffington. She was, in a word, a menace.

"And. . ." Emma gulped. "Her father and brother."

"A title doesn't make a man a gentleman!" Despite his

resolve to keep a cool head, Stephen's temper got the better of him. "I can't believe I have to spend so much time with people like that. It's such a waste, and all for the sake of appearances. Who cares? The library. . ."

Chapter 2

Paige didn't need to hear another word. She'd wandered down to sneak a peek at the library and had heard far more than she'd anticipated.

"I can't believe I have to spend so much time with people like that...." The words rang in her ears as she hurried back to her room on the fourth floor. Obviously, the earl was more than slightly peeved that he'd have to rub shoulders with commoners such as her father.

The man exemplified the vanity of his class. That type of thinking prompted her grandparents to disown her mother! How dare he judge her father without having so much as met him? Lord Freddy had urged them to take this commission, citing the new earl's love of books and lack of pomposity. Perhaps the earl was only judgmental of those from other stations.

Lord, she prayed, *I know I tend to believe the worst about those with titles, but I've just heard that the earl holds us in disdain! The condemnation in his tone angers me. How can I look*

*past words overheard when I loathe all he said? Help me to be
strong, God, and not ruin all Papa has worked for. Amen.*

◆　◆　◆

Early the next morning, Stephen sought the solace of his
library. After a dinner full of gossip, titters, innuendo, and
barely veiled animosity among some of the guests, he'd grate-
fully retired to bed last night only to have his sleep filled with
nightmares of harpies—whose faces looked suspiciously like
Arabella Poffington's—chasing him with rings.

As he strode toward his desk, the swish of a skirt caught
his attention. Not again! It wouldn't be the first time a
fortune-hunter had tracked him into an empty room to
claim she'd been compromised in order to force an engagement. Drusilla Dalrumple's attempt two months ago had
been the last. Unfortunately, retreat was the only option to
avoid the trap.

Before her partner could burst in and raise the cry, he
executed a hasty about-face to quit the room, only to run
into his sister.

"Good morning, Stephen! I knew I'd find you here. I
wanted to know why I haven't met Mr. Turner yet. I know
he and his assistant arrived, but they weren't present for dinner last night."

Stephen heard her voice trail off as he paced toward the
bookcase where his would-be fiancée hid. Now that his sister's presence gave legitimacy to the scene, he could confront
the schemer.

"What are you doing here?" As she came into view, he

realized he'd made a tactical error. This pigeon presented no threat. Her gray dress proclaimed her a servant. Was he suffering from paranoia, that he would suspect a maid of nefarious schemes? Servants were trained to be invisible, and he'd all but yelled at the poor girl. She turned, and he caught a flash in her stormy gray eyes.

"I'm sorry. I mistook you for someone else." The apology sounded lame as he found himself caught in her gaze. The anger that blazed but a moment ago faded into politeness, but he fancied he could still detect a trace of it. Why was she in here? The fire would have been lit hours ago, and he'd already overseen a full-scale cleaning of this room in preparation for the library renovation. Perhaps one of his guests sent their personal maid to check up on him. He couldn't very well interrogate her now, not after barking at her scant moments before.

"Oh," Emma interrupted, coming up behind him. "Did you suspect an intruder, Stephen?"

He nodded briefly, watching the maid's face for signs of subterfuge as his sister added kindly, "I haven't seen you before; you must be new. What's your name?"

"Paige Turner." The woman curtseyed. "Sorry to disturb you, Milord, Milady. I didn't think anyone would be here so early."

"Turner? Are you any relation of Samuel Turner?" It couldn't be. Of course, a book restorer would name his daughter Paige Turner. He appreciated the clever play on words, but it faded behind the truth he would be faced with another female. Surely Freddy would have warned him.

"Stephen, you didn't tell me his daughter served as his assistant!" Emma laughed. "Lord Freddy thinks so highly of you, and we've been looking forward to having you and your father look at our library, haven't we, Stephen?"

Grateful his sister stepped in to smooth the situation, he bowed. "A pleasure to meet you, Miss Turner. I regret that I was unable to greet you last evening. I trust your journey went well?"

"Yes, thank you, Milord. I apologize. Lord Linbrooke mentioned how extensive your collection is, and I couldn't resist a quick peek."

Well, well, Miss Turner has an independent streak, as well as an obvious enthusiasm for her work. If she gets past my abominable manners, the next few weeks in the library might well prove more interesting than I'd expected.

"What's your professional opinion, Miss Turner?" The words weren't mere courtesy; he genuinely wanted to know.

She turned her head, and her expression softened as she took in her surroundings. "From what I've seen, the collection is impressive and in fair condition. You have every right to be proud of it, and it will be a pleasure finding ways to properly display it."

Her sincerity touched him. He respected that she hadn't merely flattered his books but had given an honest appraisal that work needed to be done to do them justice.

"Has your father risen yet, Miss Turner?" Emma's voice broke in. "I'd love to meet him."

"Yes." Miss Turner's eyes clouded over again, and he wondered why. "If you'd like, I'll go fetch him."

"That won't be necessary. I'll just ring someone to request that he join us." He pulled the cord, and a maid hurried into the room.

She curtseyed. "You called, your grace?"

"Please ask Mr. Turner to join us. You'll find him in the Blue Suite on the third floor." The maid looked distinctly uncomfortable.

"Is there something wrong, Mattie?"

"Um. . .forgive my impertinence, Milord, but Miss Poffington has settled into the Blue Suite. She claimed it yesterday, saying it's where she stayed in the past. I promise she's still there, Milord. I lit the fire in that suite earlier this morning."

Stephen turned to Miss Turner. "I'm sorry the arrangements were altered without my knowledge, Miss Turner. Would you point Mattie in the right direction?"

"He'll be on the fourth floor, second room on the right-hand side of the east wing." She smiled warmly at the maid. "Thank you."

Stephen was sure Emma's frown mirrored his own. The fourth floor was much too far for an older gentleman to travel every day. The library was on the first!

"A mistake has been made. If it won't disturb you and your father, I'd like to move you closer to the library." Upon her nod, he added, "Mattie, is the Green Suite on the second floor available?"

"I believe so, Milord. I'll see to it." Mattie curtseyed and left the room.

A few moments later, Samuel Turner entered the library and dipped his head. "Good morning, Milord."

"Good morning, Mr. Turner. It's come to my attention that you were placed in the wrong quarters. I apologize for the oversight."

"Quite all right, Milord. There was nothing wrong with the rooms we were given."

"I beg to differ, Mr. Turner. I trust you will find your new arrangements more comfortable and conveniently close to the library."

"Thank you, Milord. I see you've already met my daughter."

"Indeed. May I present my sister, Miss Emma."

"Lovely to meet you, Miss Emma."

"And you." Emma curtseyed. "I'm afraid I'll have to be off. Mother will be wanting me. Things are so hectic, what with the unexpected houseguests who also arrived yesterday. I'm sure I'll see you both at luncheon, so I'll leave you to your business."

Chapter 3

Paige watched the earl's sister leave with regret. The young woman was unaffected and sincere, a refreshing contrast to the earl.

From the snippet of conversation she'd heard last night, Paige had thought he'd be older. This man's discerning gaze took her aback. Even more disconcerting was her own dismay that he'd thought her a maid. The Earl of Pemberton was a walking contradiction—self-absorbed and careless with the feelings of those of lower station, yet polite and concerned for the welfare of his library and her father. Which was reality and which the facade? Even now, as her thoughts roiled back and forth, he led her father to what was surely the most comfortable chair in the room and began enthusiastically discussing the library.

As the next few hours passed with the three of them exchanging ideas and information, Paige decided she must have been mistaken. After all, she'd only overheard the middle of a conversation, and it was the earl's right to question any strangers who wandered around his home. Besides, he treated her father with respect, and there was no denying the enthusiasm lighting his features as he spoke of his books.

Before they'd even looked over most of the extensive library or taken stock of the more valuable pieces, the butler regally announced luncheon.

Paige smiled at the butler. "Where is the kitchen?"

"You misunderstand," the earl clipped in an affronted tone. "Did you eat with the servants at Lord Linbrooke's?"

"No, Milord. Lord Linbrooke was most welcoming, but he wasn't formally entertaining a house full of guests at the time." Paige quickly realized her mistake and tried to rectify it. It wasn't as though the assumption was unwarranted. They had been hired to complete a project, not to attend a house party.

"You are to eat with the rest of the guests and family." His smile erased all doubts. "Be assured your company will only add to the quality of our table."

"Thank you. We'd be pleased to join you," Papa agreed.

"No, Papa," she whispered in protest as her father whisked her out of the library. "Lord Freddy's was one thing, with just his parents and aunt, but a whole room full of strangers? I didn't bring anything to wear. Wait, I don't own anything suitable to wear!" She knew she was babbling, but if she didn't do something, she'd have to face a table of people looking down their collective aristocratic noses at her and her father at least twice a day for the duration of their visit.

"Nonsense. Weren't you telling me how there was nothing

wrong with your wardrobe?" Her father trapped her neatly. "I don't want you worrying. You're just as good as anyone else, and I want you to remember it, Paige."

The earl led them to the dining room. It appeared as though almost everyone was already seated for a casual, buffet-style luncheon.

A servant handed her a plate, and she stared blankly at the table filled with delicacies. Delicate steam wafted from various dishes, the tempting aromas of seasoned potatoes and succulent ham making her mouth water.

"It all looks wonderful, doesn't it?" The earl's sister stood beside her and reached for a bun as Paige selected some fresh fruit, cheese, and sliced ham.

"It certainly does, Miss Emma." Faltering a bit as she looked at the long dining table, Paige was relieved to see her father already pulling out a chair for Emma, then gesturing to the one on his other side. Her father shot her an I-told-you-they-were-just-people-and-they-would-like-you grin as the earl took his seat at the head of the table—right next to Paige.

She began to relax and took a bite of the ham, surveying the other guests. She'd already met the earl and his sister, and the dowager countess at the far end of the table seemed genial enough.

The earl noticed her inspection and began a whispered list of the guests.

"Miss Turner, you've already met my sister, Emma. The fellow to her left. . ." He nodded toward a rather rotund gentleman. "Is Sir Ruthbert, who accompanied his cousin,

Miss Abercombe." The bespectacled young lady, Paige noted with interest, wore gray.

A soft voice to the earl's right carried on the litany. "The next is Mr. Flitwit, Sir Ruthbert's brother." The woman gave a titter. "Such a shame he couldn't pick a better hairpiece. . . ."

Paige was shocked to hear such venom come from such beauty. The speaker boasted golden hair teased into ringlets around a face blessed with sparkling hazel eyes and rosy cheeks. It brought to mind how just the Lord was to look within rather than upon outward appearances.

"This, of course, is Miss Arabella Poffington," the earl interjected grimly, "accompanied by her brother, Lord Arnold Poffington. Their father holds the place next to my mother at the end." His dry tone left Paige no doubt he disapproved of the girl's vicious remarks.

Her brother, Lord Poffington, had the effrontery to peruse Paige through a quizzing glass, then drop it with a dismissive snort. Paige could see why her plain attire wouldn't garner the approval of a gentleman dressed to the nines in canary yellow. Curious to see what sort of father raised children so lacking in manners, Paige saw a sallow man with a haughty expression. *Well, that explains it*, she thought uncharitably. Determined not to sink to the level of a snob, she asked, "And the kindly looking lady in purple?"

"Lady Pertelote. She accompanies her granddaughters, the Misses Pertelote." The Misses Pertelote were twins blessed with blue eyes and auburn hair. Paige couldn't suppress a smile when she realized they were the only ones presented without their first name. Perhaps she wouldn't be the only one who found it difficult to tell them apart.

One of the twins caught her smile and gave a jaunty little wave before turning back to her grandmother. Overall, Paige decided, with the exception of the three Poffingtons, it looked to be a pleasant group.

At that moment, Miss Poffington, apparently unused to being ignored for long, captured the earl's attention. "Now that you've introduced your little friend to all of us, perhaps you'd share her name?" The sweet voice warred with the sharp glance she shot at Paige.

"Certainly," the earl obliged stiffly. "I'm most pleased to introduce Mr. Samuel Turner and his daughter, Miss Paige Turner."

Paige noticed a hint of a smile playing around the edges of the earl's mouth. Good. She loved her name and was glad to see he appreciated her father's whimsy.

"Mr. Turner," the girl murmured thoughtfully. "Odd, but I'm certain I've never heard that name before. And to think, I've practically memorized *Debrette's Peerage!*" She gave another mirthless laugh, and Paige felt anger rise.

"That's quite all right, Miss Poffington. Perhaps you've heard of Paige's mother, Miss Fortescue." Her father's comment fell on fertile ground.

Miss Poffington smiled eagerly, an avaricious gleam in her eyes. "That does sound familiar. If I'm not mistaken, there was a bit of a scandal years ago—"

Paige closed out the malicious woman's delighted recitation

and quickly prayed, *Lord, please help me to hold my temper and not give this woman any cause to malign my father for his daughter's behavior. The way the aristocracy relishes tearing apart those who saw past class issues to find love angers me. You know Mama served You as best she could. Help me to remember that I must do the same.*

"I'm delighted to have enlisted the Turners' expert advice in renovating the library this month." The earl's quick intervention halted Miss Poffington's gossip.

"The library, you say? And I believe I heard the woman's name is *Paige Turner*. Why how provincial! Don't you think it quaint, Arnold?"

Emma leaned forward. "It really is quite clever, but then, one would expect such inventiveness from people who are well read. It is refreshing to have an original name, is it not?" Emma smoothly supported Paige.

"Why, yes. I do prize originality. It is so wearying to see the same old thing time and again." Miss Poffington glanced toward the twins. "To my way of thinking, gloves, shoes, and horses are the only things that should come in pairs."

Paige couldn't take it any longer. She opened her mouth to respond to the vicious comment, only to be silenced by a sharp elbow in the ribs from a papa who knew her only too well. She wasn't the only one outraged by the girl's spite. As the last of the spread was carried away and the desserts brought out, the earl took advantage of the opportunity.

"I disagree, Miss Poffington. After all, two helpings of sweet is far more desirable than one of sour."

Chapter 4

P lease?" The next day, Arabella Poffington peeked up at him through lowered lashes. Stephen supposed she was attempting to look sweet and demure, but the overall effect was closer to a nearsighted squint that anything else.

"I'm afraid not, Miss Poffington. I've been planning the restoration of the library for months now." Her resulting scowl confirmed his opinion of her changeable disposition.

"But Stephen, I already have the servants setting up the croquet field on the south lawn."

How like her to order *his* servants and then demand his approval. "I hope you enjoy yourself." He disentangled his arm from her grasp, gave a slight bow, and left the room. He gladly escaped to the library. Paige stood by a large oak shelf on the east wall, frowning.

"Is something wrong, Miss Turner?" He strode over to meet her.

"Do you see anything wrong with this bookcase?" She

looked at the large oak piece enigmatically.

Stephen scrutinized it carefully, seeing no cracks or splits in the wood. He stepped back to see whether any shelves had bowed due to too much weight, and suddenly, he understood.

"It doesn't match the other bookcases in the room. The stain is a lighter hue." Odd how he'd never noticed before. She certainly had an eye for detail.

"Exactly. It's also narrower than any of the others. Is there a reason why this was added?"

"It's been there for as long as I can remember."

Samuel Turner came over to join them and studied the fixture at considerable length. Stephen watched in fascination as father shot daughter a questioning look and received a slight nod in answer.

"Would you object to removing it, Milord?" Samuel asked.

"No, but why?" He was obviously missing something.

"This wall receives the least amount of direct sunlight. If these shelves were removed, it would be easy to construct a display case for some of the older manuscripts you mentioned," Miss Turner explained.

Her father added, "Since we're going to need very special displays, it's best to order them from the beginning of the process, so they're ready along with the rest of the room."

"All right," Stephen readily agreed, "but I'm afraid my collection is far more extensive than you know. It will require more than one fixture this size. We'll empty this one and remove it today. After the remainder of my books arrive tomorrow, we'll decide how many others need to be removed."

With that arranged, they went about emptying the highest shelves first. Not about to let a lady or her older father upon the rolling ladder, Stephen climbed up. Carefully, he passed the books down for Miss Turner's inspection, and she then gave them to her father for sorting.

"You have marvelous taste," she applauded when he handed her a copy of *The Decameron*.

"Thank you. Of course, some of these have been here for decades, and I had no part in their selection. I'm particularly interested in legends, fables, and tales passed down through centuries." He found a copy of *Beowulf*. Their thumbs brushed as she took it, sending a wave of heat up his arm. He cleared his throat. "Shakespeare and Marlowe shouldn't be ignored, though." He hoped she hadn't noticed his distraction.

"I enjoy the contemporaries, but I must admit, the older the manuscript, the more fascinating I find it." She gestured toward a stack by her father. "*The Rape of the Lock* is wonderful satirization."

"I agree, though if you want something a bit out of the ordinary, I'd recommend John Donne. Especially—"

"*The Flea!*" She spoke the title just as he did, and their eyes met. The shared humor made the time pass quickly as he and Miss Turner enthusiastically took down the plethora of volumes occupying the space while her father began separating them according to subject. They'd already agreed to organize first by genre, then by author as was necessary. Any sets would remain with their fellows and be placed in a separate section. The older and more valuable volumes that were the crowning glory of his collection would fill the new cases they'd design.

Hours later, Stephen had a greater appreciation for the sheer time that would be involved completing the process. This was the smallest bookcase, but it still stood as high as all the others, which stretched to the sixteen-foot-high ceiling.

As they finished the last row, Emma swept into the library, closely followed by a servant carrying a pitcher of lemonade and four glasses.

"Perfect timing, Emma!" Stephen grinned as Miss Turner eyed the lemonade longingly. "How'd you know?"

"I didn't. I simply couldn't take any more of Miss Poffington's croquet tournament. After Miss Abercombe won the first game, Miss Poffington decided that whoever won the most out of five earned the status of grand champion. So at the end of game four, I hit my ball over the hill. I'll have to apologize to the groundskeeper later. They're still searching for it." She looked around. "Why did you start in the middle of the wall?"

"We plan to remove this shelf and install display cases for more delicate manuscripts," Miss Turner explained, accepting a glass. "Thank you."

"The collection itself is magnificent and well preserved," Mr. Turner offered. "The real work won't be in restoration but organization. By the time we've catalogued and separated the books, little else will need to be done. Aside from the display cases, the layout already provides ample space."

"I'd thought we'd be doing a bit more than adding display

cases," Stephen broke in. This was his favorite room in the house, but the ancient furniture gave off an oppressive air. The large walnut desk situated beneath the window boasted sharp corners and clawed feet. Uncomfortable high-backed wooden chairs flanked the massive stone fireplace. The real draw of the room would always be the knowledge and mystery it contained, but he'd like to make it more inviting.

"I want to make this room. . .better. Less depressing," he clarified.

"I'd hoped you'd say that!" Miss Turner burst out. "I know just what it needs." Stephen didn't miss the conspiratorial grin she shot at Emma.

"Wait a minute. I didn't mean lace and rocking chairs or little glass whatnots!" He put his foot down before further damage could be done.

"Credit us with better taste than that!" Miss Turner folded her arms across her bosom, but the sparkle in her eyes let him know she wasn't insulted.

"What will happen if I unleash the two of them?" Stephen sought wiser counsel from Samuel Turner, who smiled and shook his head.

"It's too late, Milord. But I wouldn't worry. Paige always did have a knack for making a place comfortable."

"The key is going to be color," Emma assured him.

Stephen wasn't sure he approved of the direction things were taking. He gazed suspiciously at his sister's lavender daydress.

"No pastels," he ordered.

"I should think not. I said the room should be inviting." Miss Turner scanned the room. "I wasn't thinking it should appear feminine."

He was grateful for her support until his gaze fell on the drab muslin of her gown. Would bland be any better than frills? "What did you have in mind, Miss Turner?" He figured that forewarned was forearmed.

"No pastels, nor white nor black. More along the lines of reds, blues, and browns. I was thinking of maybe a burgundy plush rug trimmed with deep blue in front of the fire, to set off armchairs in soft tanned leather. The tables would be a bit darker, perhaps mahogany, with plenty of candles for extra light." The picture she painted was warm, cozy, and masculine without being oppressive.

The sparkle in her eyes made him wonder why he'd ever thought gray could be bland, and he found himself smiling. Her enthusiasm pleased him. She'd lost the stiff formality of this morning and the tight expression she'd maintained through lunch. He suspected she'd been restraining herself from giving Arabella a putdown she'd never forget.

"Supper will be served in one hour." The butler's voice echoed solemnly from the doorway. Anything else would have to wait, as they filed out the door to freshen up.

◆ ◆ ◆

The next day, they resumed their conversation, tying up loose ends.

"That leaves only one question. A single display case won't bear the entirety of my collection. We'll need to construct some others. Where would you want to place them, Miss Turner?" the earl asked as he turned around, surveying the room in its entirety.

"How much room will be needed?" She stepped back hurriedly as the footmen, having removed the shelves from the bookcase, hefted the emptied shell and made for the door.

"I've several manuscripts I'd like to see displayed. If at all possible, they should be opened, face up. . . ." He let his thoughts trail off as he realized she no longer paid attention to him. While he spoke, she'd made her way to the far end of the room, standing where the irregular bookcase once had been.

"What's this?" she asked as she gestured to the wall. He noticed the small door for the first time as she grasped the handle and turned.

Chapter 5

L ocked." Paige couldn't quite keep the disappointment from her voice. "Do you know what it is?"

"No, I've never seen it before. That old bookshelf stood in front of this door for as long as I can remember. It hasn't been opened in decades."

The surprise in his voice sparked her imagination. After all, it wasn't every day one stood in an ancient manor house in front of—

"A secret room! How wonderful!" Emma's exclamation voiced Paige's own excitement.

"I wonder," Paige's father murmured. "Not to be a wet blanket, but is there another entrance?"

The earl shook his head. "The music room is on the other side. It may just be a connecting door." Everyone followed as he strode to the music room, where silk hangings obscured the wall in question. Paige watched in fascination as the earl began thumping along the wall, searching for a doorframe.

"Don't just stand there!" Paige exhorted as she joined him. It didn't take long to ascertain the wall possessed no door. Her excitement rising, Paige watched as the earl walked the length of the room, then counted the paces again from the hall.

"Well?" Emma burst out.

"After counting the steps and taking into account the library measurements we gathered earlier, I'm certain that is no connecting door. There must be a small room, about eight feet wide. The rooms on either side are so large, it wouldn't be apparent unless someone actually measured. It could be an old storage room." Everyone trooped back to the library to stare at the mysterious door.

He pulled the bell, and another maid appeared immediately. She scampered off to fetch the housekeeper. A few moments later, an older woman bustled into the room, brandishing a large brass key ring.

"What may I do for ye, Milord?" she asked breathlessly after a rather creaking curtsey.

"Do you know anything about this door, Mrs. O'Leary?" The earl's gentle, unhurried tone impressed Paige even as she fought her own impatient nature. So many of the nobles they'd visited hardly even bothered to glance at the help.

"Nay, M'lord. I've ne'er seen it afore. Here are the keys. I reckon ye'd like to see if we con open it?" Affection warmed her Scottish burr as she offered the earl her key ring.

"Thank you, Mrs. O'Leary. This may take awhile." He fingered dozens of keys, searching for those made of iron.

"But if we can open the door, we will have need of light. It would be a great help if you'd fetch some lamps and such." He began trying various keys as she left the room.

Paige held her breath as key after key failed, until she resorted to counting to pass the time. It was either that or pass out for wont of air, which certainly wouldn't do. She would be ready when the door opened.

Meanwhile, Mrs. O'Leary rejoined them. It appeared as though word of the secret room had spread, since she brought along enough candles to light a chapel—each one with its own attendant. The library became quite crowded, and Paige couldn't help but smile. Twenty-two keys after the first, a sort of sharp *snick* sounded, and the earl cautiously pushed the door open. A rush of stale air greeted the onlookers but thankfully carried no hint of damp or mold.

"Candle." The earl reached back without taking his focus from the dark doorway, only to be practically pushed off his feet as no fewer than six servants hastened to light his way. Regaining his balance, he straightened to his full height and turned around. The glare faded quickly as he shook his head and gave in to a grin.

"All right." He accepted the nearest candle. "Thank you for your earnest dedication, one and all. Now, I'd appreciate it if everyone but the Turners would step back. And snuff most of those candles, lest we loose the library!" Everyone obeyed, good-naturedly jockeying for position as the earl, Paige, and her father moved in to explore.

Heart pounding, Paige followed the earl closely. She

raised her candle as high as possible, trying to see everything at once. Instead, she bumped into him as he stopped suddenly, her candle dripping hot wax onto the nape of his neck.

"Watch it!" he hissed, rubbing the back of his neck.

Paige's apology faded from her lips as her eyes began adjusting to the dim light. Old trunks and crates littered the floor, tossed in with old pieces of furniture leaning glumly against the walls. A large chest lay directly before them, the cause of the earl's sudden stop.

"What a mess." The earl obviously didn't share her enthusiasm. Incredible how one family could lock up a room full of possessions and forget them while others lived in simple cottages scarcely larger than this secret room. Paige couldn't contain her excitement. Who knew what they'd find in one of these trunks?

Paige knelt in the dust to open the chest and pulled out a leather-bound copy of *L'Morte d'Arthur*. Opening the manuscript, she noted the date proclaimed it to be more than a century old. The earl strode by, snuffing her spluttering flame.

"I'll have the servants clean the place out. We'll burn whatever is in bad shape and put the rest in the attic," he decided aloud. "Then we may be able to put this room to use."

"You must be joking!" Paige couldn't stop the exclamation, although she practically felt her father's warning glare. *Ouch!* Well, she certainly felt the warning elbow, at any rate.

"I beg your pardon, Miss Turner?" The chill tone belied the earl's polite words. Luckily, she was spared the devastating effect of his expression with so little light to illuminate it. Even so, she could feel the heat radiating from him.

"My apologies, Milord. I just. . ." She gave up as he raised his lantern to peer at her. It was no use trying to explain away her impetuous outburst. Dissembling never was her forte. She sighed. "Aren't you at all curious? I can't imagine finding a room that's been sealed for a century or more only to shovel its contents into the attic and use antique furniture for kindling." Silence greeted her, and Paige wondered miserably how soon they'd be asked to leave as the earl frowned at her.

Why were the upper classes so full of their own importance they couldn't abide listening to the opinions of others, even when honestly and sincerely expressed? She meant no offense. The anger rose even as she desperately tried to tamp it down before she gave their employer a serious reason to dismiss them.

"Please forgive her, Milord. It's my own fault I never made her learn to keep her thoughts to herself." Her papa's voice only fanned the flame. Why should he have to apologize for a comment she'd made just to appease wounded vanity?

"Not at all. Maybe your daughter has a point." The softly spoken words startled her out of her silent reflections. What? She was right? Well, of course she was right, but an earl was admitting he was wrong? She peered up at him in the glow of the lantern, realizing the frown she'd seen as condemning was really thoughtful. He swung his arm around to better illuminate the contents of the room.

"What made you say a century?" The question was sincere.

"I know some of it's old, but I'm not sure it's all that old. Are you an expert on furniture as well as books, Miss Turner?" He sounded genuinely interested rather than mocking, and appreciation for his lack of pomposity flooded her. It wasn't often a nobleman valued her input. Most of them pretended she didn't exist, preferring to address only her father.

"This." She held her find up to the light. "The print date is 1697, Milord." He gently took it from her, his thumb brushing her palm. The shivers racing up her spine owed nothing to the temperature of the room. The light of the lantern bathed his face in a soft glow as he perused the book, showing an expression of wonder.

"It's beautiful. And in the original French." His enthusiasm warmed her heart even as the look of respect in his eyes as he spoke to her roused something more dangerous. She realized she'd been holding her breath as he shifted his gaze to her father.

"Would you mind helping me go through these trunks? Your daughter has a keen eye, and we may yet find more treasures. I know it's not part of the original commission, but I'd like to see this room as an addition to the library." Rather than order them to perform more work, he invited them to explore a treasure trove of family possessions, asking whether or not they had the time and inclination.

Now was Paige's turn to not-so-subtly grab her father's arm. She let go when she caught sight of his self-satisfied grin.

"To be honest, Milord, my joints aren't what they used to

be, and sitting on the floor opening old crates isn't wise at my age. It would be time well spent, though. Since this room has no windows, it would be perfect for your older and more valuable collectibles. We've spoken enough that I feel I've a good idea what you'd like done, so what say you and Paige go through this room while I continue on in the library?"

That's why he looked so pleased. Paige vowed she'd speak to him later about his matchmaking. She should have known he'd jump on the opportunity. Well, he had a surprise coming. After lunch, Emma had confided the reason for the house party, and Paige knew the last thing his grace wanted to do was spend time alone in a dark room with an unattached female. She waited for the earl's response, wondering how he would phrase it. Something like, "I'd really appreciate your expert opinion, Mr. Turner." Or, "You could probably use your daughter more than I. My sister would be delighted to help, you know."

"That sounds like a fine idea to me. Shall we continue tomorrow? I'm certain it's almost time to change for dinner." His deep voice, slightly amplified in the small room, sounded anything but horrified or desperate to be rid of her. On the contrary, he sounded almost excited.

Her brow furrowed as she followed her father out of the room and thought over the situation. The conclusion she reached sent pangs through her heart. Obviously, the earl did not consider her a threat to his bachelorhood. *Is it because I'm of lower station or simply that I'm old and plain?*

Chapter 6

Stephen whistled as he changed for dinner. Things were definitely looking up. Just yesterday he'd decided the next week would be horrendous. It was a forgivable assumption, given that he'd been facing days on end filled with prospective brides whom he thought held no prospects. Of course, that was before he'd cornered a feisty miss whose intriguing eyes discovered a secret room and a valuable volume languishing in an old trunk.

At first, he'd been angry. He'd realized that, even in the sanctuary of his library, he wouldn't be able to avoid eligible females. How had his friend managed to forget mentioning that the talented and knowledgeable Mr. Turner brought his daughter with him?

Her fire delighted him. How long had it been since someone bothered to disagree with him? Not while he commanded his troops, and certainly not since he'd joined the ranks of a society only too pleased to fawn all over him due to a title and fortune he'd never earned. No. This was no simpering debutante or sly diamond he need tread carefully around.

Miss Paige had spunk, in addition to an active mind and an honest streak. Not to mention abominable fashion taste. It would be interesting to see what she'd look like with that heavy, dark hair curling around her shoulders instead of pulled back so tightly. The candlelight in their secret room picked out rich strands of mahogany in her brown tresses even as she glowered at him, brandishing a book.

His gaze fell on the volume he'd carried up to his chambers. One thing was for certain. Even if they found nothing else of value the next day, he would enjoy the search. He could feel the grin spread across his face.

"You look awfully pleased with yourself." Freddy Linbrooke strolled into the room and sprawled on a chair.

"So you had the nerve to show up, after all," Stephen countered lightly.

"Well, I thought I'd give you a day or so to get over the surprise before I showed up." Freddy let loose a grin of his own. "Still, I assure you there will be no cause for disappointment. I'd forgotten what it was like to enjoy an intelligent conversation without innuendo and being rapped with a fan. Paige Turner's a most. . .unusual young lady. Bang-up to the echo, if you ask me."

"I noticed." Stephen quelled a spark of jealousy over the fact that his friend had gotten to know Miss Turner so well. "But you should have prepared me."

"You wouldn't have hired Mr. Turner if I'd told you he'd bring his daughter." Freddy idly twirled his pocket watch.

"Seems you've suffered a bit of paranoia regarding the fairer sex lately."

"Paranoia, eh?" Stephen muttered grimly. "Wait until dinner."

"I already told you she's not that kind."

"And I agree. My mother made other plans."

"Your mama's a worthy opponent," Freddy agreed. "But she won't find an ally in Miss Turner. Not angling for a rich husband."

"Reassuring as that is, you mistook my meaning. Mother knew I'd be here to oversee the library, so she planned a surprise house party—an intimate gathering of eligible women and their escorts." Stephen relished watching as comprehension darkened Freddy's face.

"Stormed the manor, have they? Sorry, old chap." He heaved a sigh. "Bother. Now I'll have to do the pretty, too." Horror widened his eyes as he asked, "Miss Merryweather wasn't invited, was she?" Freddy, as another eligible peer of the realm, had his own share of female admirers. Estelle Merryweather made no secret about the fact she'd set her cap for the wealthy viscount.

"Now who's overanxious?" Stephen teased, then shook his head. "No, but Arabella Poffington wrangled an invitation."

"Well, on to the battle, I say." A relieved Freddy marched out of the room. "It should be an interesting stay."

◆　◆　◆

There'd be reckoning for this bit of matchmaking, Stephen vowed. Now that the numbers were even, his mother had taken over the seating arrangements. Rather than a casual buffet as they'd enjoyed at luncheon, he'd have to endure a seven-course meal. How had she not realized he'd need to be next to the Turners, since they were his honored guests?

He eyed Freddy enviously. Sure, he could enjoy himself, sandwiched between Emma and Miss Turner. To be fair, Stephen himself enjoyed the place on his sister's other side, but the menace of Miss Poffington to his left far overshadowed that comfort. *Two courses down, five to go.*

Stephen winced as Arabella daintily slurped another bit of split-pea soup. He'd withstood cannon fire. How could the challenge of stoically enduring Arabella's piercing titter prove a heavier burden? He wasn't sure, but he knew it to be true.

Silently, he disparaged the social dictates allowing one only to politely converse with the guests seated directly to one's left or right. How long could a man feign interest in his plate? The footman placed a serving of capon in front of him, and he stabbed it with his fork with far more violence than necessary.

He struggled to pay attention as Arabella recited various snide on-dits with malicious glee, but found his mind wandering until the words *hidden for ages* brought him back. He realized immediately what had happened.

Miss Turner had mentioned the secret storage room, and Emma enthusiastically corroborated the report to an interested Lord Freddy—along with everyone else at the table. Despite the convention of concentrating solely on the conversation of one's partners, everyone stilled at the mention of a secret room.

Stephen suppressed a groan. Why hadn't he warned everyone not to mention it? He should have known better. Now everyone at the table began buzzing excitedly. He caught the words *heirlooms*, *treasure hunt*, and *mystery* at random.

"Ooooh, how interesting." Arabella laid her hand on his arm, ostensibly overwhelmed with excitement. "You're so clever to find a secret room everyone else missed."

He reached for his glass to dislodge her touch. "Actually, Miss Turner found it." He wanted to give credit where credit was due, and after Arabella's catty words the night before, he would not pass up an opportunity to praise Paige.

"But I'm sure you were the first one to look inside. You're so brave." He couldn't believe she was actually batting her eyelashes at him.

"Yes," he replied shortly, manfully resisting the urge to spill his water as a pretext to leave the table when she scooched her chair nearer.

"I'd love to explore it. It's so exciting to see things no one has for years."

He briefly considered offering to avoid her for the next twenty years in a gallant attempt to please her, then discarded the tempting notion. Instead, he pasted a concerned expression on his face.

"Why, Miss Poffington, I must say I'm rather surprised. I'd hate to think of your ruining one of your lovely gowns in the dust."

"You're right." A frown wrinkled her brow. "I haven't

anything suitable. Perhaps I could borrow something from Miss Turncoat." She cast a disdainful look at the second gray dress Paige wore in the same day.

Stephen wasn't fooled. If Arabella considered Miss Turner to be competition, she knew her rival's name. It was a deliberate insult, just as was the remark about her dress. Such idiocy made his blood boil.

"Why, Miss Poffington, I doubt that would do." He stabbed another bit of succulent capon. "The two of you are as different as night and day." She preened at the comment, though Stephen thought she would do better to remedy that as soon as possible. This stuck-up wench would do well to cultivate the sincerity and intelligence Miss Turner displayed. True, Paige had spoken before she thought earlier, yet her artless honesty and conviction were to her credit, in sharp contrast to Arabella's blatantly catty remarks.

"Besides," Stephen spoke loudly enough to garner the attention of the entire table, "I wouldn't permit anyone access to the room until we ascertain both its condition and contents. We have yet to find proof that the floorboards are in good shape and the place isn't infested with spiders and other distasteful insects that thrive in such places." He disciplined himself not to grin at the expressions of terror gracing the faces of his guests.

"You know we are in the process of renovating the library. I'll be more than happy to give everyone a detailed tour after the work has been completed." This promise placated even the most recalcitrant of his guests, whose romantic ideals of treasure hunting easily gave way in the face of cobwebs. At least he could rest assured that he and the Turners would be able to proceed with the library in peace.

Mother rose, signaling the end of the seemingly interminable meal, and the women followed her into the parlor as he led the gentlemen to the billiard room. He vastly enjoyed the reprieve until Sir Ruthbert cornered him, asking when he planned to lead them on a hunt. Making some vague response, he headed for the door.

"About time we joined the ladies, don't you think?" When he walked into the parlor, he noted Emma's harassed look as she sat between Miss Turner and Miss Poffington. Miss Turner's snapping gaze betrayed her bland expression as Arabella nattered on.

"Why, it's so interesting to talk to someone who *works* for a living. You know, Father has always shielded me from any of the tradesmen at our home, so I never had the opportunity to interact with someone like you before."

Stephen realized he'd caught the tail end of what must have been an unbearably long and insulting monologue. Arabella excelled at that dubious skill.

Miss Turner pasted on a smile and turned to face Arabella. "And I do not hesitate to tell you, I've never enjoyed company such as yours."

Stephen suspected the words were not intended as a compliment, yet they could be interpreted as such. He had to credit her for being clever enough to avoid falsehood while avoiding a faux pas.

"Now, as I've so much to do tomorrow," Miss Turner said as she rose, "I think I'll excuse myself to get a good night's sleep."

At least Miss Turner could hold her own. Stephen envied her easy escape even as he wondered whether he'd fare so well as she had for the remainder of the evening.

Chapter 7

I can't believe we've already been here almost two weeks! Paige stretched as she awoke. She and her father had established a sort of pattern during the days, although by no means had they settled into anything mundane.

Since the discovery of the secret room, a certain anticipation colored their work. Before anything else could be done, a day was lost airing out the room. Then the process continued at an agonizingly slow pace. The servants, already overly busy meeting the needs of the houseguests, came only in pairs rather than the excited crowd present for what Paige thought of as the grand opening.

Another five days plodded by as the servants scrubbed the walls free of dirt and cobwebs, attached wall sconces to provide adequate lighting, then dusted items and moved them to rest against the walls before the hardwood floor could be swept and mopped.

Paige jumped out of bed, relishing the warmth provided by the fire as she dressed. Finally, she and the earl could begin looking through the mysterious trunks! The long wait hadn't been the only test of her patience. The rest of the work in the main library did not show the typical progress. The sheer size factored into this, but most of the cause lay with the time wasted on social niceties. The servants delivered breakfast directly to their chambers. Luncheon, however, took more time, although since they'd begun adjourning to the cheerier morning room, the company improved.

The three smaller tables provided a welcome change, as Paige enjoyed the company of Lady Emma, Lord Freddy, and Miss Abercombe. Whenever possible, the earl joined them, but Arabella Poffington and her party determinedly waylaid him on a regular basis. Paige couldn't help but sympathize with the distressed and longing looks he sent toward their table as Arabella let loose her high-pitched titter. By now, Paige knew this signaled a cutting observation or direct insult aimed at some poor, maligned soul.

The elaborate multi-course dinners and requisite entertainments, varying from cards to music, monopolized the entire evening. She even lost a precious hour having to "dress" every night for the formal ordeal. What with all the distraction of the house party, she and her father lost almost half of every day! She harbored a sneaking suspicion the earl shared this sentiment with her, although her father certainly didn't mind foisting her into the company of "others of her station."

It did no good to dwell on what Arabella Poffington would say to that idea! Paige shook her head. It didn't really matter—not when the earl and a dozen mysterious trunks awaited her belowstairs.

She resisted the impulse to scurry down the staircase, instead choosing a more decorous pace. Her heart sank when she realized the earl wasn't in the library yet. *Of course, that's only because I was so ready to explore, and he has to be here.* She ignored the small voice in the back of her head that tsk-tsked and remembered all the kind things he'd done.

Long ago, she'd decided she must have misunderstood the first words she'd overheard him speak. The earl exhibited none of the snobbery she'd braced herself for. Instead, he not only let the servants know he appreciated their efforts, but he also called each one by name. He displayed no patience for Arabella's snide comments and went out of his way to make Paige and her father feel welcome among his upper-class guests.

She let her thoughts continue along this vein as she wandered toward the secret room. The earl's uncommon enthusiasm for knowledge and books warmed her heart. Why, she could almost see those fascinating green eyes light with interest—

"Good morning, Miss Turner." The deep timbre of his voice pulled her out of her reverie, and she realized she hadn't been imagining those intriguing depths—she'd been staring into them.

"I'm so glad you're here!" she blurted out without thinking. At his wide grin, she swiftly amended, "When I didn't see you in the library, I thought I'd have to wait, and I must confess, my patience is at an end. Have you already begun?"

"I'm hurt, Miss Turner. I wouldn't dream of beginning our exploration without you. After all, if you hadn't such a keen eye, we wouldn't be standing here. Shall we?" He gestured toward the trunks.

"Yes, please." She resisted the urge to peer over his shoulder as he opened the first trunk. Instead, she walked a short ways over and picked another.

"Hmm. . . Old ledgers and accounting records in this one. How about yours?"

Paige smiled at him. She should have known that he'd share his findings immediately rather than make her wait. "It looks like old primers. Yes, here's an English text. . .math problems. . ." She laughed. "One of your ancestors had horrible penmanship!" She passed the practice sheet to the earl.

"Wait a minute. This looks a lot like mine!" He chuckled. "One of the reasons I became so fascinated with older, hand-written manuscripts is that I could never duplicate them."

Paige vividly imagined a young earl painstakingly copying lines, frustrated and intrigued to find something he couldn't master. She moved to the next trunk.

"You write beautifully, Paige. I've peeked at some of your notes. It's an enviable talent."

"It's more of a skill," she consoled. "One needs a deft hand to restore and mimic script, and I practiced for years at our old shop." She hoped he didn't hear the wistfulness that crept into her tone. If he had, he gallantly ignored it.

"Before we search any others, I should move these aside."

She watched as he hefted the heavy-looking trunk, noticing the breadth of his strong shoulders as he carried it across the room. After he repeated the feat, they continued.

So many choices. Each chest held a promise she couldn't wait to reveal. She reached for another, only to pull up short at his disappointed groan.

"Ugh. Clothes. Why would anyone put clothes in an old teaching room next to a library?"

She reached out to stop him when he made as if to close the lid and move on. "Wait a minute! I never thought you'd give up so easily. You have to look through the entire thing."

He pulled out article after article of clothing. Layers of doublets, gloves, voluminous folds of farthingale dresses appeared. She ignored the I-told-you-so look he shot her as he reached to stuff the beautiful fabrics back inside. Something clunked as he dislodged a hat from the top of the pile.

"What do we have here?" Paige picked it up and looked inside. After fishing out a small black bundle, she tossed the discarded velvet cap toward the earl.

"Ahem!"

She looked up from unraveling the fabric to see she'd hit her target: The cap hung drunkenly on his head and over one eye.

She tilted her head and surveyed him critically. "I suppose we should be grateful your valet has a more refined sense of style than you do." Through teasing him, she plucked it from his head and dropped it into the chest. His deep rumble of laughter caught her off guard. She'd thought his rare smiles to be special, but when he gave happiness free rein, the result took her breath away.

After his laughter had run its course, he gestured to the bundle in her hands. "So, what treasure did you find?"

She hastily finished unwrapping it to discover two small paintings. "Miniatures. I'd say this fellow was an ancestor of yours."

When he looked at the brown eyes and blond hair depicted, he shot her a doubtful glance. She elaborated, "The shape of the nose and chin are similar. It looks like his young bride gave you your green eyes." The lovely woman, rather than staring solemnly as was customary, had been painted smiling. She looked happy and radiant.

"I'll bet these dresses belonged to her," Paige murmured, "and you're right. It's a bit odd they were stored here."

"Maybe not. Old rooms collect the strangest things."

"Like what?" The overly warm voice sent chills down Paige's spine as Arabella Poffington invaded their secret room. Her cloying perfume filled the air, the heavy scent making it difficult not to sneeze. Out of the corner of her eye, Paige saw the earl surreptitiously shut the lid on the chest of clothes.

"We've found stacks and stacks of old papers and ledgers," he answered. "Boring things no one bothered to get rid of but didn't actually want to read. So tell me, to what do we owe the pleasure of your company?"

"Well," Arabella heaved a dramatic sigh, "I suffered an absolutely dreadful headache all night and simply couldn't sleep. No one else is up and about, so I hoped for some pleasant company." The adoring look she shot at the earl made it clear Paige wasn't included in her estimation of "pleasant company."

Something had to be done, lest they be saddled with the harpy for the rest of the day, nay—the remainder of the party! Arabella Poffington would spend one hour in their workroom and consider it open ground from then on.

"Oh, dear." Paige stifled a pang of guilt. *Lord, forgive me for believing the worst of this woman. Maybe I can help.* "No wonder you're so pale. Do you know, the cook kindly made my father a headache draught a few nights ago, and I'm sure she'd be glad to do the same for you."

"How sweet." The fire in Arabella's eyes proved Paige's hunch that the headache was only a pretext to win some attention.

"You do look a bit peaked, Miss Poffington," the earl joined in, the very picture of concern. "I know fair complexions are all the rage, but it won't do for any of my guests to become ill. Why don't you make your way back to the comfort of your room?"

"All alone?" The tremulous note positively rang with vulnerability and demanded a knight in shining armor.

"It wouldn't be proper for me to escort you to your chambers. You really must be ill to so forget, Miss Poffington. I'm certain Miss Turner would assist you if you wish."

"Oh, such a fuss is hardly necessary," Arabella gushed, and Paige felt a spurt of gratitude toward her for the first time. "Your concern is so kind, Milord."

"Of course, I'll immediately send word to the kitchen, ordering the cook to make all due haste with that healing draught. I trust you'll be much recovered by supper."

Paige watched the solicitous manner in which he herded the intruder out of the library with a mix of admiration and, at the sight of Arabella leaning heavily on his supporting arm, a hint of jealousy. She ignored it. She'd never willingly play the role of cosseted-beauty-turned-manipulative-harridan. Why the upper classes rewarded physical charm over kindness, compassion, or intelligence was beyond her understanding. For now, while the earl rid them of the problem, she would practice patience rather than give in to her curiosity and explore the contents of that promising crate in the corner.

She grinned at the earl as he returned to the library.

"I don't suppose," he drawled lazily as he leaned against the doorsill, "that draught Cook is making for Arabella is a tasty beverage?"

"Sadly, though its restorative powers are undeniable, Papa did lament its acrid flavor."

"Well, imagine my surprise," the countess spoke from the doorway, "when I went down to confirm tonight's menu and Cook told me Miss Poffington is ill. The news is so distressing, I knew the other guests would be in sore need of cheering up." The sparkle in her eyes belied the words. "I decided it's a fine day for a picnic luncheon. Follow me."

After our long wait, we hardly even began to explore this

162

room before being dragged away! Paige stifled a groan, and she respectfully followed her hostess toward a dismal afternoon of fresh air and delicacies.

Chapter 8

The next morning, Stephen strode into the library to find Paige staring wistfully at the door to their secret room. Stephen held the only key, and the room was always locked to prevent the likes of Arabella pawing through things and causing irreparable damage.

He smiled, remembering the previous morning and Paige's outburst of "I'm so glad you're here!" Her thoughts mirrored his so often, yet she constantly surprised him. For a routine library renovation, the past two weeks had been anything but dull.

"Good morning." She shot a conspiratorial smile at him. "If we continue this trend of getting here a little earlier every day, maybe we can actually finish! You know, since he begged off the picnic yesterday, Father is almost done cataloguing your collection already."

"Could you believe that picnic took up the whole afternoon?" The earl shook his head in disbelief. The trek to the old abbey ruins made it so everyone returned to the manor just in time to change for supper. The only bright spot was Arabella's absence.

He noticed the daisies Paige had picked yesterday now graced the mantel. The other women snatched up lilacs and roses for their own bedchambers, but it was so like her to leave the simple blossoms where others could appreciate them.

"I enjoyed the abbey, but I must confess to some frustration that we waited six days to open these trunks, and we only managed to get through three before stopping." Paige traipsed in behind him as he unlocked the door. They fell to the task at hand with unbridled enthusiasm.

"Let's try that one." She gestured to a rather long crate resting in the corner under a stack of other boxes.

"We'll have to get to it first." He hefted another box off the pile and set it on the old school table.

Paige couldn't resist peeking inside. "Oh, look at this!" The china doll with its exquisite painted features, beautifully stitched clothing, and tiny ringlets deserved admiration. Paige held it up to catch the candlelight.

"A doll?"

"Sorry, but there are a few things in here you might find interesting." Paige moved aside to allow him room. In moments, Stephen animatedly dug around in what looked to be an old toy chest. He set down a spinning top, some crooked samplers, and a few carved animals before pausing.

"Would you look at this? Someone had a talent for whittling." He drew out handfuls of figures, each about three inches tall.

"What are they? Toy soldiers?"

"Prussian soldiers. Look at the detail! Their uniforms are perfect right down to the last detail. And these chess pieces— Wait a minute. . . ." He dove into the toy chest once more and emerged with more chessmen and a board of contrasting light- and dark-hued wood.

"Truly exceptional workmanship," she agreed. "We should find a place for this in the library."

Years fell away from him as he pulled out an intricately carved, life-size sword. "The one I played with as a child couldn't hope to compare with this." Stephen ran an admiring hand down the dull blade. "We'll have to find a place to display this, too." He placed both beside the doll on the table, which would hold the wonderful things they found. The next crate proved more difficult to open.

"I think Mrs. O'Leary left a crowbar in here, just in case." He watched as Paige rummaged in the corner and emerged triumphantly.

With her hair slightly mussed, a streak of dirt across her cheek, and her right arm enthusiastically brandishing a heavy crowbar, she looked like a librarian warrior queen. If every other trunk held only clothing, it didn't matter. Stephen knew he'd already found the most precious thing in the entire manor. He took the crowbar and worked at the lid until it popped off.

"I think it's more clothes. Let's look at them later and move on." He shook his head as she pulled at the cloth. What was it about women and clothes? Reaching for another chest, he pulled up short at her admiring gasp. He turned to find a real warrior queen, complete with helmet and shield, woven into an intricate tapestry Paige held aloft. She came back into view as she laid the piece on the table.

"You really do have to stop rejecting anything that isn't paper, Milord! Isn't she magnificent?" The same glee as had been evident when she waved the crowbar lit her face, and he couldn't help but smile.

"I've never seen anything so wonderful." His reply had less to do with the tapestry than its champion, but Paige didn't notice.

"I think it's Deborah, one of only two female judges to rule Israel. Am I right?" Her question made him take a closer look.

"I believe so. This would be a depiction of when she rode with Barak to defeat Sisera. She was supposed to be his talisman of God's favor."

"See? Behind every great man is a determined woman." Paige's eyes sparkled with humor.

No self-respecting man could leave it at that. "The trick is that the man chooses the woman."

She chuckled in acknowledgment of his comeback. "Deborah would look marvelous over the mantel, don't you think?"

"Certainly. I wonder who made this and where she came from." He lifted the now-empty crate to make room for the next and found a slim volume sliding around. "What's this? I can't read it, but it looks like German."

Paige came to read over his shoulder as he opened the

book. He caught a whiff of sunshine and honeysuckle as concentration furrowed her brow.

"It's a diary. And you're right; it is German. Wait a minute! Annalisa of Ravenhurst," she murmured and scurried off to one of the trunks they'd opened yesterday. "Yes, that's right." She brought over the miniature of the woman and traced the name on the back.

"It's her diary, and she probably wove the tapestry!"

"It makes sense. Germany has a strong warrior heritage." He flipped through the diary, curious. "Why don't you read it to me?" He handed her the diary, and she perched on the edge of the table next to the tapestry. He caught a glimpse of trim ankles and dainty feet enclosed in worn leather half-boots before she adjusted her skirts. He settled on one of the sturdier trunks as she began to translate.

"Fifth of April, Year of Our Lord, 1763
   Today the Mother Superior called me to her office. After Papa's death, I was certain I'd stay here the rest of my life as I have no other relatives.
   I did not know Papa arranged a betrothal for me until this afternoon. This diary is a gift from my intended, the first Earl of Pemberton, whom I am told received his title in service to his king.
   It is kind of him, and I hope bodes well for the future. He also sent a miniature of himself. He seems a handsome man, not dissolute, so I pray he not be given to drinking, gambling, or any other vice. . . ."

An elusive memory niggled in the back of Stephen's mind. He concentrated, content just to hear the soothing tones of her voice. Then he remembered.

"Wait a minute!" His sudden exclamation startled her, and she almost dropped the diary.

"What?" Disgruntled, she was absolutely adorable. He completely understood; whenever he began reading, the world faded away.

"This is family legend. I remember my grandfather telling me when I was just a boy." Interest flashed in her silver eyes, encouraging him to continue.

"The first earl of Pemberton was appointed in the early eighteenth century for service to the crown. I believe he uncovered an assassination plot. This manor always belonged to the family, but we only bore a viscountcy until then. As the story goes, the first earl, my great-grandfather, agreed to a diplomatic, arranged marriage with a younger German noblewoman whose father bore no sons. It's rather poetic that a woman with no more family was given a new family with a new name—almost like they'd start off on more of an equal footing."

"So the miniatures are the very first earl and his young bride?" Paige clutched the diary in her excitement.

"It looks like that's the case," he agreed.

"How wonderful. To think all of this came from Germany when they were wed." A troubled frown creased her brow. "But why would everything be locked in here?"

"My ancestor went to fetch his bride in autumn, and they

were wed immediately in Germany. They stayed for the winter rather than travel and didn't leave for England until late summer, after she'd born his heir. Supposedly they loved each other deeply, but she died on the trip to England. By all accounts, losing her grieved the first earl deeply, and he never remarried."

"That's terrible." Regret lined her expressive face. "Well, now we know the secret of the hidden room. I imagine he couldn't bear to look at the things that reminded him of her, so he sealed them in a spare room. Such a pity. She seemed like a lovely woman." Paige traced the flowing script with one finger.

"Why don't you read a bit more before we continue looking through the trunks?" he encouraged, loathe to leave the story on such a disheartening note. It made the place a bittersweet treasure—bitter from its poignant past, but sweet because he shared it with Paige. Stephen didn't want her to regret their special room, especially not the time they spent in it together.

Paige began translating again:

"Seventh of April, Year of Our Lord, 1763
My betrothed is on his way to fetch me. I pray daily for peace and strive to give my concern to the Lord, though it is difficult when I think of how I will be marrying a man I've never spoken with and moving to another country.
The tapestry of Deborah I began takes on a new

meaning for me. Since my Great-Great Grandmother Lorice, weaving has been a skill and comfort to the women of our family. Now, the task deepens, reminding me to trust in God's plans for my life. I take comfort that Deborah was another woman the Lord took far away from everything she knew to lead her country to victory on the battlefield.

My marriage is to strengthen my country, and I, too, will be going someplace I'd never imagined I'd belong. I hope to finish the tapestry before the earl arrives. I harbor hopes it will hang in our home someday. I do not bring much to this man save a good name and my determination to be a good wife.

I have a few baubles, this tapestry, and my most precious possession—the Gutenberg Bible passed down through our family for generations. I cherish the thought that I may have children who will use it to further their walk with the Lord. . . ."

Paige's voice trailed off as she looked up from the diary to meet his gaze.

"If he really did put everything of hers in this room, then is it possible the other items mentioned are in here, as well?" Even in her excitement, she didn't articulate the hope of finding an original Gutenberg Bible.

"There's only one way to find out." He followed as she hopped off the table and headed for the remaining unopened trunks.

"This one. I don't know why, but I'm positive." Paige shoved a large trunk off the smaller crate she'd singled out earlier.

"Move back a second."

She stepped back as he used the crowbar to open the crate. Paige couldn't help but notice the play of strong muscles beneath his blue superfine overcoat. When he moved aside, she squeezed in for a better look, her heart pounding.

Chapter 9

They'd found it. She reached for the large object at the same time he did. She tried to convince herself the tingles racing up her spine were due to the excitement over finding such a treasure. He held it as she unwound the old cloth, revealing brown leather.

Beautifully made, the leather-covered studs across the front formed a cross. Awestruck, she touched them, smiling as his hand covered hers. Neither of them spoke, their silence a mark of reverence for the cherished Bible.

Papa walked into the room. "It's awfully quiet in here." His voice boomed around them.

"Papa, look!"

"What's this?" Her father became quieter as he suspected the magnitude of the find. "Can it be?"

"An original Gutenberg," the earl confirmed. He opened it, and the pages fell to Psalms.

" 'Thy word is a lamp unto my feet, and a light unto my path.' " Paige translated the Latin aloud, marveling that they should find this verse so naturally.

The first letter of each chapter was written in red, with exquisite rubrication in still-vivid hues of green and gold embellishing the thick pages.

"Here." Stephen gently flipped through the volume until he reached the verse he sought. " 'Let the word of Christ dwell in you richly in all wisdom'—Colossians."

"Surely the Lord intended for you find it," Papa said softly. He reached out and returned to the front of the volume. " 'The fear of the Lord is the beginning of wisdom: and the knowledge of the holy is understanding'—Proverbs."

"That brings to mind another of my favorite verses." Stephen turned a few precious leaves. " 'A wise man is strong; a man of knowledge yea, increaseth strength.' Also Proverbs. Wisdom and understanding from the Lord strengthens us not only as individuals, but as His children."

"Turn to Romans chapter nine, verses thirty-eight through thirty-nine," Paige requested. She laughed. "I forgot they hadn't numbered the verses yet."

The earl scanned through the book of Romans and finally read aloud, " 'For I am persuaded, that neither death, nor life, nor angels, nor principalities, nor powers, nor things present, nor things to come, nor height, nor depth, nor any other creature, shall be able to separate us from the love of God, which is in Christ Jesus our Lord.' "

"This is one of my favorites because it reminds me that no matter where I am, He is with me," Paige said.

"And He loves us," Papa added. "Let's see if we can find

First John chapter four, verses seven through eight, please."

"No need." Stephen closed his eyes. "I know them by heart: 'Beloved, let us love one another: for love is of God; and every one that loveth is born of God, and knoweth God. He that loveth not knoweth not God; for God is love.'"

The holy words of love spoken in Stephen's deep bass sent tingles down Paige's spine once more. She darted a look at Papa, and his raised eyebrows told her he'd intentionally brought up the subject of love.

"Oh, you know your favorite verse isn't here, Papa. After all, the commandment, 'Honour thy father and thy mother' is in Exodus." She ended the disturbing topic of love, only to realize something. "The diary only mentions the Gutenberg Bible. I wonder if she possessed both volumes, or if she refers to this alone."

"I don't know. There's not another in the crate, and I'd imagine they would be packed together to prevent separation if she owned both."

"But they were traveling. Could it have been to prevent the loss of both if one went missing?" She hated to sound as though she were ungrateful for what they'd been given, for they now held a blessing from heaven.

"We'll write to the abbey where she stayed and see if they know anything about it. I don't see any other matching crates." Stephen still didn't sound disappointed, merely fascinated.

"Paige! I knew I'd find you here." Emma shattered the tranquil feeling.

"Look at this, Em!" Stephen tried to show her the precious

Bible, but Emma would have none of it.

"We haven't the time right now, Brother." She caught Paige's arm and headed for the door. "The ball is tonight, and we must get ready!"

Alarm shot through Paige as she dug in her heels. How could it already be afternoon? "I'm not going to the ball! It isn't my place!"

"Balderdash." Stephen stopped his perusal of the Gutenberg to glower at her. "You're a lady through and through. Besides. . ." His smile banished any thoughts of arguing. "I want you to be there."

"But, um, I. . ."

Emma marched her toward the door as Paige struggled for a plausible reason to avoid her fate. Desperate, she played for time. "It's hours before the ball! Surely we could wait a bit."

"Every lady takes hours for her toilette before such an occasion."

"Why?" The question escaped before Paige could think it over. Her curiosity always managed to find her at the most deplorable times.

"You'll see." With a gamine grin, Emma whisked Paige upstairs before she could utter another word of protest.

◆　◆　◆

"I haven't a thing to wear." Paige spoke the realization aloud as she stood before the armoire, looking critically at a sea of gray cotton and serge.

"I know." Emma's self-satisfied pronouncement held no

reassurance. She opened the door to the sitting room between Paige's room and her father's.

"Miss Rosebrawn will see to it that this isn't a problem. I gave her your measurements as best I could figure them. I borrowed one of your other gowns, but I've noticed they're a bit large on you. Of course, there will be a few alterations needed, so she'll have just enough time to finish it for tonight!"

Miss Rosebrawn held up a shimmering creation of white cloth overlaid with sheer silver.

"Come on, Love. We'll have it on in a trice, then you'll let old Rosey see what needs be done!"

Paige couldn't voice the protests welling up inside her: It was too expensive, she didn't deserve it, they were too kind. . . . The simple truth was, she couldn't stop imagining what it would be like to meet Stephen at a ball dressed in this ethereal gown.

"Oooh, how marvelous!" Emma gave a little clap as Paige twirled a bit.

Fit for a princess, the high-waisted gown fitted closely at the bodice, then gathered beneath her bosom to fall in graceful folds to the floor. Tiny, ruched sleeves, which Paige would have thought simply ridiculous in their frivolity, flattered the line of her neck and gave dignity to her height. *Really*, Paige mused, turning to look in the large cheval mirror Emma had thoughtfully produced, *it's not all that different from what I usually wear. Silver just sparkles a bit more than gray, and it's slightly tighter in the chest than I'm used to, but it's not overly fitted. . . .*

"It's too large in the waist," Rosey muttered, pinching the fabric and sticking in a pin.

Paige couldn't stifle the gasp of dismay at the dramatic change. "No, that won't be necessary. I love it just the way it is." Paige groped in vain to find the mischievous pin wreaking havoc on her dress. "This way it's simply too. . ." For the first time in her life, words failed her.

"Flattering?" Emma supplied helpfully, amusement coloring the word. "Really, Paige. It's neither improper nor ostentatious, though it showcases your figure quite nicely. Why have you been hiding behind those old gray dresses? This suits you far better. I can't wait to see Stephen's reaction!"

Paige couldn't respond, didn't know how to explain that the dress made her feel vulnerable. Simply by cinching in the fabric at the waist, Miss Rosebrawn turned the garment from lovely to stunning. The dress, no longer the focus of the ensemble, served to accentuate. . .her. Although, if she were to be perfectly honest, it wasn't overly revealing, nor did the fabric cling because the overdress skimmed the other fabric.

Coward, Paige chided herself. *Who are you to dictate fashion, anyway?* She remembered how Stephen had at first thought her to be a maid. Then her mind filled with other memories. Stephen, his eyes alight with earnest interest when she spoke. How he never made her feel like a giant when he stood next to her and how he valued her company. *"I want you to be there."* The words echoed sweetly in her thoughts, and she realized for the first time how much she wanted to be there for him. In this dress.

She squared her shoulders, stifled her qualms, and smiled at Emma and Rosey. "It's perfect. Thank you so much for your kindness." Tears swam in her eyes as Emma enveloped her in a hug.

"Here, now!" Rosey pushed them apart. "It won't do to wrinkle it afore you ever wear it!"

"That's right." Emma composed herself. "We'd best get on with it. Please tell Alice to come in, Miss Rosebrawn."

For the next three hours, Paige gave up protesting. The mysterious Alice smeared some concoction—smelling suspiciously of cucumbers—all over Paige's face, instructing her to let it sit as she luxuriated in a warm bath. Before her hair dried, the formidable lady's maid wielded a pair of scissors. Here, Paige wouldn't be overruled. She allowed only a trim rather than a more stylish cut. After her hair dried, she regretted her stubbornness, for surely if she had less hair it wouldn't have taken so long to curl.

Finally, after she'd been primped, powdered, draped in her mother's pearls, and popped into a pair of Emma's slippers, Paige allowed the maid to help her into the lovely gown. As she made her way toward the receiving platform at the top of the grand staircase, she felt a strong kinship with Deborah and Annalisa, all of them women venturing where they felt they didn't belong.

Chapter 10

"Tonight's the night, Freddy." Stephen threw the sixth ruined cravat on the bedside table, narrowly missing his friend. He just couldn't concentrate.

"So you've finally figured out you're in love with her?" Freddy took mercy on him and constructed an elaborate knot.

"I asked Samuel's blessing this afternoon while Emma kept her busy, and Mother gave me the Pemberton engagement ring, looking like the cat who swallowed a canary." Amazing how not even that bothered him. After Emma stole Paige, he'd read their Bible for hours. But every chapter somehow reminded him of her.

He ran across the "noble woman" passage in Proverbs and felt a stab of longing to be the man who gave her children. Flipping the pages, he came to verses about love. "Love is patient. . . ." He felt anything but patient. He couldn't wait to see her again.

"You couldn't do better than Paige, old man. Still piqued I didn't warn you?"

Stephen decided he must be in love, since the I-knew-it-all-along tone of his friend's voice didn't bother him. He left the room to join his mother and sister in the receiving line. His mother must have invited every neighbor within five miles.

Stephen's smile froze after twenty minutes, and his mind wandered. Where was Paige? He'd seen no glimpse of her since Emma had whisked her off. She should have been among the first ones in the receiving line.

Of course, part of her beauty lay in her unpredictability. No other woman he knew would allow dirt to smudge her cheek, traipse around in baggy gray dresses, brandish crowbars, discover secret rooms, enthuse over books, care diligently for her father, and love the Lord like his Paige. Her versatility reflected in those marvelous gray eyes of hers, stormy, deep, lit with the fire of her inner loveliness. A man could get lost in such eyes.

He welcomed the news that this would be the last guest. He bowed to yet another debutante, the shining silver of her gown reminding him faintly of Paige. He smiled into her gray eyes, and his own widened in shock.

Behind this shimmering creature, the epitome of sophisticated elegance and taste, lurked the mischievous minx he'd come to love.

"Good evening, Milord." Her dulcet tones sent his pulse racing as she curtseyed gracefully. He longed to rip the ribbons from her hair and run his fingers through those mahogany curls. The style, while lovely and all that was proper, did not showcase her uniqueness as did the queenly braided coronet she typically wore. How could a man want a woman's hair to be up and down at the same time?

He offered her his arm and escorted her as they descended the grand stairwell toward the ballroom. Tonight, he'd ask her to be with him forever. He knew exactly where he'd propose, too—in the place he'd first seen her: their library.

◆　◆　◆

Heart hammering a wild beat, Paige concentrated on the steps. It simply wouldn't do to fall down the stairs, no matter how Stephen made her head spin.

Papa led her to the ballroom, and she hardly knew where to look. The chandeliers gave a glow reflected in the fabulous jewels and clothes of the guests. She smiled, remembering the first time she'd seen this place, when Stephen began thumping the wall in their hunt for the secret room.

"May I request your hand for a cotillion later this evening, Miss?" She glimpsed at a freckled face blushing hotly as the youth bowed.

"Certainly." As he scrawled his name on her dance card, another fellow took his place. *Amazing what one little dress can do*, Paige thought bemusedly as her tiny card filled more rapidly than she ever would have thought possible. Years ago her mother had insisted Paige learn to dance, though she hadn't practiced in quite awhile.

"My turn." Stephen's voice cut through her reverie, and he snatched up her dance card with unneeded ferocity.

"I may not be of nobility, Milord, but even I know one isn't allowed to waltz unless given the nod by a patroness at Almack's!" Paige felt scandalized and more than a little pleased as he signed his name next to all three waltzes planned for the evening.

"That's only for young debs making their come-out." His words both thrilled her and sent a pang of regret coursing through her body. The pain of not being a lady of his class would be mitigated by the fact he'd singled her out.

"Ahem, Ahem." The orchestra stopped playing as Lord Poffington stepped onto the dais and cleared his throat purposefully.

"I just wanted to make a toast. Let's all raise our glasses to the Earl of Pemberton and his bride-to-be, my only daughter, Miss Arabella Poffington!"

Gasps met his pronouncement as Arabella stepped next to her father, simpering smile in place. "Lord Pemberton—although I suppose I can call him Stephen now," she cast a smitten look toward him, "simply insisted. Thank you all for wishing us happy."

As Stephen moved toward the platform to join his fiancée, Paige made a beeline for the door. Excited whispers buzzed in her ears as she tried to leave without bursting into tears.

"So romantic. . .they make a lovely couple."

"Perfect match, both of high station. . ."

"I'm so relieved. You know, I'd heard rumors he spent far too much time with some little commoner. Can you imagine a nobody being the next countess?"

"Of course not. He knows what's due his station."

Paige finally reached the hall and ducked into the library, closing the door and giving in to the tears. *I'm being silly. I knew he'd never choose me. "Some little commoner," "a nobody." They are right. I would never fit in, anyway. How could I have been so blind as to think he despised Arabella's catty comments? Since when did a man care about words when a woman offered beauty and status?*

She'd have to leave. It would be impossible to see him in their library, their secret room again. She couldn't pretend happiness when her heart lay shattered and her pride sorely bruised. Before she left, she'd see the Gutenberg one last time, though, as a reminder of God's love.

◆　◆　◆

The moment of frozen disbelief cost him dearly. Even as Stephen stormed toward the dais, he saw Paige make her way out the door. He longed to go after her but knew if he didn't expose this engagement as a sham, he'd be duty bound to wed Arabella Poffington.

"You are mistaken, Sir." He used his height to tower over Lord Poffington.

"Oh, no, I'm not." The older man drew his shoulders back. "I have it on very good authority you two reached an understanding after spending the afternoon unchaperoned," his voice lowered, "in the caretaker's cottage."

"Impossible. Such a situation never arose, Lord Poffington. And don't you suppose I would be gentleman enough to approach you if I desired your daughter's hand?"

Clearly, his firm tone gave Arabella's father pause, and for the first time, the older man cast an uncertain look at his daughter. "But I was told two days ago. . ." His voice trailed off.

Lord Freddy broke in. "Inconceivable. Two days ago would make the day in question Wednesday, and I personally can vouch for the fact that the earl spent the day in his library with me, the Turners, and his sister, Emma."

Stephen watched with satisfaction as the smile dropped from Arabella's face.

"How dare you accuse my son of even a hint of impropriety!" Stephen's mother rapped Poffington on the chest with her fan.

"I apologize for the. . .misunderstanding. We will, of course, be leaving immediately. My daughter. . . ," Lord Poffington spat out the word, "has some explaining to do." As they left the ballroom, everyone burst into conversation.

Stephen made for the door, only to be blocked at every turn by guests expressing their relief he'd escaped marriage to "that Poffington chit."

As each person offered condolences, he edged around them, desperately wishing for the first time there was no secret room but instead an adjoining door to the library. He would give almost anything to escape so he could find Paige and explain what happened.

He burst into the hallway and was heading for the library when he saw Samuel Turner just ahead of him. "Wait." Stephen put a restraining hand on the older man's shoulder.

Samuel turned around, shaking his head. "You don't know how bad this is. She heard all those people saying how you and Arabella were the perfect match. I warned you earlier you'd have to convince her that our station didn't matter. It may be too late."

Stephen refused to give up. "No, it's not."

The older man's eyes darkened in resignation. "I'll pray for you both. But so help me. . ." Fire flickered in his gaze. "If you make this worse, you'll hear from me, earl or no." Paige's father crossed his arms and leaned against the wall. "I'll be waiting right here."

Finally, Stephen made it to the library, and his heart stopped. She wasn't here. But the door to the secret room stood open, although he'd made sure to lock it when he left. Stepping over several bent hairpins, he strode in to check on the Gutenberg.

Paige sat on a short stool, traces of tears still on her face, with the Gutenberg on the table before her.

"Paige. . ."

"Don't." Her shoulders stiffened. "I can't hear it, not now. I'll be leaving in the morning. I–I–I wish you happy, Stephen."

His heart leapt as she spoke his name. "Paige, you don't understand. Arabella lied to her father, and they've been publicly denounced. I never wanted her. If you really wish me happy. . ." He knelt and took her hand in his. "Marry me, Paige. I love you."

"I can't." Her voice broke as she began to weep. "I heard what everyone said. They'll never accept me as your bride.

I'm unfit to be a countess."

She looked so forlorn, he wrapped his arms around her and let her cry on his perfectly knotted cravat. "Darling, I love you. You're everything I've ever wanted in a wife. The nobility is a fickle crowd, anyway. Right now they're tearing Arabella to shreds with their words. What does their opinion matter if you care for me, too? The Lord doesn't divide us by class but by the contents of our hearts. Yours is beautiful to me. Can't you make room for us?" He held his breath, waiting for her answer. If she refused him, he could never stand in this room again, never hope for a family of his own.

"I love you, too, Stephen. Are you sure?" Her eyes, once sparkling gray, stared up at him, red and puffy.

He'd never seen anything more beautiful. "I've never been more certain. Be my wife."

"Can we pray about it?" she asked. "I came in here for guidance, and I wanted to see the Bible one last time. I'm just not sure."

Stephen looked more closely at the open page and smiled as he read aloud: " 'Whoso findeth a wife findeth a good thing, and obtaineth favour of the Lord'—Proverbs." He took her into his arms. "I think God's will is quite clear." He slipped the family engagement ring on the third finger of her left hand.

"Let's go downstairs so I can show everyone my treasure." Stephen took her hand as they left the room, thanking the Lord for his blessings. God gave him not only the gift of His Word but also the love of a lifetime. Amidst the trunks of a forgotten room, he'd truly found a treasure worth keeping.

KELLY EILEEN HAKE

Kelly is a recent high school graduate who is fast aspiring to her lofty dreams of writing and teaching by attending college. She is currently majoring in English and spends her free time writing, baking, and playing with her dog, Skylar.

Of Immeasurable Worth

by Joan Croston

Chapter 1

London, 1940

Agust of wind scattered twigs along the sidewalk, then swirled around the ladder as Ann Heydon stepped on the first rung and inched her way toward the top. "I don't like heights," she muttered as her stomach churned, "but Grandpa can't climb up here to do this." She grasped the ladder with her left hand and stretched as far as she could to wipe dirt from the sign on her grandfather's shop. Her weight shifted, and the ladder began to tilt. "Oh, no!" she cried out as she and the ladder headed for the sidewalk.

"Taking flying lessons?" Below, hands steadied the ladder and helped her to the ground.

She looked up into the face of Peter Austin and felt the dreaded blush creep over her. "Oh, no, Sir. The shop sign was dirty so I climbed up to clean it, but the ladder slipped, and I. . ." She stopped in embarrassment as he chuckled at her rambling.

"After you've risked life and limb up there, the least I can do is check the results." He stepped back to inspect her work. "You did a great job!" The sign again clearly identified her grandfather's establishment:

WORTHINGTON'S BOOKSHOP
BOOK REPAIRS AND RARE EDITIONS
NIGEL WORTHINGTON, PROPRIETOR

"That's a relief! I never want to climb up there again!" Ann collected her cleaning supplies and smiled. "You haven't been by the shop for awhile, Mr. Austin. You must keep busy with that book you're writing, or is it those literature classes you teach at the university?"

"A bit of both, I'm afraid." He shook his finger at her, a teasing glint in his eyes. "But how many times do I have to remind you? My name's Peter. After all, we're fellow Americans here in jolly old London. 'Mr. Austin' makes me feel too old." He wagged his eyebrows at her. "Unless you're trying to tell me something. . . ."

She fought to keep the red from her face. "No, of course I'm not. You're not old, but I'm used to calling teachers by their more formal names. I know you're not my teacher, but you do teach at the university and—"

"Hold it!" He burst out laughing. "Don't be so serious. It's 1940. The world's not that formal anymore. It may be falling apart around us, but that's even more reason to enjoy it while we can." He picked up the ladder. "I'm here to see your grandfather about a book. I'll take this in for you."

Ann let out her breath and collapsed against the shop as a woman stepped out of her gift shop next door and bustled over.

"Are you all right, Dearie?" Mrs. Chumley stopped in front of her and peered over her glasses.

Ann brushed off her cardigan sweater. "I'm fine—at least physically. I'm not so sure about the rest of me."

Her neighbor planted her hands on her ample hips. "I saw that handsome young man rescue you. It was so romantic!"

Ann sighed. "I know I'm a dunce when it comes to men, Mrs. Chumley, but why does that man always leave me in a dither? I'm foolish to think he could be interested in a plain Jane like me. After all, he's tall, dark, and handsome, a writer, and a professor, but. . ." She twirled the empty bucket in her hands.

Mrs. Chumley folded her plump arms across her chest. "And who says you're a plain Jane?"

"I have mirrors, Mrs. Chumley. I don't look like the girls who make themselves up the way movie stars do. No pompadour. No long red nails. Mousy-colored hair. I'm just a plain Jane who's more at home with books than people."

Mrs. Chumley shook her head 'til her bright red curls bobbed on their dark roots. "So you think you need to look like a movie star to get a good man. I don't look like none of them, but my Albert says I'm classy." She gave her hair a pat. "And I do have a sense of style, if I may say so myself."

Ann looked at her neighbor's orange dress and bright red

hair and stifled a chuckle. "But you—"

"Let me finish, Dearie. Those women may look all fancy, but they're probably pretty stuck on themselves, if you ask me. Maybe your young man has better taste, like my Albert. Think about it." A woman approached her store, and she hurried away.

As Ann turned, Peter stepped out of her grandfather's shop, waved, and walked briskly toward the bus stop. With a sigh, she entered the store, her heart thumping. There were no customers, so she was startled when suddenly a raucous voice screamed and ranted from the workroom at the back of the building. When it paused, a crowd roared, *"Sieg heil! Sieg heil! Sieg heil!"* She knew her grandfather was glued to his radio, and she gave a shudder as the harangue continued. She didn't understand German, but from the sound of Hitler's voice, she knew he wasn't saying anything good. As she picked up a feather duster, the voice disappeared and her grandfather approached the counter, bristling with anger.

"There's no hope of a peace treaty?" she ventured.

He spread his hands on the counter and stood silently a moment. "No, my dear, Hitler is a liar who thinks he can grab whatever he wants." He gave a snort. "He talks about peace; then in the past two years, he's taken the Rhineland, Austria, Czechoslovakia, and Poland. In April he invaded Norway and Denmark, and now a month later he's taken Belgium, Holland, and Luxembourg with that Blitzkrieg of his." He shook his white head slowly and pounded his fist on the counter. "And mark my word. By the end of June, he'll have France. How long 'til we're not safe here in London?"

Ann watched the pain in her grandfather's face as he recited the litany of Hitler's conquests. She braced herself for what she knew was coming next.

"We've talked about this before, Ann. You must go back to America. It's not safe here." His voice was firm. "You have to leave while you can still get out."

Ann moved the feather duster back and forth over the counter. "I won't leave you over here alone, Grandpa, and that's final. Besides, why should I run away? You've always assured me God's with us."

He sighed and rubbed his hands together slowly. "And that He is, my dear, but He also gave us brains and expects us to use them. We're not to act foolishly and wait for Him to bail us out." He picked a book off the counter and returned it to a shelf.

"England's my home country, Ann. Those years I spent in America as a young man were wonderful, but it wasn't home." His face took on a nostalgic look. "That's where I met your grandmother. She returned home with me, and we lived here all those years. But when our daughter grew up, she wanted to see America, so across the ocean she went. When she met your father there, she decided to stay, and you were born American. So, we each have our homeland." He looked at her with a sad smile.

"But Grandpa, there's tradition. I have to find the love of my life in another country as you and Mom did. Don't send me away now. Please. Wait to see what happens. Maybe this war will be over soon. Hitler can't take over the whole world!"

He shook his head. "You understand so little of what's going on. We'll talk about this again. I have a book to repair; I'll be in the workroom."

Ann leaned on the counter and stared out the window. "I won't leave Grandpa," she muttered, "and I can't lose my chance to have the great adventure of my life and find the man of my dreams. After all, I'm twenty-five years old already. Nothing will make me give up and go home!"

Chapter 2

Peter Austin leaned back in the chair and rubbed his neck, enjoying the warmth of the sun's rays streaming through the windows of his flat. He sighed and tapped his pencil on the manuscript before him. He needed to do more research for his book on England in the Middle Ages, but with the country at war, it was no longer a matter of *if* he went home but *when*.

He twirled the pencil between his fingers. At the rate students were leaving school to help the war effort, he wouldn't have enough people in his classes to keep teaching here much longer. He should collect the information for his book and do the writing back home in America.

He walked to the window and stared out at the city he'd come to love. He could feel its history and tradition all around him. If he left now, how many valuable books and documents would be sacrificed to finance the Nazi cause or be destroyed when war came to London? He couldn't desert his colleagues and the efforts they were making to preserve things that couldn't be replaced.

Another image, this one soft and sweet, floated through his mind. He loved the way Ann's face turned pink at the least little thing, and he chuckled at her tendency to ramble when she was flustered, but once they began discussing books, she was relaxed and fun. Then he'd turn around and she'd start acting so. . .well, so strange—almost as if she really didn't like him. If he went home, he'd never know why she kept popping into his mind.

He walked back to the desk and stared at the manuscript. He was stuck without the material Nigel had ordered for him. If he stopped by the bookstore, it might be in—and maybe he'd have a chance to talk to Ann. He grabbed his tweed jacket and headed for the bus stop.

◆　◆　◆

Customers were in and out of the bookstore all morning, and it was midafternoon before Ann climbed the steps to the upstairs apartment she shared with her grandfather to make a list of groceries she hoped to buy. Planning meals had become a challenge with so many items either rationed or in short supply. She put the list in her purse and hurried down the stairs, poking her head into the workroom. "I'm going shopping, Grandpa. I'll stop by the bakery to see if Mrs. Wilson saved you any sweets."

He nodded and turned back to his work.

She stepped outside and slowed her pace, taking a deep breath and enjoying the warble of birds and fragrance of late spring blossoms that brought a touch of home to a country girl in the big city. She glanced up to check a street sign only to find it gone. Signposts and street names had been taken down to confuse German forces should they invade the country, more evidence that life wasn't normal these days.

She turned the corner and faced the inevitable line. With shortages, lines grew long as people waited in hopes of purchasing the items they needed. Somehow the wait seemed more tolerable when she thought of them as queues. She smiled to herself at the English expression.

Back on the sidewalk with her purchases, her ration books tucked in her purse, the air took on a sudden chill as she stared at sandbags piled high to form a protective wall in front of the post office and the bank. The city was changing from a place of adventure to one of uncertainty. She gave a shudder.

She needed a few moments to refresh her spirits, so she headed for an area of the park across the street adjacent to St. Andrew's churchyard. The park seemed eerily quiet now. No children played and shouted. A year ago, most of them had been sent to homes in northern England, where they would be safer should the Germans attack. Women were working up to sixty hours a week in the war industry.

Ann entered a sheltered corner near the churchyard, set her packages down, and plopped on a bench that offered a view of green grass and flowers. The rest of the park was marred by trenches dug to serve as quick shelters if German planes attacked, but in this corner, irises bloomed in shades of purple and lavender, and dandelions brought bits of sunshine to the lawn. At least here in her sanctuary the world seemed the same.

"Is this seat taken?"

"Oh!" Startled, Ann looked up to see Peter smiling at her. She shook her head and tried not to blush as he settled down on the bench beside her.

"I often stop here on my way to the bookshop. I'm pleased we have the same tastes." He paused and sniffed the air. "Hmm, speaking of tastes, either I smell something tasty, or you have very unusual perfume. You've been searching out some sweets, I believe." He leaned over and sniffed the bag she had set beside her.

"No, it's my new perfume," she teased. "It must have leaked. Besides, I'd never tell you if I had goodies in there. I've seen how you and Grandpa devour a tin of biscuits!" She moved the bag to the other side of her.

"Oh, ho, trying to sound English, are we? That smells like my favorite cookies to me!" He tried to reach around her for the sack. "I'll take a look to be sure. Scarce as sweets are these days, I may have to walk you home to protect them."

"Oh, no, you don't!" Ann grinned and slapped at his hand. "Mrs. Wilson has a soft spot for Grandpa and saves him treats whenever she can. If I let you see them, there won't be anything left!" She put her hand on the bag.

Peter hung his head and gave a dejected sigh, then winked at her. "It's good to see you relax and have a little fun."

The smile quickly left her face. "There's something wrong with me? How can you be so cheery when the world's falling apart, *Mr*. Austin? When I came over here, I didn't expect this." She looked down at her hands. "I know that sounds selfish when countries are being overrun by the Nazis, but I loved it here so much the way things were."

Peter leaned back and crossed his legs. He looked over at her and spoke quietly. "I do understand, Ann. Don't forget; I've come to love England, too. I'm not through with my research, so I try to hang on a little longer. I love my work, and I like the friends I've made here, especially two in a little bookshop I frequent." He patted her hand and gave her a lopsided grin.

Ann could feel the color rise in her face and took a deep breath. "Seriously, Peter, do you think Germany will attack London?"

He reached down to pick a blade of grass and twisted it between his fingers. "The signs are all around, Ann, and they're not hopeful. We're under a blackout every night. Street signs are gone. Think how long it's been since you've heard a church bell. Headlights have to be covered so no light shows at night." He looked over at her. "I don't want to frighten you, but you need to be aware of what's going on."

Ann nodded without looking at him. Her fingers played with the top of the bag.

"You do know what's happening at Dunkirk, don't you?" His tone was somber.

"Some. I guess I try to ignore as much as I can. As if that will make it go away, I suppose." She shrugged.

He paused a moment. "Ann, the Germans are taking

France. They've pushed the French and English forces to the coastal areas around Dunkirk, right across the English Channel from us. The troops are trying to defend themselves, but they won't last. There's a big operation underway to evacuate them. Fishermen in their boats and men in every kind of vessel that will float are risking their lives to bring these men home."

"But the channel separates us from the continent. Isn't that a good protection?"

Peter slapped his hand against his forehead. "You do wear blinders! Today's wars aren't like those of years ago, Ann. You read a lot. You should know that. Planes can fly over the English Channel in twenty minutes, and guns fire long distances today. France thought its Maginot Line of defense fortifications would protect them from the Nazis, but those concrete bunkers and the wooded hill country of the Ardennes were nothing to Germany's planes and tanks. By the end of June, France will no longer be free, and that's only a few weeks away. Then we'll be looking right across that channel at German troops and planes."

"If you're trying to make me feel selfish and ignorant, it's working. I know wishing won't make things the way I want—"

Suddenly the piercing wail of an air-raid siren drowned out her words. Peter grabbed her hand as she reached to pick up the groceries. "Leave everything," he shouted above the noise. "We need to get in the church!" They ran to the small old building and pulled the door open. The interior was dim and cool, but as their eyes adjusted, they could see people sitting here and there in the pews with their heads bowed.

A side door opened, and the vicar hurried into the sanctuary. "Follow me to the basement," he called out. "You'll be safer down there." He held the door while people rushed past him. Ann and Peter were halfway down the aisle when the all-clear signal sounded. A sigh of relief passed through the church as people came back into the sanctuary and stopped to gather items they had left in the pews.

Peter followed Ann from the church, still holding her hand as she tried to stop trembling. "Are you all right?" He looked at her with concern. "It was probably just a drill."

She nodded, enjoying the security in Peter's hand covering hers.

"After we pick up your groceries, I'll walk you back to the shop." He led her to the bench where they had left her packages. He was loading his arms when she reached over to grab the bag with her grandfather's sweets. "Hey, don't you trust me?" He looked at her, crestfallen.

Ann shook her head. "Not on your life. That would be like asking the fox to give the chicken a lift home. I'm carrying these, *Mr.* Austin!"

Peter chuckled. "I guess I'll have to consider your company my sweet treat for the day then." He shifted the bags of groceries and grinned at her, and she felt her cheeks flush.

The breeze was soft as they walked along the sidewalk. Lofty chestnut trees arched over the walk, leaving it dappled with sunshine. Ann looked up at the sturdy branches. "Just think of the stories they could tell."

Peter's eyes followed her gaze. "They've survived for many years. That's a hopeful sign."

Ann watched the changing patterns of the shadows on the sidewalk. "When I sat in the park, everything was so peaceful and beautiful that I had one of my *now* moments— like I was completely in the present and it would never change. It was so real." She smiled sheepishly. "That probably sounds stupid."

Peter stopped at the curb and glanced down the street before starting across. He smiled at her. "Not at all. I've always thought you had poetry in your soul."

Ann stepped onto the sidewalk and looked up at the sky. "It doesn't happen often, but sometimes the moment seems to spread and connect with other times in my life when I've had that same feeling. Then they run together, and it becomes so real the rest of the world fades and becomes unreal. I'd like to stay in that moment forever." She laughed softly. "Grandpa would say it's a little taste of heaven." Embarrassed at revealing so much of herself, she concentrated on the displays in the shop windows with their diminishing supplies of watches and clocks, fabrics and clothes.

Suddenly Peter grabbed her elbow and pointed to a notice. "Look—a poetry reading! Would you like to go? I said you have poetry in your soul, so how can you refuse?" He grinned at her.

She hesitated, wondering if he was teasing or really asking for a date. "I, uh, well, I—"

"You don't have to go, but I thought we'd both enjoy it. If it's no good, we can take a walk or do something else." Peter looked at her, uncertainty on his face.

She took a deep breath and smiled. "I'd like that."

"Good. We'll call it a date then." He gave her a smile, and her heart raced.

As they approached the shop, a short, middle-aged man stood on the sidewalk staring at the building. "Are you looking for something?" she asked when they walked up to him.

He gave them a quick glance. "I see this is the shop of Mr. Worthington. He's known far and wide for the rare and valuable books he's able to procure for his customers. No one else has his connections." He spoke briskly with the touch of an accent she couldn't place.

Ann felt uncomfortable, but knowing she needed to be polite to a potential customer, she took a deep breath. "Is there something I can help you with, Sir? I work at the shop; Mr. Worthington's my grandfather."

The man continued to inspect the building. "I'm told Mr. Worthington's ancestry goes back to persons of position in Germany. Rare books must run in the family." One side of his mouth turned up in more of a smirk than a smile.

Peter shifted the packages. "Come inside, Sir. We'll get Mr. Worthington for you."

"Another day, I think." The man glanced at his watch. "I just wanted to know where to come when it's time." He tipped his hat and hurried away.

"An odd man," Ann remarked as she opened the shop

door. After a trying afternoon, the comforting smell of old books wrapped around her, giving her a sense of warmth and security. She motioned toward the counter. "Leave the groceries there. I'll put them away."

Footsteps approached from the back of the shop, and her grandfather hurried into the room. "My good friend, I was hoping you'd come by. I've gotten in some books you'll want to see."

Peter placed the packages on the counter and smiled at Ann. "I enjoyed our afternoon. Don't forget our date."

Ann returned the smile and turned to pick up the groceries, hoping he couldn't hear her heart pounding. She couldn't believe it! Peter hadn't made fun of her when she shared her special feelings, and he'd even asked her for a date!

Chapter 3

Peter followed his friend to the workroom, where Nigel handed him a book. "It's perfect," Peter said as he sat down and leafed through the volume. "As always, you've come to my rescue."

Nigel sat at his cluttered worktable, books stacked all around him in various stages of repair and an open Bible in front of him. He rested his elbows on the table and brought his fingers together, tapping them lightly, then resting them under his chin. "I want to thank you for walking Ann home today. I was afraid for her when the sirens sounded." He shook his head. "I've tried to convince her to return to America, but she's stubborn." He winked at Peter. "She gets that from her grandmother."

Peter laughed and ran his hand over the book. "I refuse to touch that one, Sir. But I do understand your concerns; I have the same ones. To stay or not to stay; that's the question. I have research to finish, and I don't want to desert our project."

Nigel nodded. "Your help has been invaluable. With the

Nazis stealing art treasures to finance their war, it's important we get valuable books and materials to places of safe-keeping. And if bombs should fall, I shudder to think of the treasures we'd lose."

"I'm honored to serve as a link with our colleagues at the university who are working to preserve materials from either disaster," Peter replied. "I hope my coming here for research material has kept me above suspicion."

Nigel sighed and moved a stack of books to the side. "And if you leave, I'll not only lose your help, I'll lose a good friend."

Peter rested the book in his lap and glanced around the room. Books were everywhere. "It's easy to see you consider books your friends as well as your treasures. Did I ever tell you about the collection of Bibles my grandmother left me? Some go back several generations."

Nigel studied him for a moment. "That Bible collection. You've read the books as well?"

Peter felt a stab of guilt. "I can't say I've read them as much as I should have. They've been more a treasure to preserve than something to read. Not that I don't believe them," he added quickly, "but I've been so busy with other things I. . ." He felt as if Nigel were looking into his soul and finding it wanting.

Nigel leaned forward. "Since rationing and shortages, the value of food has become more apparent. Would you stock your cupboards and leave the food on the shelves only to look at?"

Peter felt Nigel watching his response and shifted in his chair. "You're talking about food for the soul. You sound like my grandmother. She said the body couldn't be nourished by cream puffs, nor would the soul be nourished by the fluff we try to feed it."

Nigel nodded. "A wise woman." He rubbed his hands together. "Peter, you have that collection because men risked their lives to translate and preserve God's Word many years ago. They didn't sacrifice themselves so the Bible could be collected. They wanted people to read it and store it in their hearts, not their bookcases." He peered over his glasses.

Peter raised his hands. "I admit I have no excuse. The world is too much with us, as they say, and too often it takes times like the present to try men's souls and make them think of things spiritual."

"Every generation is the custodian of God's Word, Peter, and must see that His truths are learned and passed on. When that doesn't happen, we have the violence that's in our world today." Nigel paused as if making a decision before closing the workroom door. He walked to a bookcase and rolled it aside. Behind it, he pushed on a part of the wall, and a narrow door popped open to reveal a tall safe.

Peter stared at him and had opened his mouth to speak when Nigel continued.

"I keep the most valuable books in here. Some are priceless, but there are people willing to pay any amount for what they want. I protect them here until they go to their new owners. And some of these are my own family treasures." He took out a bundle secured with a cord.

Peter watched as Nigel placed it on his worktable and removed the paper. Inside lay a large, worn book with a brown leather cover. Nigel carefully opened it at random. Peter stared, and words caught in his throat. "That's. . .it's. . . it couldn't be what I think it is." He blinked and looked up to see Nigel smiling gently. "It is, isn't it? It's a Gutenberg Bible!" He let out his breath and stared at it in awe.

"Yes, Peter, it's one of the first books produced by a printing press, somewhere around 1455. It's been in my family for many generations. I'm its guardian in this time. Ann will have to protect it after me, in these times perhaps a dangerous task."

"May I?" Peter looked at his friend.

Nigel nodded, and Peter reached out to touch the book, feeling overwhelmed as he leafed through it. Two columns of Latin ran down each page. Some of the pages were plain. On others, curling vines decorated the sides along with colorful birds and flowers, or vines curled down the center between the columns. The letters at the beginning of each book were elaborate designs done in shades of green, blue, and red. Peter stared at the book, mesmerized.

"This is volume two," Nigel explained. "Somewhere along the line the first volume was lost. The Gutenberg Bible was so large, it was usually bound in two volumes— sometimes three. Mine includes Proverbs through the rest of the Old Testament and the entire New Testament." Nigel rewrapped the book and put it in the safe, and Peter moved the bookcase to its place in front of the panel Nigel had opened. Neither spoke as they worked.

Peter let out his breath and picked up his book. "I feel as if I've been on holy ground."

Nigel smiled. "You have been but not because of the Gutenberg Bible, old and rare as it is. With any Bible, you're on holy ground. This is God's Word to us, written so we can know Him. Through it, He reveals His love, comes into our hearts to redeem us, and then shows us how to live. Just knowing that should bring a sense of awe."

Nigel studied him a moment. "Your Bible collection. I think you take it for granted. Have you ever thought about the men who preserved God's Word for you? What they sacrificed? Men like William Tyndale, one of the first to translate most of the Bible into English in 1526? He dedicated his life to the task but had to flee England for his safety, was finally betrayed in Antwerp, strangled, and burned at the stake—just for putting the Word into our language. And yet all many people do with Bibles is collect them."

Peter felt his face take on a sheepish look.

"I'm not chastising you, my friend, but there are forces today trying to destroy this Word or, in the case of my treasure, use it to finance their evil purposes. The Bible I have would bring a lot of money. And so I have to ask, 'Who is willing to defend God's Word in our time?' When you go home, Peter, spend some time in your Bible."

Peter nodded and extended his hand. "I will, Sir. Thank you for sharing this with me. I feel very honored."

Nigel placed his other hand over Peter's. "I didn't do it for that reason, my friend, though I knew what the book would mean to you. Someone needs to know about my Bible besides Ann. I won't always be here, and with the country at war, I want someone trustworthy to help her with it if need be." He walked with Peter to the workroom door. "I shudder to think what would happen if the Nazis knew of that book."

At the words, Peter felt a chill. "Is the book in danger? Are you?"

Nigel shook his head. "I pray not. My name is English, and the family lost its connection with Germany many years ago, but we must always take precautions."

They walked into the shop, where Ann was handing a customer his purchase. Peter put his hand on Nigel's shoulder. "Thank you again, my friend. You've shared with me an experience I'll always cherish. And I will go home to spend some time in my own Bible." He gave Ann a warm smile and followed the customer out the door.

Ann glanced quickly at her grandfather. "What experience? What's this about his Bible?"

He turned toward her. "I showed him our Bible, Ann. Someone besides you needs to know. We live in dangerous times."

"You trust him that much?" Ann was astounded.

He nodded. "My friend at the university trusts him completely, and he's been a loyal friend to me. He knows the value of the book, and I think he went home to ponder the value of its contents as well."

◆ ◆ ◆

Peter walked toward the bus stop, thinking about the treasure he'd seen. When he looked up, he saw he had passed his stop and quickly retraced his steps as the bus pulled up and he scrambled on.

He took a seat and stared out the window as thoughts and questions assailed him. Why had this Bible had such an impact on him? He'd touched many old books and had held many Bibles. Nigel had chided him for collecting Bibles but not being fed by their content. His face felt warm as a thought nagged at him. If all Bibles disappeared, would it matter to him? Would it change his life?

The bus pulled up to his stop, and he got off, carrying the bag of books Nigel had sent with him. He entered his flat and absently put the books on the table. Nigel had told him about the man who died for translating the Bible. War was coming to London, and he could die. What had he stood for that would matter?

The troublesome thoughts continued as he sorted through the books and put them away for safekeeping until he could deliver them to his colleagues. He walked over to the bookcase, picked up a Bible his grandmother had given him, and frowned. If the Bible was holy ground, why wasn't he feeling the same awe from this one that he did from the Gutenberg Bible? Was he in awe of the book's age instead of its contents?

He paced the floor and stopped suddenly as a Bible verse he'd learned in Sunday school popped into his mind. "*For where your treasure is, there will your heart be also.*" He swallowed hard as he thought about things that were treasures in his life—even Ann settled comfortably among them—but the list didn't include God's Word.

"I think I understand," he spoke aloud as he stared at the book. "The Gutenberg Bible is a reminder of the value men placed on the Word and what they were willing to give up for it. I could sense their commitment. The man holding this book hasn't made such a commitment. It's not the treasure of his heart; he doesn't even read it."

Peter sat down in the overstuffed chair by the window and opened the book. In his twenty-nine years of life, this would be the first time he had read the Bible as God's Word to him.

Chapter 4

Ann had unlocked the glass case beneath the counter and bent down to run the feather duster along the shelves when the bell over the door jangled. She peered through the glass case as a man entered the shop. Peter! He looked so handsome, her heart beat faster, and she straightened quickly, banging her head on the frame of the case. Taking a deep breath and squeezing back tears, she stood as Peter approached the counter.

"Good afternoon, Miss Heydon. Ready for the poetry reading?" Peter smiled at her and folded his umbrella. "I know I'm early. I need to speak to your grandfather before we leave."

Her heart gave a flip, and she smiled. "I'll get ready and meet you in here." She hurried upstairs to change and run a comb through her hair, taking care to avoid the bump that had formed.

A date with Peter! Her stomach had a strange, nervous feeling, and she hoped she wouldn't babble or, even worse, have nothing to say! She added a fresh coat of pink lipstick and returned to the shop, where Peter was examining the books in the glass case. "I'm ready," she announced. He offered her his arm, and they stepped out of the shop and into the rain.

◆ ◆ ◆

Peter quickly raised his umbrella and pulled Ann close so they could share its protection. The patter of raindrops on the umbrella grew loud as Ann's nearness left him tongue-tied. He looked down at her, and all he could think of was flowers. Her perfume smelled like some kind of spring blossom, and in her pink blouse, she reminded him of the delicate blooms he saw in window boxes near his flat. Her light brown hair and the pink in her cheeks added to the soft look. He swallowed hard as she smiled up at him.

"Watch the puddle!" He pulled her to the side but not before her right foot splashed into the water. "Do you need to change shoes?" he asked apologetically.

Ann shook her head. "I'm fine. I don't want to make us late."

"We'll let it go then—unless you start quacking," he teased as her shoe sloshed with each step.

Ann wrinkled her nose at him and gave him a gentle push toward a puddle.

"Truce!" he declared. "From henceforth I promise to carry you across all puddles."

They approached their destination and saw a notice taped on the door. "Poetry reading canceled," Peter read. "So much for that. And it's not a good day for a walk, so how about a cup of coffee? There's a shop right around the corner."

"I'd like that." Ann smiled at him.

Inside, they sat down at a table and soon held cups of steaming coffee. Peter took a careful sip and watched as Ann wrapped her hands around the cup. Her blue eyes sparkled and seemed to hint at something deeper within, something he longed to know better. He cleared his throat. "So tell me. Why did you come to England to work in a bookshop?"

Ann carefully twirled the cup. "I'd always wanted an adventure. When Grandma died, I talked my parents into letting me come over to stay with Grandpa. It's been the most wonderful time of my life. I love books, and I'd like to learn enough so I could take over the shop someday." Her face grew red, and she looked down at her cup. "That's one reason going back to America upsets me so much."

Peter reached out and squeezed her hand. "Believe me, I understand. I don't want to leave, either. I know it doesn't feel like much consolation, but at least we have a safe country to return to."

Ann nodded. "I know all that. And I know God will watch out for Grandpa better than I can, but leaving him and the shop would be so hard. I keep hoping a miracle will change the direction the world's headed." She looked up at him and smiled. "Pray and think positive, you know."

"A miracle's certainly what we need." Peter swallowed the last of his coffee and picked up the umbrella. "Ready to brave the elements?"

They stepped out into the rain and hurried along the wet sidewalk. At the shop door, Peter suddenly dropped the umbrella and scooped her up in his arms, making an exaggerated step across a small puddle. "I keep my promises!" he said with a chuckle.

Laughing, Ann reached for the doorknob. He stepped inside and set her down as the bell jangled. "Would you like to go out again sometime?" He raised his eyebrows, and she nodded. "I'll try to find something interesting and let you know."

Footsteps could be heard coming from the back room as Peter bent to give her a quick kiss before her grandfather appeared. "I had a great time," he said softly. "Watch those puddles!" He touched the tip of her nose gently and stepped outside.

A warm sense of Ann's presence stayed with him as he walked along the sidewalk, trying to figure out why she fascinated him so. She was a surprising mix of spunk and softness, and they had a mutual love of books, but there was something more, something about the way she captured special moments and stored them inside to enjoy on bleaker days. He ambled along, oblivious to the raindrops until they trickled down his collar. The umbrella! He quickly retraced his steps and paused at the shop window, hoping for a glimpse of Ann, but the room was empty. He picked up the umbrella. *What's that woman doing to my mind? Or is it my heart?*

◆　◆　◆

The next morning, Ann's grandfather was rearranging a shelf of books when she came downstairs after completing her morning chores. He looked up and smiled. "I'm pleased you had a good time with Peter yesterday. He's a fine young man."

Ann felt her face grow hot. "I. . ." She paused as the bell jangled and a man entered the store. From his clothing and stocky build, he looked like someone who spent much of his time outdoors.

"What can I do for you?" her grandfather inquired as he stepped down from a stool.

The man walked up to the counter and looked around. "I'm interested in old Bibles. Ones like that Gutenberg Bible. You don't have one of them I could look at, do you?" He looked her grandfather in the eye without smiling.

Ann could feel her heart beat faster and watched her grandfather take a quick breath. "There aren't many of those left, Sir, and most are in museums," he answered truthfully, watching the man's face.

"I heard there are still some around. They were made in Germany. Too bad they're scattered around the world instead of staying in their own land." He ran his hand over the counter, his mouth smiling slightly, but his eyes remaining cold.

"I'm sorry I can't help you. Would you like to order some information on the subject?" her grandfather offered.

"No, just asking." The man turned and left the shop.

Ann let out her breath. "Grandpa, you don't think. . ."

He shook his head. "Just a coincidence, I'm sure." He climbed back on the stool and searched through the books on the top shelf.

Ann stepped to the window and looked out to see the

man a short distance down the sidewalk in a conversation with. . .Peter Austin? Her heart gave a flip. Peter would be here in a few minutes! She busied herself at a bookshelf as minutes ticked by, but Peter didn't appear. Finally she walked to the window and looked out. The sidewalk was empty. Why had he been out there if he didn't come in the shop?

She was jolted back to reality as her grandfather called out, "Ann, unload the box of books that arrived yesterday and stack them on the counter. I need to take a look at them." He climbed down from the stool and stepped out the shop door.

Ann worked absently, seeing Peter's soft hazel eyes instead of the books she took from the box. Sharing her thoughts with him had seemed so natural, even her dreams and her feelings deep down inside. And when he picked her up to step across the puddle, it felt so right to be in his arms. She jumped as the shop door slammed.

"I knew it would happen!" Her grandfather entered the room, staring at the day's newspaper. "France has fallen! They signed the surrender yesterday. Now England stands alone between Hitler and the free world!"

Ann stared at him in disbelief.

"I've been trying to get you a ticket home, Ann, but we've waited too long. Everything's booked. It won't be long before German submarines make it unsafe for ships to cross the Atlantic." He slapped the paper against his leg.

"It's June twenty-third, and nothing's happened here in London, Grandpa. Maybe Hitler will stop with France."

"If wishes were horses, beggars would ride," he snorted.

He picked up a small package and handed it to her along with some money. "Take this to the post office for me, please. It needs to go out right away." He rubbed his forehead and sighed.

Ann stopped to pat him tenderly on the shoulder. "We'll be all right, Grandpa." She opened the door and stepped out onto the sidewalk.

"Yoo-hoo, Ann," Mrs. Chumley called out. "How's the romance coming along?" She wore a bright purple dress, and her red curls bobbed as she swept the sidewalk in front of her shop.

Ann stopped to tell her about the date. "And he wants to take me out again!"

"What did I tell you? You come talk to me if you need advice on romance," she said smugly. "That's what my Albert always says."

Ann chuckled. "I'll remember that." She glanced at her watch. "I have to get this package to the post office. Talk to you later, Mrs. Chumley."

◆ ◆ ◆

A frown creased Peter's brow as he hurried along the side-walk and entered the bookstore. "We need to talk," he said to Nigel abruptly and looked around. "Is Ann here?"

Nigel shook his head. "She went to the post office. Come, have a seat by my desk."

Peter joined him and took off his hat. "Things have been happening that make me uneasy. Did Ann tell you about the man we talked to on the sidewalk awhile back?"

Nigel put down his pencil. "She told me."

"A few days ago, a man stopped me in front of your shop and asked if I worked here. I told him I'm doing research for a book, and you help me find material. Then he asked if I had heard of a Baron Ravenhurst or the Earl of Pembroke. I had no idea what he was talking about and told him so."

Nigel paled as Peter completed his story. "What did he look like?"

"Stocky, sportsman type. I was afraid he suspected I help move valuable materials to safekeeping. I didn't want to jeopardize our work, so I went on home."

Nigel got up and paced, a deep frown on his face. He let out a sigh. "Peter, those men he named were my ancestors. It's through their line I received the Gutenberg Bible." He pounded his fist into the palm of his hand.

"You think someone suspects you have the Bible?" Peter watched his friend carefully.

"I'm concerned, Peter, but I won't let anyone use the Bible to finance an evil cause. It must stay with the family." He continued to pace. "I've been praying for a way. . ."

"Sit down, my friend. Let's talk about this."

Nigel joined him and put his head in his hands. "I'm not worried for myself, Peter, but I don't want either the Bible or my granddaughter hurt. Why didn't I get her a ticket and make her go back to America with the Bible?" His voice was filled with anguish.

Peter thought a moment. "Maybe there's a way. I also came to tell you I sail for America in September. My colleague got me the ticket and is sending boxes of material with me for safekeeping. I'd be honored to take your Gutenberg Bible along—if you'd trust me with it."

Nigel took off his glasses and rubbed his eyes. "I trust you completely, Peter, but that would solve only half my problem. How do I get Ann to leave? There won't be more chances soon."

"I could give her my ticket," Peter began.

Nigel shook his head. "No, you need to go home. And even if I had a ticket, how would I get her to leave?"

"Convince her she has to take the Bible to America to keep it out of Nazi hands?"

Nigel looked doubtful. "But would she leave me to save the Bible? And if she knows you're leaving, she'll tell me to send it with you. I need to get both of them to America."

Peter stood. "My colleague got my ticket. Maybe he can come up with one more to save the Bible. I won't reveal the item we're talking about, but if I hint at its importance, maybe he'll do something."

Nigel grasped his hand. "I'd be so grateful, Peter. The Bible and my granddaughter are of immeasurable worth to me. It will be hard to part with them, but my heart will be at peace knowing both my treasures are safe. Let's keep this from Ann for now."

Peter nodded. "I'll talk to my colleague this afternoon and let you know if I find out anything." He walked to the door, then turned. "Oh, I haven't had a chance to tell you, but I've been reading my grandmother's Bible. It's become more than something I collect. The road ahead may be rough, but the Word is a light for my path in this very dark world. Thanks, my friend."

Nigel looked pleased. "Let God's Word keep you focused on the One who holds the world in His hands. And indeed the days ahead will get rough. The Germans have taken the Channel Islands, and they're bombing airfields and industrial plants in the south of England. I'll be praying He puts a ticket into your hands soon."

Chapter 5

The last customer had left the shop, and Ann was collecting the day's receipts when the aroma of fresh bread filled the room. Mrs. Wilson stepped through the doorway, carrying two large loaves, and smiled at Ann's grandfather. "I brought your favorite bread," she said. "We didn't have sugar to make anything sweet today."

He got up and walked to the counter. "Thank you. We'll enjoy it as a special treat." He took the bread and smiled at the dainty, white-haired woman.

Pink appeared on Mrs. Wilson's cheeks. "If I can find enough meat to buy, I wondered if you and Ann would share a pot of stew with me. Maybe after church one Sunday?" Her hands clutched her purse tightly.

He glanced over at Ann, and she nodded. "We'd be delighted. And we'll bring some tea for the occasion."

Mrs. Wilson walked to the door. "So many things are scarce these days. I'll let you know when I'm able to buy the meat." She gave a small wave and stepped outside.

Ann watched her grandfather return to his work with a quiet smile on his face. She'd been hoping he would find someone with whom to share his life, and, as a widow, Mrs. Wilson would be perfect. She got up to lock the shop door, hoping meat wouldn't be so scarce it would take all year before they got together!

◆　◆　◆

Midsummer arrived. To Ann, the shop had become stuffy, and she fanned herself with a book from the shelf she was rearranging. As she worked, her mind drifted to the afternoon they had spent with Mrs. Wilson. Peter had been invited to join them, and after the delicious stew, the four went for a stroll. She and Peter had found a grassy spot in the park, where they talked while her grandfather strolled along the paths with Mrs. Wilson holding his arm. The day had been so fresh and peaceful, one she'd always cherish.

She stepped down from the stool and looked through a pile of books. The constant blare from her grandfather's radio frayed her nerves as unearthly screams from Germany's Stuka dive bombers shrieked from the back room. As he worked, her grandfather was listening to BBC reports of the German Luftwaffe sinking British merchant ships in the English Channel and attacking navy bases and airfields in the south of England.

And where was Peter? He hadn't been by the shop lately. Suddenly she felt suffocated and hurried to the workroom. "I need some air, Grandpa. I'm going for a walk."

His face reflected concern. "Be careful, my dear, and be

ready to take cover at a moment's notice."

Ann nodded and hurried out the door. She walked along block after block, looking in store windows at the meager selection of goods now available and remembering the days when window-shopping was a pleasant pastime. Around her, the English went about their daily routines and searched the stores for the rapidly diminishing items they needed. She sighed and turned toward the bakery for a chat with Mrs. Wilson, who had become a dear friend.

◆　◆　◆

Peter entered the bookshop as Nigel was turning off the radio. "Hello, my friend." He smiled and looked around for Ann.

Nigel walked to the counter and placed his hands on it. "She went out for some air. The shop felt stuffy, and the radio broadcasts were too much for her."

A look of disappointment crossed Peter's face.

Nigel's forehead creased in an anxious expression. "Do you bring me good news, my friend?"

Peter shook his head. "People know time is running out, and everyone wants a ticket to go home. I'm sorry."

Nigel slapped his hands on the counter. "Please keep trying, Peter. There must be some way."

Peter paused a moment. "I'd like your permission to try one last thing. I haven't told my colleague about the Bible, just that Ann has something of value to take to America. He says everyone else does, too." Peter stopped and looked at Nigel. "If I could tell him about the Bible, he might be willing to pull some strings to get her a ticket. I can't think of any-thing else."

Nigel paced, praying softly, then stopped and faced Peter. "I don't see we have a choice, but reveal as little as possible." He gave a deep sigh.

"These people know how to keep quiet," Peter reassured him. "I'll be here for another month, and I'll keep working on it. Now, I have to run. I'm trying to do as much as I can in the time I have left." He paused. "Tell Ann I haven't for-gotten her."

When Peter left the shop, he hurried toward the bench in the park to spend some time in his quiet place. He had sat down and bowed his head when a sound on the sidewalk caused him to look up. Ann stood there, looking uncertain.

"I don't mean to intrude," she began.

He smiled at her and patted the bench. "I'm always glad to see you."

Ann sat down, and he reached for her hand. Pink appeared in her cheeks as she looked up at him. "It's coming, isn't it? The attack on London, I mean. Even I can't pretend any longer."

Peter nodded.

"Grandpa tried to make me leave, but I refused to look at reality."

"Are you sorry you stayed?" Peter raised his eyebrows.

"I'm glad to be here for Grandpa; he'll never leave. I have to admit I'm afraid, though." She looked up into the leaves above them. "Sometimes I can't take any more of the news about the war, and I come here. This place has become my sanctuary." She looked over at him. "Are you sorry you didn't make arrangements to leave when you could?"

Peter paused, remembering Nigel's request that he not tell Ann about his ticket. "I'm not sorry to spend more time with someone who's become very special to me," he answered evasively. "And you have become very important to me, you know. When I pray, I ask that I not lose the opportunity to know you better and find out what happens from here. War is not the easiest time to develop a relationship!"

Ann's face filled with color as he squeezed her hand. "I've. . .we've missed seeing you at the shop lately." She looked at him with questions in her eyes.

Peter picked a leaf and smoothed its surface. "I've had to take on more responsibilities at the university." He stood and pulled her to her feet, gently putting his arms around her and resting his chin on the top of her head. As she nestled against his chest, the world faded away, leaving nothing but the two of them in their sanctuary.

He sighed when she pulled away and spoke. "I'd better go. I've been gone so long, Grandpa will be worried." They looked at each other silently, the uncertainty of the times hanging between them.

"I'll walk you back." Peter reached down and picked a daisy to tuck in her hair. "A beautiful flower for a lovely lady. I've been praying I'll have the opportunity to give you many morc." He lifted her chin and gave her a soft kiss, then took her arm and walked her to the shop.

Chapter 6

As the weeks of summer passed, Ann tried to avoid the incessant radio broadcasts. Her grandfather listened to them religiously, so she no longer minded the hours she spent waiting in long lines for the food they needed. German air attacks had now reached the outer suburbs of London. As she walked through the city, she couldn't ignore the sandbags piled high in front of most stores.

Again it seemed so long since she'd seen Peter. She sighed as she remembered the walks they'd taken, sharing their thoughts and dreams as they ambled along, and the day they took a picnic lunch to the park to enjoy their favorite poetry. Why did he disappear for periods of time?

The August day felt warm as she hurried home with her few purchases. She entered the shop, relieved to be met by quiet as her grandfather sat with his Bible open. "I bought what I could," she told him. "We won't starve, but meals may be strange."

He nodded. "And Mrs. Wilson brought some bread. We

should invite her to share a meal with us; she's been very kind." He gave a soft smile.

"I agree." Ann hesitated a moment. "Has Peter been here lately? I've been standing in line so much, I thought perhaps I'd missed him." She shifted the packages with exaggerated concentration.

Her grandfather looked up at her, his eyes tender. "You don't need to pretend, my dear. I can see how much you care for him, and I certainly approve. He's a young man I'd be honored to have in the family. And yes, he has come by while you've been running errands." He rummaged through the desk. "He left something for you. I forgot all about it."

Ann took the package he handed her and hurried to the door to their living quarters. "I'll take these upstairs and see what I can fix for dinner." She ran up the steps and pulled out a small book, *Poems for the Heart*. She opened it to see a note in Peter's handwriting. "We missed the poetry reading, so I hope you'll enjoy reading some poetry on your own. When I read this one, I thought of you. Peter."

She quickly looked at the pages where Peter had placed the paper. On the left she saw one of her favorite poems by William Wordsworth. Peter had remembered! She skimmed to enjoy the lines she loved:

I wandered lonely as a cloud
. . . .
When all at once I saw a crowd,
*   A host of golden daffodils;*

She ran her finger down the page to the last verse:

For oft, when on my couch I lie
In vacant or in pensive mood,
They flash upon the inward eye
Which is the bliss of solitude;
And then my heart with pleasure fills,
And dances with the daffodils.

She caught her breath. Peter understood! He knew she spent time in quiet places like her sanctuary near St. Andrew's, reflecting on memories to refresh her mind and spirit! She ran her hand over the page. Peter hadn't laughed at her when she'd shared her deepest feelings. Instead he said she had poetry in her soul. Peter was the man she'd longed for all her life. Did she dare hope he'd be more than her friend?

She shifted her glance to the page on the right and stared. *"How do I love thee? Let me count the ways. . . ."*

A shiver ran through her as the words of Elizabeth Barrett Browning leaped from the page. *He couldn't mean this one, could he?* She tried to catch her breath as her grandfather's footsteps sounded on the stairs. She quickly took the book to her room and started on the evening meal. Which poem did Peter mean?

◆　◆　◆

On the morning of August 24, Ann opened the blackout curtains and stared at a wall of white: Fog had spread across London. She had straightened the shop and was getting ready for the day's business when the bell on the door jangled and a man stepped into the room. "Peter! What are you doing here so early?" She smiled and put down the keys to the cabinet as her heart beat faster.

"I didn't know I was on a schedule." He raised an eyebrow and grinned. "After struggling to get here in this pea soup, that's all the welcome I get?"

"No, you don't need a schedule. You're welcome anytime. This is a business. It's just that we weren't expecting you. Grandpa's in the back." Ann stopped as Peter chuckled at her rambling. *Which poem did he mean?*

"I thought we could—" Peter stopped suddenly as the air-raid sirens began to wail.

"Follow me!" her grandfather called out as he hurried into the room. "We need to take cover, just in case!" He led them to the storeroom in the basement, where he closed the door and turned on a light. "We'll be as safe in here as anywhere." He reached for their hands and asked God's protection as the piercing sounds continued above. Then he took a Bible from a shelf and opened it.

Ann and Peter sat down on a small sofa. He put his arm around her and drew her close so her head rested on his shoulder. She could feel his heart beating rapidly and hoped it was because of her nearness as well as the sirens.

Time dragged while the wailing continued. Suddenly there was a loud silence. Her grandfather listened a moment before he opened the door. "Stay here. I'm going up to see what's happened."

Ann stood quickly. "We're not letting you go up there by yourself!" They followed him up the stairs.

Her grandfather opened the shop door, and they stepped out, relieved to find their street unchanged. The fog had thinned, and they anxiously scanned the skyline through a wispy veil. In the distance, smoke billowed above the tree-tops, and a church spire pointed toward the sky in the midst of boiling black clouds.

"The city was hit," her grandfather said softly. "People over there need our prayers."

As they stared in disbelief, Mrs. Chumley stomped out of her shop and scanned the skies. In spite of the disaster, Ann chuckled at their neighbor. Her red hair stuck out in all directions, and she had two different kinds of shoes on her feet. Her bright green summer dress was buttoned with one side hanging lower than the other. As she searched the skyline, her red curls bobbed and her glasses moved up and down on her nose. "If those Germans think they're going to march in here and find us quaking in fear, they don't know the English!" she declared, then looked around and gave a huff. "Well, what are you standing here for? This is a business day. Let's get to it!" She turned and marched into her shop.

Peter stared after her and shook his head. "I'd better get back to the university to see if all's well. We'll plan to do something another day when things are quieter, Ann. I'll try to come by soon." He touched her cheek gently and hurried down the walk.

◆　◆　◆

On Monday morning, Ann finished the breakfast dishes and came downstairs to find her grandfather hunched over the newspaper. "The situation is about to get worse, mark my word. British planes made a raid on a Berlin suburb last night in retaliation for what the Germans did here. Hitler won't let this pass. He'll be back!"

Ann shuddered at the danger that lay ahead for the city and people she loved.

Tense days followed. To Ann, they crept by as she waited impatiently for Peter to appear. She was sweeping the stockroom when the bell jangled and a customer entered. As she had so often lately, she paused to listen for that familiar voice.

"Peter!" she heard her grandfather exclaim. "Ann and I were beginning to worry about you."

She dropped the broom and hurried into the shop. "Where have you been?" she blurted out. "I was afraid you'd gone back home and hadn't had time to tell us." She stared at him as her heart thudded and the warmth came into her face.

"I've been busy at the university. I'm sorry I worried you." Peter quickly glanced at her grandfather.

"Why don't you fix some tea, Ann? We've been saving it to enjoy at a time like this." Her grandfather smiled at her.

Ann nodded and hurried from the room.

Peter sat down and put his hat on the desk. "I told our friend about the Bible, Nigel, and he met with those higher up in our work. They were astounded at what you have and very concerned for its safely. It took time, but they were able to pull strings and book passage for Ann on the same ship I'm leaving on." He reached in his pocket and took out an envelope. "Keep this ticket safe. I couldn't get either of us passage until the middle of September, but things seem to have calmed down for awhile anyway."

Nigel reached out to grasp Peter's hand firmly. "The Lord's been good to us, and you have my deep gratitude, my friend, but let's not tell Ann about this yet. The less she knows, the better. I'll tell her at the last minute, and it's essential she not discover you're on board until she gets there." They could hear the rattle of teacups and Ann's footsteps on the stairs. "Come by late Wednesday morning," Nigel said. "I'll see that Ann's out on an errand, and we'll plan the details."

Peter nodded as Ann came into the room carrying a tray. He hurried to take it from her and smiled into her eyes. The room was quiet as she poured the hot but weak tea and handed Peter a cup.

Nigel cleared his throat. "I have a book I need to work on. I'll leave you two to solve the world's problems." He took his cup of tea and left the room.

"I'm sorry I worried you." Peter set his cup on the desk, reached over, and took her hand. "There's much going on at the university that takes my time. With the war moving closer, we need to insure records and important items will be safe."

Ann drew a deep breath. "I was afraid you'd left for America." As she looked at him, tears filled her eyes.

"You can't get rid of me that easily!" He smiled and handed her a small bag. "Here. Sweets for someone sweet."

Ann sniffed. "Cookies! Where did you get them?" She peered into the sack. "One for each of us!"

"My friend at the university gave them to me. I wanted to share them with the most special people in my life." He put his hand on the sack and winked. "One's for your grandfather, don't forget."

She handed him a cookie, and they ate slowly, savoring each bite. "When I was little, I'd raid the cookie jar and eat until my stomach hurt." She sighed.

Peter chuckled. "And I remember one time my grandma taught me a lesson. I'd been eating cookies she'd baked for her ladies' group, so she put extra salt in the next batch. Was that awful! I was a more cautious cookie thief after that!" He smiled at the memory and wiped the crumbs from his hand. "Ann, I—"

The bell jangled as a customer walked in, and Peter stood. "Your help is needed. I'll come by as soon as I can. " He smiled at her and headed for the door.

Ann's heart dropped as she watched Peter leave. Something felt different, but she couldn't put her finger on it. She sighed and turned to help the customer.

Chapter 7

On Wednesday morning, Peter arrived at the shop to find Ann out running errands as Nigel had promised. He took a seat beside the desk. "So, how do we get Ann to the ship without arousing suspicion?"

Nigel sat back in his chair. "I've thought of nothing else, Peter. I've decided to tell her about the ticket right away. The ship leaves in a few weeks, and we need her possessions taken from here a bit at a time in case the shop's being watched. We'll want her to slip away from here at night. I'm hoping you can arrange all that."

Peter nodded. "I'll work on it with our friends. They've reserved a very small but private room for her aboard ship. Now we have to decide how to protect the Bible. Ann will be transporting it, but we don't want to put her in jeopardy. We can always keep it in the ship's safe, if we can trust those with access to it, but these days there are too many people who will do anything for money."

Nigel got up and paced to the counter, rubbing his chin.

"She'll have her suitcases with her. We can ship some books on her ticket, but we want the Bible to remain in her possession." He paused. "Maybe I can disguise it so it looks like some ordinary book that wouldn't arouse suspicion."

"How about Shakespeare?" Peter suggested.

Nigel tapped his fingers together. "An excellent idea!"

Peter paused. "But the Gutenberg Bible's twelve-by-seventeen inches and thick. That's too large for her to carry as casual reading."

Nigel was silent a moment. "Mrs. Wilson keeps her knitting in a large cloth bag. Maybe she has an extra one that would hold the Bible."

"And we could fill it with knitting supplies so the book wouldn't show," Peter added. "Mrs. Wilson could teach her to knit—"

"Perfect!" Nigel's eyes gleamed. "I'll talk to Mrs. Wilson and start on the false cover right away."

"Passengers will be carrying all their possessions on this trip, so a bag that's a bit heavy won't be out of place," Peter commented.

Nigel placed his hand on Peter's shoulder. "I want you to know how much I appreciate this, and if I may speak out of turn, you and Ann have my blessing. . . ." He paused and looked at Peter.

Peter smiled broadly. "I was hoping to hear those words before we left. But how I wish you were going with us. Ann will be very sad to leave you, and I'll miss a dear friend."

"We'll be together again one day, Peter. If it's not until

heaven, take good care of Ann for me."

"You know I will." He looked at Nigel solemnly and stood to warmly clasp his friend's shoulder.

"If you have time, Peter, stop by late this afternoon. I should have the information you ordered, and maybe I can talk Ann into fixing us something to eat," Nigel suggested. "We need to enjoy an evening together while we can."

Peter's face lit up. "A real dinner? Tell her I'll be there!" He was smiling in anticipation as he hurried out the door.

◆   ◆   ◆

Ann finished the errands and returned to find her grandfather again listening to his radio, a Bible in his lap. He looked up as she walked in. "The fighting's fierce and the bombing heavy in the south of the country," he reported. "And with the Germans bombing areas around London, be sure the basement is well stocked with food and water." He paused to listen again before he said, "Oh, and Peter will be by later to look at some materials. I invited him to join us for dinner. I didn't think you'd mind. Mrs. Wilson will be here, too."

Peter was coming! Ann hurried upstairs to plan the menu, hoping she had enough food on hand to make a decent meal. The afternoon passed quickly, and soon she heard her grandfather leading Peter and Mrs. Wilson up the stairs. The table was set, and she was dishing up the food as they walked in. Her grandfather seated Mrs. Wilson, and Peter joined them at the table, smiling at Ann warmly.

"This isn't fancy, but at least there was plenty of fish available when I shopped this morning," she explained as she set the platter on the table, then added bowls of potatoes and green beans and the plate of bread Mrs. Wilson had brought. "I wish we had butter, but we've used our ration coupons. We'll have fresh fruit for dessert; I didn't have sugar to make anything."

"No need to apologize." Peter chuckled. "You wouldn't want to know what I usually eat for dinner!" He bowed his head for the prayer her grandfather offered. The conversation was light as they enjoyed the meal, and Ann felt her spirits lift as thoughts of war faded.

When they finished, her grandfather ushered Peter and Mrs. Wilson into the sitting room, where they discussed England in more peaceful times. As Ann was bringing a pot of the tea they had saved for special occasions, she paused and looked at the three people so dear to her. Maybe some-day she and Peter could invite her grandfather and Mrs. Wilson to dinner at their apartment. Suddenly her face grew warm. Where had that idea come from?

She served the tea as Peter told stories about his family in America, and Mrs. Wilson and her grandfather shared tales of their childhood days in nineteenth-century England. Mrs. Wilson worked on her knitting and offered to teach Ann how to make an afghan. "I volunteer to be your first victim, er, recipient," Peter teased. He chuckled as she flicked a piece of yarn at him.

Finally her grandfather left to walk Mrs. Wilson home, and Peter stood. "I have to catch the bus. Will you see me out?" At the shop door, he turned to her. "The dinner was delicious, Ann. Imagine, a poet who can cook! I'm impressed!"

She smiled. "Thank you for the compliment, but I only read poetry."

"I wish we had time to share our special poem, but this will have to do." He bent to give her a long, warm kiss and smiled into her eyes. "I'll see you soon."

Ann closed the door behind him and tried to catch her breath. *Which poem did he mean?*

Upstairs, she cleaned the kitchen, then headed for her room to get ready for bed. She paused at the book of poetry and turned to the pages where Peter had placed the note. What was he trying to tell her? She fell asleep, her dreams filled with images of a bookshop and a cozy home with Peter.

Suddenly, she sat straight up as the air-raid siren wailed, a feeling of terror racing through her at the deafening sound of antiaircraft guns and exploding bombs. "Let's get to the basement!" her grandfather called out over the noise. He reached for her hand, and they hurried downstairs, where he closed the door carefully and turned on a small light.

Explosions sounded in the distance, and Ann felt the terror build in the pit of her stomach. Even down here, she could hear the planes overhead, some droning and some like a swarm of bees buzzing in terrible anger.

She sat on the edge of the sofa and clasped her hands tightly to keep them from trembling as she prayed for their safety. Trying to escape the sounds, she closed her eyes to picture Peter's teasing smile and his hazel eyes that seemed to say he understood her deepest thoughts. Her heart ached for the security of his presence.

Her grandfather got out a kerosene lamp. "We'll need this if the power goes out." He sat next to her on the sofa and put his arm around her. Ann laid her head on his shoulder and closed her eyes as he stroked her hair gently. After reading the Twenty-third Psalm and praying, they listened to the terrifying sounds until both fell asleep.

Suddenly Ann awoke. Silence! The light was still on, and she could see the room was unchanged. She touched her grandfather's shoulder, and he sat up quickly, looking around in confusion for a moment before hurrying to the door. All was quiet above. He motioned to her, and they ascended the stairs to find the first floor unscathed. Ann breathed a sigh of relief.

"But others somewhere will not be so fortunate this morning," he remarked as he unlocked the door. "We need to check on Mrs. Wilson today."

In the early morning light, they could see thick, dark clouds of smoke billowing above the trees. Their neighbors' homes, however, appeared undamaged. They were staring at the scene when Mrs. Chumley tromped out of her shop, dressed in her nightclothes. Her red hair stuck out from under a green hat with a feathered plume, and she wore work boots on her feet. She shook her fist at the sky and tromped back inside.

Ann chuckled. "Leave it to Mrs. Chumley to bring us a smile at a time like this!"

"Let's thank the Lord for His protection and pray He extends it to others in the days ahead," her grandfather said as he stepped back inside. "Then you work in the shop this morning, Ann. With the attacks increasing, I have things to do in the workroom."

Throughout the day, Ann looked up quickly whenever the shop bell jangled, but Peter didn't appear. When she expressed her fears, her grandfather reminded her Peter had said he'd be very busy for awhile, but she knew she wouldn't have peace until he walked through their shop door unscathed.

With night raids occurring on a regular basis, her grandfather set up cots in the basement, where they would sleep until the bombing raids ceased. She spent the afternoon moving their bedding down from upstairs and seeing there was a supply of food and water.

After their dinner of scrambled eggs and toast, her grandfather stood. "Leave the dishes for now, Ann. We need to talk." He walked to their sitting room and sat in his over-stuffed chair. When Ann was seated, he stared at his hands for a moment, then looked up at her. "It's about our Gutenberg Bible." He ran his hand over the arm of the chair slowly. "We can't let it be destroyed by the bombs, and we can't let it fall into the hands of evil men."

Ann watched him carefully. The conversation seemed to be very difficult for him.

He looked at her and took a breath. "I think some men know I have it, and now in the confusion of the bombing, I'm afraid someone will try to steal it. We can't let that happen."

Ann caught her breath.

Quietly, he continued. "The book has to be taken to America. I can't do it. If someone is watching the shop and I leave, they'll know I have the Bible with me, and it would be in jeopardy. I don't like putting you in danger, my Ann, but it's also your possession. You have to be the one to save it." He reached in his pocket and took out an envelope. "I was finally able to obtain a ticket to America. You need to take our Bible to safety."

Ann stared at him. "You expect me to leave you here alone? I've told you before I will not do that, Grandpa! Can't you ship it?"

He shook his head. "Boxes can be searched. It needs to travel with someone who will have it in her possession and look out for it." He stood. "I have a plan. Come downstairs with me."

Protesting, Ann followed him to the workroom, where he opened the safe and took out a book. She stared at a worn copy of *The Works of William Shakespeare* and frowned. "I don't understand."

He smiled. "I'm pleased to see you're confused. I put a false cover on the Bible."

"It doesn't look like the Gutenberg Bible at all." She touched the metal latches he had added at the opening to secure the closure.

He breathed deeply. "I hope others will think so, too." He returned the book to the safe and handed her a large cloth bag. "You'll carry the Bible in this, and we'll add balls of yarn to conceal the book. When you're aboard ship, you'll need to work on the afghan whenever people are around so they'll believe this really is your knitting bag."

All Ann could do was stare.

He rubbed his chin. "Now, we need to have your possessions taken from here a bit at a time so nothing will look suspicious. Your ship sails in two weeks, so we need to get started."

She tried to speak but couldn't seem to get any words out.

He looked at her, waiting. "Don't be afraid, my Ann. I'll be praying for you. And don't worry about leaving me here. You couldn't protect me from the bombs anyway. Only God can do that. The truth is I'll be safer when the Bible's on its way to America."

Ann took a deep breath and swallowed hard. "I didn't realize you'd be in danger if I refused." She nodded. "I'll go. I love you too much to see you hurt, Grandpa, and I couldn't live with myself if I helped the Nazi cause." Her heart felt like a leaded weight. She blinked back tears as she patted his shoulder and forced a mischievous wink. "Besides, Mrs. Wilson will be more than happy to see you're well fed." She noticed a spot of pink appear in his cheeks.

He turned quickly. "Good. Then it's settled. Now we need to pack your things." He headed to the basement. "I'll get your trunk and suitcases."

Chapter 8

Peter sat at his desk, reviewing the plans. Arrangements had been made for the removal of Ann's possessions, and she would be spirited away at night for the journey to the ocean liner. He felt guilty knowing he could make the trip in the safety of daylight while Ann would be at risk from night raids and vehicles with covered headlights.

He ran his hand over his forehead and walked to the window. In the far distance lay areas of the city that had been bombed, and he remembered the day he had walked through the streets to view the damage. Walls jutted into the sky, and the ruins resembled archeological sites with remnants left here and there. Smoke rose from smoldering fires. People picked through the rubble for any belongings that survived, and some were staying in the remains of their houses without windows or walls.

"Hitler's wrong if he thinks he can crush the English spirit," he said aloud. "He'll only make them fight harder. They're carrying on with remarkable courage." He turned to finish packing before he made one last trip to the bookshop to say good-bye to Nigel and review the plans.

When he entered the store, Ann looked up quickly, a big smile spreading over her face. "Peter! It's so good to see you! Where have you been?" She hurried over to greet him. "Grandpa, Peter's here!"

"I'll stay away more often if this is the welcome I get!" He smiled at her and took her hand. She looked so trusting and happy to see him, he hated to think what lay ahead.

Nigel hurried into the shop. "Peter, my friend, come, see what I've found for you." Peter smiled at her and followed him into the workroom, where Nigel handed him some papers. They reviewed the plans, prayed together, and said their good-byes.

As they returned to the shop, Peter turned to Nigel. "Now, may I borrow your granddaughter?"

He nodded. "Keep her safe."

"We can go to our special spot for a bit of peace and quiet." Peter paused with his hand on the doorknob.

Ann gave him a shaky smile. "I'd like that."

◆　◆　◆

They were quiet as they walked to the park. Ann's heart ached, knowing she might never see Peter again. They entered their secluded spot and sat on the bench. The place that had been such a solace now seemed strange and different, she thought as she stared at the late-summer flowers, not trusting herself to speak. The wind rustled the leaves above them and moved through the trees with a mournful sigh. To Ann, it was the sound of her heart being broadcast for all to hear.

Peter picked up a wilted daisy and straightened the petals. "I'll be praying for you, Ann. Your grandfather told me about your plans to go home." He leaned forward with his elbows on his knees. "I wish. . . ." He paused and looked up at the trees and sky. "Maybe when this is over, we'll be back here someday."

Ann couldn't hold back the tears. She pulled a handkerchief from her pocket and mopped at her eyes. "It will be so hard to leave. I'll worry about you and Grandpa and the city, but this is something I have to do. Others have sacrificed things they cared about. Now it's my turn, and I have to give up all this for something I believe is right. I just didn't expect it to be so hard." She wiped her eyes again.

Peter reached over and took her hand. "Courage is doing the right thing even when it breaks your heart. Think how sad it would be if you could leave everything without caring." He pulled her into his arms and stroked her hair gently. His chin rested on her head, and her tears made wet splotches on his shirt.

Ann sat up and wiped her nose. "Please take care of Grandpa for me, Peter. I know Mrs. Wilson will see that he has food. They care about each other so he'll have someone after I'm gone, but promise me you'll come by often and see that he's safe. You've been a dear friend to him; I'll never forget that."

Peter stared at her, then looked down. "I'll, uh, I'll get

there as often. . .as I can. I'm sure Mrs. Wilson will do a better job than I could, though." He stood quickly and pulled her to her feet. "Now, you need to stop worrying and enjoy the rest of your time here. I miss that smile of yours." He lifted her chin. "We'll see each other again, I promise. You can't get rid of me that easily."

Ann couldn't stop the tears that streamed down her face. Peter took her in his arms and kissed the top of her head. "Okay, Kiddo, time to get you back to the shop before we have a flood here. I didn't bring a boat!" He grinned at her, and she managed a wet smile. He bent to give her a tender kiss, then took her arm and walked her home.

When Peter left her at the shop, Ann went to the window to watch him walk away. Instead he approached a tall man she'd seen out there before. Why would Peter be talking to him? By the time Peter had finished the conversation, curiosity had replaced her tears.

◆ ◆ ◆

The following days passed quickly, and most of Ann's possessions had been sent ahead. As she made a last tour of the neighborhood and talked to people she had grown fond of, she chuckled to herself. Mrs. Chumley felt something was up and decided Ann was eloping with Peter. "You can't fool me," she insisted. "I know romance when I see it!" She thrust an object at Ann. "From Albert and me." Ann stared at the framed picture of King George VI. "Deserves a place of honor in every proper home," her neighbor declared proudly.

Ann took a deep breath. "I can't take it now. Please keep

it for me." She tried to make her smile sincere.

"Sure thing, Dearie." Mrs. Chumley gave a wink. "A person don't need much on a trip like that. It'll be here when you get back."

Bombing raids had continued every night starting at dusk, so Ann was thankful their area of town remained unscathed. She glanced at the clock—one hour left. Now she had to face the good-bye she dreaded, and she hurried into the workroom, where her grandfather was repairing a book. Keeping busy was his way of handling the pain of her leaving, she realized.

"Grandpa, please stay safe and let Mrs. Wilson see that you're properly fed. She cares for you very much, and I have a feeling it's mutual. You have my blessing." They spent the hour reminiscing, and her grandfather reviewed important points for the safety of both her and the Bible.

Ann clasped and unclasped her hands. "I thought Peter would come by one last time. Tell him—" Suddenly, there was a soft tap on the back door, and she jumped.

Her grandfather stood. "Ann, your ride is here." He put his arms around her, and she hugged his neck, fighting back tears. "Grandpa, I can't leave you here. Come with me. Please."

He patted her hair gently. "God will watch over me—and I'm sure Mrs. Wilson will, too. I'll be praying for your safety, as you will mine. God will keep us safe." He reached out to wipe a tear from her cheek. "Now you must go. And do what these people tell you; I'm trusting them completely with my two greatest treasures."

Her grandfather turned and opened the door to admit a man who reached for Ann's suitcases. "We need to leave right away, Miss." Ann nodded and hugged her grandfather one last time before following the man out the door and into the night, carrying the knitting bag into which was tucked a well-worn copy of Shakespeare.

Chapter 9

Ann stepped into the ocean liner's tourist-class entrance and stared at the chaos around her. Everyone in London seemed to be boarding the ship. How would she ever find her cabin in this confusion? She spotted a ship steward and quickly asked directions.

"Follow me, Miss." Looking relieved to get away from the clamor, the steward took her suitcases and led her down the grand staircase to her corridor, finally stopping at her cabin door. "As you can see, this won't be a normal passage. We're carrying as many refugees as we can hold, so you'll find cots set up in the ballroom, lounges, and everywhere we can put them. People want to get to America while they can." He unlocked the door and set her suitcases inside.

Ann took a deep breath and asked the question that had been plaguing her. "Will the ship be in much danger from German submarines?"

He paused at the door. "We'll be escorted by a convoy of navy ships until we're several hundred miles from the English coast," he explained briskly. "Then we'll be on our own until we approach North America and pick up another convoy. The United States is still neutral in this war, so the Germans haven't been targeting her passenger liners. Once we're on our own, we'll do everything we can to make it clear we're hauling civilians and not military personnel."

Ann let out her breath. "So, there's no danger?"

"We can't guarantee that." He gave a frown. "There have been maverick attacks against neutral ships, but the captain will do all he can to make this a safe trip." He took some papers from a folder. "We're carrying so many extra passengers, meals will be served in shifts. We ask that you come to the tourist-class dining room promptly at your assigned hour." He handed her a schedule and a list of wartime regulations and hurried down the hall.

Ann put the bag on the bed and looked around the small cabin. It was compact with a single bed, dressing table, a tiny closet, and bathroom. How did her grandfather get her a cabin of her own, especially one this nice? She had come over third class. She glanced at the beautiful wood finish of the furnishings and paneled walls.

The ship rocked gently. This didn't seem real. One day she was in London, and now she was on a ship sailing for America in the middle of a war. The old worry nagged at her as she thought of leaving her grandfather and Peter to the mercy of the bombing raids.

After hanging her clothes in the closet, she set her suitcase on the dressing table and put her smaller travel bag on the floor of the closet. Now what? Her grandfather had said to keep the Bible with her at all times. There was no place she'd be more comfortable than in the ship's library, and she had time to locate it before dinner. She checked a map of the ship she had found on the dresser and picked up the knitting bag.

After carefully locking the cabin door, she hurried down the corridor and up the grand staircase. To the left, she could see the main lounge filled with row after row of mattresses and cots. People sat against the walls with their possessions and children around them. Ann swallowed hard and turned in the opposite direction to the library.

Inside, she walked around the small room, checking the titles before sitting down and taking out the afghan she had started with Mrs. Wilson's help. As she struggled to remember the instructions, the door opened and a distinguished-looking gentleman entered. He nodded to her and picked up a magazine.

She fumbled with the knitting and was relieved when she glanced at her watch and saw it was almost time for her dinner hour. She put the afghan in the bag and hurried down the staircase. Suddenly her heart gave a lurch, and she gasped as she saw the back of a man's head standing out above the crowd. Her eyes had to be playing tricks on her! The man looked like Peter! He quickly turned a corner, and she lost sight of him. Suddenly she felt very alone.

When she finally arrived at the spacious dining room, she found long rows of tables had been set up to accommodate the increased number of passengers. She took a seat and was inspecting the lovely room when a voice spoke at her left. "Is this seat taken?" Looking up, she saw it was the gentleman from the library and shook her head. With his white hair and blue eyes, he reminded her of her grandfather. Somehow she didn't feel as alone when someone seemed familiar.

"You're the lady from the library," he said as he sat down. "When I travel, I spend most of my time in the ship's library, too, though not to knit." He smiled. "I'm Winston Humbolt, and you're. . . ?"

"Ann Heydon," she replied. "I notice you don't have an accent; you're American?"

"Yes, I'm returning from a business trip. I'm an importer."

As she unfolded her napkin, a woman took the empty seat across from them. Her hair was smartly coifed, and her face carefully made up. She smiled across at Mr. Humbolt and gushed, "I'm so glad to find an empty seat at your table. I can see you're a person of quality." She sniffed. "I can't believe I'm stuck with these. . .these. . ." She waved her hand toward the other passengers as her perfume engulfed the table. "Who did they think they were, denying me first class!" Voices around them grew still. The woman reached out her hand as large gems sparkled on her fingers. "I'm Mrs. Van Peldt. My late husband was Herbert Van Peldt, the shipping magnate. I'm sure you've heard of him."

Mr. Humbolt took her hand and introduced himself, and the woman chattered on about her social status. The food was soon served, and conversations again buzzed around them.

"An adequate meal but not up to their usual," he commented. "And I don't enjoy having my meals rushed."

"I do agree," Mrs. Van Peldt replied. "We have so much in common."

Ann finished her dinner, picked up the knitting bag, and stood, almost colliding with another diner as she stared at a man leaving the room. He could be Peter's twin! She hurried to the corridor, but the man was nowhere in sight. With a sigh, she headed for the staircase, her feeling of loneliness deepening as she entered her dark cabin and switched on the light. All windows on board were tightly covered to help the ship proceed undetected for this part of the voyage.

Her nerves felt frazzled, so she decided to stay in her cabin. Maybe Peter wouldn't feel as far away if she read the book of poems he'd given her. As she opened her suitcase to pick out clothes more comfortable for lounging, she gasped. Someone had searched through her suitcase and left everything in a mess! A jolt of fear ran through her.

Her hands shook as she carefully checked each item; nothing seemed to be missing. What was happening to her? She had imagined she saw Peter on the ship and now this! Were worry about the war and the responsibility for the Bible weighing heavier than she thought?

She sat on the bed and tried to read, but her thoughts drifted from the mess in her suitcase to her grandfather and Peter. The ship's motion was comforting, and her eyes grew heavy. At least she felt rocked instead of seasick! Her mind drifted back to the days she and Peter had spent in their special place in the park. The memories brought a warm feeling, but too quickly the worry intruded. Was Peter safe, and was their part of town still undamaged? Finally she fell asleep, longing for the security she had found in Peter's arms.

◆　◆　◆

That was close! Peter closed the door to his cabin and threw the key on the bed. He never dreamed he'd be assigned to the same meal schedule as Ann. He had promised Nigel he wouldn't let her know he was on the ship until they were a day out at sea. He'd have to be more careful.

He paced the room, trying to quell another worry nagging him. Ann was going to feel he'd deceived her when she learned he was on board. He couldn't let that destroy their relationship.

Pacing wasn't going to help, he realized. He got out his grandmother's Bible and turned to the Psalms to calm his spirit, something he'd never have done a few months ago. Now with so many things he couldn't handle on his own, it had become a comforting habit.

Chapter 10

The next morning, Ann woke late and rushed into the dining room. Looking around for an empty seat, she ran into the back of a steward carrying a loaded tray. "Oh, no!" The contents began to slip, and she gasped as a man's hands grabbed the tray to steady it.

When the steward bent to set it on the table, Ann looked into Peter's face. "Peter! It *is* you! What are you doing here?" All she could do was stare. He had known she was leaving. If he had gotten a last-minute ticket, why hadn't he told her? Something was very strange.

"Ann." Peter finally spoke up. "I, uh, you. . .you'll have to be seated, or you'll miss breakfast. The next group will be here in a few minutes." He thrust his hands into his pockets and jingled some coins.

Ann's stomach knotted, and she shook her head. "I'm not hungry anymore, Peter, but I do want to know what's going on. The last I knew, you were in London. How did you get here, and why didn't you tell me?"

People around them were staring as Peter took her arm and led her from the room. "There's a small lounge down this hall. We can talk there."

Neither spoke as Ann followed him down the corridor. Suspicious scenes flitted through her mind. Peter talking to the men who seemed to be watching the shop. Peter avoiding the shop for so long. Peter being the only one on board who knew she was taking the Bible to America. *Who is Peter Austin?*

When they were seated in the lounge, Ann couldn't hold her thoughts in any longer. "Something strange is going on, Peter, and I want an explanation. Does Grandpa know you're here? You knew which ship I was sailing on; why didn't you contact me?" She frowned at him and held the bag tightly.

Peter took a deep breath. "I was able to get a ticket, and I planned to find you, but there are a lot of people on this ship. The staff is overworked, so I thought I'd wait until things settled down."

Ann continued to frown at him. "Not good enough, Peter. I thought. . ." She paused. Even under these circumstances, she could feel the red start to cover her face, and her eyes filled with tears, so she quickly looked down.

Peter reached out to cover her hand, but she pulled it away. He let out his breath. "We're far enough out at sea that I guess I can tell you. I promised your grandfather I wouldn't say anything until we were well underway."

Ann's head jerked up. "Promised Grandpa? What's he got to do with this?"

Peter sat back and rubbed the arm of the chair slowly. "I've had my ticket for a long time, Ann. Your grandfather wanted you to go home, and the Bible needed to be taken to safety, but you wouldn't leave. He was afraid if you knew I had a ticket, you'd have me take the Bible. He wanted both his treasures safe, so he had to send the Bible to America with you. And I had to promise I wouldn't let you know until we were far enough out that you couldn't change your mind."

"And what did you think I was going to do? Swim back?" Ann spat out. She grabbed the knitting bag and hurried from the room as tears ran down her cheeks.

She stumbled along the corridor, her mind full of disturbing questions. Was Peter ever who she thought he was? Who were those men he talked to outside the shop? A chilling thought ran through her mind. Peter was the only one on board who knew she had the Bible. Did he go through her luggage last night? Was he connected with those men hoping to steal it?

Her heart felt torn as she opened her cabin door. She couldn't let the Bible fall into the wrong hands. Whom could she trust? *Lord, please show me what to do!* She stared at the knitting bag. Her grandfather always said the Bible wouldn't do her any good if she didn't read it. She washed the tears from her face, then took her own copy out of the suitcase and opened it to the Twenty-third Psalm. It brought a sad comfort as she remembered the night her grandfather had read it aloud while the bombs fell on London.

◆　◆　◆

"I really blew that!" Peter muttered as he walked back to his room. "And I must admit the situation looks pretty suspicious." He nodded at a distinguished, white-haired gentleman who turned toward Ann's corridor. He could show Nigel's letter to Ann and clear up the misunderstanding, but he needed to know if she really trusted him. He stopped and turned around. He couldn't take a chance on losing her. They had to talk this out, and he had an idea where he'd find her.

◆ ◆ ◆

Ann checked her suitcases again, memorizing the position of the contents. If anyone went through her possessions, she'd know for sure. She locked the suitcase, picked up the knitting bag, and headed for the library. When she entered the room, Mr. Humbolt was reading a newspaper. "So, we meet again, my dear. Are you enjoying the voyage?"

Ann started to reply, when suddenly the door opened and Peter stepped into the room. She stiffened and quickly looked down. As he took a seat beside her, she could feel Mr. Humbolt watching them before he got up and left the room.

"Ann, please listen. I'm telling you the truth. Your grandfather is doing what he thinks is best for you. He loves you so much and so do I. . . ." He stopped as if shocked at his own words.

He loves me! The puzzling scenes and Peter's words jumbled together in Ann's mind—the suspicions on one hand and their precious moments together on the other. Of all the times to hear the words she'd been hoping for!

Peter grabbed her hand and wouldn't let go. "Ann, this is a dangerous trip. The convoy has left us, and the ship's on its own. They're turning all the lights on, windows are being uncovered, and spotlights will be turned on the ship's name and the American flag so the Germans will know this is a passenger ship, but it's still dangerous. I don't want to be fighting with you under these circumstances."

Ann looked down at their hands and spoke in a whisper. "Peter, you're the only one who knows what I'm carrying. If you didn't go through my suitcase, who did?" She looked up and stared at him.

Peter's mouth dropped open. "Someone went through your suitcase? When?"

"Yesterday when I came back from dinner, I opened it and found everything in a jumble."

"Ann, if I wanted to take the Bible, I'd know where to look. I wouldn't have to rummage through your suitcase. Apparently someone suspects you have it, and that puts you in jeopardy."

Ann longed to believe his words. "But I saw you talk to those men watching the shop. Who were they?"

Peter let out his breath. "Your grandfather and I were part of a group working to keep valuable materials both from the Nazis and from being destroyed by bombs. When we realized someone might be watching the shop, we arranged for a man from our side to keep an eye on things. That was the tall, thin man. We assume the others were looking for treasures to steal, either to sell to the Nazis or because they were Nazis."

"Oh." Ann swallowed hard, suddenly feeling foolish as she remembered her grandfather had told Peter about their plans for keeping the Bible safe. "What should I do now?"

"Check your suitcases when you get back to your room and let me know what you find. I'll keep running into you. People can think I'm the ship's Romeo chasing after a beautiful girl.

And the last part's true." He smiled and winked.

Ann felt herself blush. "I'll check my luggage and then come back to the library. I feel more comfortable here." Peter nodded and she left the room.

Back in her cabin, she went straight to her suitcase and opened it to find the contents as she had left them. Quickly, she pulled her travel bag out of the closet and placed it on the bed. As she opened it, she gasped. Someone had rummaged through it and left everything in a jumble! Her hands were shaking as she picked up the knitting bag and hurried to the library.

No one was in the room. She had taken out the afghan when the door opened, and Mr. Humbolt walked in. "Ah, so we meet again." He smiled at her. "And how is the afghan coming?"

Ann greeted him, and as she shifted in the chair, her foot caught the knitting bag. It plopped on its side with a *thud,* and balls of yarn rolled across the floor. "Oh, no!" She quickly grabbed as many as she could and turned to stuff them in the bag but instead stared in horror when she saw the copy of Shakespeare lying exposed.

She felt Mr. Humbolt stop beside her with the yarn he'd collected and looked up to see him staring at the book. "I see you enjoy Shakespeare." He motioned toward the book. "It must be very special to carry it with your knitting."

Prickles ran down Ann's spine. "It was a gift from my grandfather."

Mr. Humbolt bent over. "I collect old books. This one's very unusual. May I—"

As he reached out to pick it up, the door burst open and a wave of heavy perfume filled the air. "There you are, Winston!" Mrs. Van Peldt stalked into the room. "I saw you turn down this corridor." She gave a haughty smile and put her arm through his. "Let's leave the tourist class to itself." She patted his arm with a hand covered in sparkling rings.

Ann smiled weakly as she watched Mr. Humbolt's face turn a dark red and a frown cover his brow. The woman pulled on his arm and led him to the door. Ann sighed in relief. In the Bible God had used some unusual characters to accomplish His purposes; it looked like He still did!

When the door opened a moment later, Ann quickly reached for the knitting bag, then let out her breath as Peter stepped into the room. "I saw the gentleman leave and hoped you'd be alone." He took a seat and peered at her. "You look pale. Was something wrong with your suitcases?" As Ann related what she had found in her cabin, Peter gave a deep sigh. "Someone knows there isn't much time left to steal the Bible. Fortunately, no one realizes what you carry in that knitting bag."

"Oh, but now someone does!" She told him about spilling the contents of the bag and Mr. Humbolt's attempt to examine the book.

Peter was quiet a moment. "Ann, do you trust me? You know how much I care about you, but are you really convinced I'm who I say I am?"

The question caught Ann by surprise, and her suspicions and feelings struggled with each other. She knew she loved him, but did she believe him and trust him? It was true; he could have stolen the Bible a long time ago, and he'd been nothing but a help to her grandfather and her. She said a prayer for guidance, then nodded. "I trust you, Peter. What do you want me to do?"

"Let me take the book. If you don't have it, you won't be in danger." He watched her face carefully.

Ann couldn't breathe for a moment. *Lord, this is Your Word. Don't let anything happen to it!* She hesitated, then handed him the knitting bag.

Peter looked relieved and took an envelope from his pocket. "Your grandfather asked me to give you this when we met on the ship."

Ann blinked in surprise as she opened it and read the brief message. Relief washed over her, and she looked up at Peter. "Grandpa confirmed what you told me. I'm so sorry I suspected you." She flashed him a mischievous smile and motioned toward the bag. "Ready for some knitting lessons?"

"Knitting lessons, no, but I am counting on lots of hugs and kisses to even the score!" Grinning, Peter pulled her to her feet for a tender embrace. "You won't have to worry about the Bible now, so let's pretend this is a pleasure cruise and enjoy the rest of the trip. Those Germans are supposed to think this is a normal voyage. Let's show 'em!"

She felt her heart racing. "That sounds wonderful!"

"I need to take care of the Bible. You get ready, and I'll meet you by the main lounge in an hour." He lifted her chin and smiled into her eyes.

Chapter 11

For the rest of the voyage, Ann and Peter tried to forget the war as they swam in the pool and lounged on deck chairs. They strolled the enclosed promenade hand in hand, admiring the ocean view outside the sliding-glass windows. As they turned at the class barrier isolating the tourist-class promenade from that of first class, Ann chuckled. "Any minute I expect to see Mrs. Van Peldt leaping the class barrier so she can be on the first-class side."

Peter stopped at the windows, and they watched the ocean moving in rhythmic waves before he spoke. "Ann, when we dock, I don't intend to have you disappear from my life. I want some promises made between us." He glanced over at her. "Your grandfather said he'd welcome me into the family—if you so desire."

Ann's heart was pounding, and she could feel the red start to cover her face.

Peter held her close, then glanced at his watch and sighed. "I'll walk you to your cabin. We dock this afternoon, so we both need to pack. Then we'll continue this conversation and thank the Lord for a safe journey both for us and the treasure we carry."

"And let's ask Him to keep Grandpa and Mrs. Wilson safe," she added as they headed for her corridor. "I pray constantly their area of town has remained undamaged."

Back in her cabin, Ann rechecked the room, then closed her suitcases. She was putting the keys to her luggage in her purse when a knock sounded at the door. She opened it to find Mr. Humbolt standing there. "What are you doing here?" she asked as he entered and shut the door.

"Since we're about to disembark, I didn't want to miss my chance to inspect your unusual book," he said with a smirk. "I've never seen one like it. It's odd how you always kept it with your knitting but never read it. So, how about a look for a fellow book lover?"

Ann stood speechless. "But I don't have it anymore. I gave it to someone who wanted a book for the voyage."

"And who might that be? Mr. Peter Austin? Is he keeping it safe for you? My, my, you are clever, my dear. But he'll find he has a choice to make—you or the book. Which do you think he'll choose?" Mr. Humbolt looked at her with cold eyes.

Ann couldn't catch her breath. *Lord, please help me!* She jumped at a sudden knock on the door.

"Stay where you are. I'll answer it." He jerked the door open and stared.

"So this is where I find you!" Mrs. Van Peldt stalked into

the room, bristling with anger. She glared at Ann, then turned her ire on Winston. "All that sweet talk, and here you are chasing some young floozy. I've seen you come here before. Don't think you can take me for a fool!" She jabbed him in the chest with her long red nails.

Despite the serious situation, Ann chuckled to herself.

"It will take more than an apology before I forgive you, Winston." She pulled him toward the door. "We need to talk before the ship docks."

As she opened the door, Peter stepped inside, followed by a ship's officer, who quickly grasped Mr. Humbolt's arms. "You're not going anywhere, Humbolt. We checked you out and found you're nothing but a thief who preys on people aboard ship." Winston Humbolt struggled, but the officer kept a firm hold. "After a tip from Mr. Austin, we followed you here."

Mrs. Van Peldt gasped. "Winston, a thief? He can't be! I. . .uh. . .we. . .well, I never! That's what I get for lowering myself to traveling tourist class!" She thrust her chin in the air and stalked out of the room as the officer led Mr. Humbolt away.

Shaking, Ann sank against the wall. "How did he know I had the Bible?"

Peter shuddered as he let out his breath. "It's worth a lot of money, and word gets around. I'm sure those men outside your grandfather's shop weren't working alone. Someone must have had access to the passenger lists."

"The Bible! Peter, where is it?" Ann straightened quickly

and stared at him in alarm.

"In a box with a note on it," he said with a smug grin.

Ann frowned. "I don't understand."

Peter picked up her suitcases and headed to his cabin. "I put it in a box I got at the ship's gift shop." He opened the door and pointed to a box sitting on his suitcase. His coat was carelessly thrown on the pile. "I disguised it as a gift to someone special."

He picked up the box and turned it so she could read the label: *Kramer's Nativity Scenes—authentic reproductions of original works; 15"x20" set includes ceramic figurines, manger, and stable.* He placed the box in the knitting bag, then repacked the yarn around it. "I took out the heavy figurines and laid the Bible on the bottom, then put the stable walls on top and ended with straw and the small figures." He chuckled. "It's true; the box does contain nativity scenes!" He handed her the cloth bag, then led them back to the promenade, where they set their possessions on a bench.

Ann frowned. "But the box looked as if it had never been opened."

"Ah, another of my hidden talents, my dear." He winked and reached in the bag to retrieve a paper that lay on top of the box. "I said this was a gift for someone special. Read the note I left on it. It's addressed to you."

Ann took the paper. *"To the one who makes my life complete. Will you enjoy this nativity scene with me every Christmas for the rest of our lives? I love you with all my heart. Peter."*

Ann couldn't speak as she blinked back tears. Peter raised

an eyebrow, and she nodded her answer.

He took her in his arms. "There are two treasures in my life that are of immeasurable worth—God's Word and you. I don't intend to live without either again."

Ann nestled against his chest. "Peter, haven't you guessed why I blush whenever I'm around you? I've loved for you for a long time, but I knew I was a plain Jane while you're handsome, a writer, and a prof—"

"Hmm, keep talking!" He wagged his eyebrows at her. "Seriously, my love, you're anything but plain. And your sweet blush is what attracted me in the first place. Never change it."

She looked up at him and took a deep breath. "That note you left in the poetry book. Which poem made you think of me?"

His lips curved into a teasing grin. "Which do you want it to be?"

She felt her face grow warm as she answered softly, "I'd like to hear you count the ways you love me."

He smiled into her eyes. "My dear, I promise to spend the rest of my life telling you all the ways I love you, but for now I'll let Elizabeth Browning say it for me: 'I love thee with the breath, smiles, tears, of all my life! . . .' " He lifted her chin. "The only thing I can add is a kiss for punctuation!"

JOAN CROSTON

Joan lives with her husband Lee in the beautiful Missouri Ozarks. They have two married daughters and two lively young grandsons. She looks forward to snowy winter days that allow more time for her special interests—reading, writing, and family history. Correspondence with a distant cousin in Norway has helped her fill over forty notebooks with family history so far. This winter she hopes to connect the ancestry of her husband's fourth-great-grandfather who served with George Washington's troops at Valley Forge to the family's roots in Croston, England.

The Long
Road Home

by Joyce Livingston

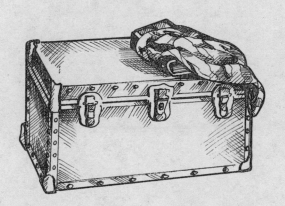

Chapter 1

Buzz Greeley plopped his muscular body onto the dormitory bed amid a clump of mingled sheets and grinned from the opposite side of the room. "About time. I need to get some z's. I gotta make a presentation in engineering class tomorrow morning on corona discharge."

He yanked off an expensive running shoe and tossed it in the direction of the wastebasket across the Dallas Technical College dorm room. The size-twelve shoe missed and hit the floor with a *kerplunk*. The other shoe followed with the same fate.

Nick held his nose, bent, and picked up both shoes, carefully placing them in Buzz's side of the closet before closing the door. "Anything I can do to help?"

Buzz pulled off his heavily soiled white socks and shoved them under his bed. "Go to class for me?"

"Hey, you need that class for your major."

"I know—but that class is hard. You wouldn't believe the stuff we're supposed to read. I never—"

"Engineers need to know that stuff."

"You take school too seriously, old buddy." Buzz lifted the pair of hand weights a few times, then dropped them onto the bed as he eyed his roommate. "How do you stay so fit, Nick? You hardly ever exercise, but look at you. You ain't got an ounce of fat on you, and your muscles are toned. I don't get it."

Nick sat down on his bed and leaned back on his hands, crossing his ankles. "Maybe it's because I walk to my classes instead of driving, and I don't drink beer or that sugar-laden stuff you drink. I'm lucky if I get one good meal a day." He gave Buzz a friendly smile. "But I do work out every day."

"You do? I've never seen you on the equipment at the rec center."

"Yep, sure do. Instead of taking the elevator the eight flights to our room, I take the stairs. That'll work the fat off you in no time."

"Eight flights? No wonder you ain't got no blubber on you."

"I haven't got any blubber on me," Nick said, correcting him with a grin.

Buzz frowned. "That's what I said." He reached his hand beneath the crumpled sheets in search of the TV control. "You oughtta be more like me. You gotta live a little before you're too old to enjoy it."

"Not me. I got plans." He slipped the chemistry book into the backpack hanging from his desk chair before turning to face Buzz again. "I'm gonna make my life count for something."

Buzz gave a snort. "What you need is a woman. I told you I'd be happy to fix you up with one of the girls in my class. There's this little cutie in my English—"

Nick cut him off midsentence. "Forget it! Someday I'd like to meet a nice girl and get married, but women take time and money, and right now, I have neither." With one quick swoop of his hand, he gathered up the change from the desktop, where he'd placed it when he'd showered, and stuffed it into the side pocket of his blue jeans. "I'm strictly here for an education. Period. That's it."

"You don't know what you're missing. How about going to the sports bar with me Saturday night? My treat!"

"How about spending the evening here in our room studying for a change, and I'll treat you to a diet drink from the machine in the hallway?"

Buzz lifted an arm, proudly displaying a flexed bicep. "And ruin my reputation? Never!"

"Beats failing."

"They wouldn't dare fail me. Not with the kind of money my dad pumps into this school. The Greeley name means something around here. If you don't believe me, check out the name on the new library."

Nick shook his head and pulled the door closed behind him.

He took the steps, two at a time, down the stairs, then jogged across the campus. *God, I'm trying. I really am. I just can't seem to reach Buzz. I know You put me with him as a witness for You, but—*

He glanced both directions, then bolted across the street toward the little all-night diner a couple of blocks away. The street was nearly deserted. His pace slowed and dwindled to a walk as his mind mulled over the facts he'd tried to absorb from his chemistry class. He liked chemistry. To think God put so many checks and balances in His creation was nothing short of a miracle. Why couldn't people like Buzz see that?

The clapper on the little brass bell fastened to the top of the door of Al's Diner clanged his arrival as he entered. Al, himself, waved his spatula and sent a smile. "Hiya, Nick. Didn't expect to see you here tonight. Been studying, huh?"

Nick nodded, looked around, and settled for one of the empty stools at the counter. "You alone tonight, Al?"

The pudgy man left the grill and joined him. "Naw, finally got me a new waitress. She's in the back lookin' for a jar of dill pickles. Hard to keep good help these days."

Nick playfully rammed his fist into the man's bicep. "Maybe they don't like working for a cranky old man."

Before Al could respond with a quip of his own, the swinging café doors to the storeroom swung open, and a pretty, dark-haired woman, who looked to be in her early twenties and was using enough makeup to keep a cosmetic counter in the profit margin, stepped through. She was wearing an extremely short, white uniform with a red apron tied around her slender waist and a pair of long, dangling red earrings. She stood smiling at Nick while balancing two one-gallon jars of pickles in her arms, her dazzling white teeth framed by an oval of deep red lipstick.

He leaped to assist her, but she shook her head and carefully turned and placed them on a shelf.

Nick couldn't help but stare. She was not at all like the last waitress he'd seen at the diner. That one had gotten furious with Al and quit. She'd looked as if she'd tried to cram her size-eighteen body into a size-twelve uniform and hadn't quite succeeded. *No,* he thought, keeping his eyes trained on the woman, *this waitress is nothing like the last one.*

With the pickle jars in place, she sauntered toward him, pad and pencil in hand, and, chomping on a wad of gum, asked, "What'll it be, Honey? We've got a great special tonight, just for you. Orange juice, two sausages, a nice slice of sugar-cured ham, two eggs, two pancakes, and all the hot coffee you can put in that flat tummy of yours. All for only four ninety-five."

Nick stared at the woman. How could anyone be that cheery at eleven-thirty on a weeknight? His hands went to his pockets as he fingered the change he'd put there earlier. Without checking, he knew exactly what was there. Three quarters, two dimes, a nickel, and two pennies. Certainly not enough for the special she'd touted. "Just coffee."

She tilted her head a bit. "How about a nice piece of warm apple pie with a big round scoop of creamy vanilla ice cream on top? Doesn't that sound good?"

Yes, it sounds wonderful, especially since I haven't had any supper. "Just coffee, thank you," he mumbled, wishing he could afford the pie. Al's Diner was famous for its homemade pies, made by Al's wife herself.

With a wink, the woman slipped the order pad into her apron pocket and stuck the pencil over her ear. "Coffee coming right up, but if you change your mind about that pie, you just sing out *Angela,* and I'll bring it right over. I'm sure a handsome young man like you would enjoy that pie."

Angela? Nice name. He watched as she turned and reached for the stainless steel pot, grabbed a cup from the shelf, and filled it with the steaming hot liquid. It smelled good. Just what he needed after an evening of intense studying. Why was an attractive young woman like Angela working the late shift at Al's Diner? Surely there were better jobs for a pretty woman like her.

"Cream, Handsome?"

"Ah. . .cream?" Her question caught him looking at her, and he felt himself blushing. He shook his head as his hands wrapped around the cup. "I–I like it black."

He couldn't help noticing once again her exceptionally short skirt as she turned her back on him to return the pot to the warmer. Knowing he should, he quickly turned away and stared out the window.

She gave him a coy smile. "You live around here, Honey?"

"No. I mean yes." He knew he sounded like a bumpkin, but for some reason, his brain went fuzzy. Maybe he'd been missing too much sleep, studying into the wee hours of the morning. Or maybe it was from going without proper food.

"I'm a student," he finally blurted out. "I graduate this spring."

"Wow!" Her dark eyes rounded with interest. "At that

fancy college down the street?"

He had to laugh. No one he knew had ever used that term to describe Dallas Tech. Not with the type of classes they taught there. "Yes, at the college down the street," he answered, trying to conceal his amusement.

Al let out a generous chuckle. "Hey, Angela, that school Nick goes to's not fancy, just expensive."

Angela smiled over her shoulder at her employer, but immediately turned her attention back to her customer. "You're Nick, huh?"

Nick felt himself smiling. "Yeah, Nick."

"Well, Nick," Angela began, drawling out his name like a southern belle would pronounce it, "you some rich kid?"

Nick couldn't keep himself from responding with a boisterous laugh. "Hardly! I'm barely scraping by."

She eyed his simple T-shirt suspiciously and glanced down at his worn sneakers. "Then why are you going to school there? Seems you could find a cheaper school somewhere else."

"Not with the kind of training as a structural engineer I'm getting here at Dallas Tech. They're famous worldwide," he explained with pride. "Coming to DT is a dream come true for me."

"So what are they teaching you? To be some big executive? You gonna make big bucks someday?"

"Executive? Me?" The corners of his mouth turned up, and he was sure she could read the amusement on his face. "No," he said evenly, masking a laugh at the ridiculous idea.

"Some students may end up being executives, but certainly not me."

She reached for the pot and refilled his cup, although he'd barely taken two sips. "Why not you? You're a handsome guy, and you seem smart enough. I'll bet you make good grades, don't you? All As and Bs, or whatever letters of the alphabet they use in college."

Before he could answer, an elderly couple entered and seated themselves in a booth by the window. Angela scurried over to hand them a menu, then stood by touting the evening's special.

Nick shifted in his seat to watch. She reminded him of the girls he'd grown up with in the Bronx. Brassy. Confident. Heavily made up. Dresses too tight and too revealing for their own good. He'd known what the guys were thinking. He'd been one of them. They'd made no secret of it. The terms they'd used to describe women like Angela left no doubt as to what they thought of them.

He bit his lip as she bent over the table to point out something on the menu, then stared at her for an unguarded moment before turning away again, busying himself by reading a newspaper someone had left on the counter. He'd promised himself, when and if he dated, the girls would always be ones he could marry, with the same high standards he'd set for himself. One look at Angela told him this woman was not dating or marrying material. At least, not for him.

Although he kept his eyes trained on the paper, he listened, despite his resolve, as she patiently explained the menu's items to her customers. Her tone was light and friendly, and she had an easy way about her. A likeable way.

"Pretty cute, isn't she?" Al asked as he poured himself another cup of coffee and rejoined Nick at the counter. "The minute that girl came through that door and filled out her application, I knew the customers would like her. That one's got a way about her."

Nick tried to appear nonchalant, as if he wasn't aware of Angela's beauty. "She's all right, I guess. I really didn't notice."

He felt Al's elbow jab at his ribs. "Sure you didn't."

"She from around here?" *Why did I ask that? It's none of my business where she lives.*

Al shrugged. "Here. There. Arkansas. New York. That one's been around. I get the feeling she's had a hard life."

"Oh? How so?" Nick found himself wanting to know more about this woman he'd met only minutes ago. Something about her fascinated him.

"Can't say for sure. Just a feeling the wife and I got when we looked over her application."

Nick folded up the newspaper and placed it on the counter. "Well, from the looks that couple are giving her, I think you picked a winner. They like her."

"She's a good worker, too. Been waitressing since she started high school. You're right. She sure knows how to handle people."

"That she does," Nick agreed, his attention once again fastened on the dark-haired beauty. "I'm surprised she doesn't work in a department store or someplace like that."

Al gave a harrumph. "And miss out on the tips? Not that one. She knows a good deal when she sees it. Hard to find good help with the wages we can afford to pay. I was lucky to get her. But tips? She'll clean up like one of them one-armed bandits in Las Vegas."

"Tips? She makes that good on tips?"

"Guess you poor college boys don't know much about tipping. Most waitresses make fifteen percent tips, but a good waitress with personality? One who gives good service? I've seen guys order a single eighty-nine-cent cup of coffee and leave a five-dollar tip. If a cute little gal gives good service, a friendly smile, and a bit of chitchat, she can do real good. I'll bet some nights Angela makes as much as a hundred and fifty dollars in tips. Even more on weekends."

Nick rested his elbows on the counter and took a slow sip of his coffee, savoring the soothing liquid and remembering the little amount of change he had in his pocket. *If the coffee costs eighty-nine cents, and I have to pay six percent tax, that's ninety-five cents, leaving enough left over for a seven-cent tip.* A frown creased his forehead. *I can't even make the fifteen percent minimum!*

"She probably won't be here long," Al was saying. "The good ones always move on. Usually get hired by one of my competitors or some fancy restaurant."

"More coffee, Sugar?"

Nick swiveled around and nearly collided with the stainless steel pot in Angela's hand as he slid off the stool. "No, thanks. I've had my fill. I have to get back to my dorm room. Still got some studying to do yet tonight."

"Looks like you're out of here, too, Angela," Al said with a sigh as he rang Nick's coffee up on the old brass cash register. "It's midnight."

Angela glanced at the wall clock. "Sure is." She deposited Nick's empty cup in the gray plastic container already loaded with dirty dishes, then untied her apron before reaching beneath the counter and pulling out a macramé shoulder bag and slinging it over her shoulder.

Nick awkwardly fumbled with the change still left in his pocket. He wanted to leave her a tip. But now instead of leaving it beside his empty cup, he'd have to either hand it to her or forget about leaving one.

"Good night, Al. You, too, Honey," she called back over her shoulder as she made her way toward the door, stooping long enough to pick up a paper napkin someone had dropped on the floor and tossing it into the little wastebasket by the gum machine.

Nick raced to beat her to the door, pulling it open for her before she could reach the handle.

She gave him a demure smile. "Well, a gentleman! Thank you, Sweetie."

He followed her out, fully expecting to see her crawl into one of the few cars that dotted the parking lot's broken blacktop. But instead, she turned in the direction of the narrow sidewalk that led along the road and through the mostly residential neighborhood that surrounded the little strip mall. Since the college was in the same direction, Nick didn't know whether he should catch up and walk beside her or hang back and let her wonder if he was following her.

She made the decision for him. "Going my way, Darlin'?"

Nick nodded and moved up beside her, his finger pointing straight ahead. "My dorm is just up there a few blocks."

"Well then, walk with me. My apartment is this way." She took his arm and smiled up into his face. "Been a long time since a handsome young man has walked me home."

Nick fumbled for words, but none came. All he could think about was the pretty, bubbly woman who was tightly clutching his arm.

"So? What you wanna be when you grow up, Nick?"

She grinned, and even in the dim light from the streetlights, he could see the whites of her perfect teeth and her sparkling blue eyes shining up at him.

"An engineer. That's my major."

Her tinkling laughter pierced the silence of the surrounding darkness of the midnight hour. "You're gonna drive a train?"

He threw back his head with a raucous laugh, something he seldom did these days with the pressure of school and the workload he carried. "No! Not that kind of engineer."

Her fingers tightened about his arm, and he had to admit it felt good to have female companionship. He'd denied himself such relationships since he'd left New York. He went on to explain the kinds of jobs for which his degree in engineering would qualify him, summing it all up with, "So you see, four years of hard work and sacrifice will pay off in the end. I graduate this coming May."

Angela seemed impressed. As they walked along, she asked other questions pertaining to his studies and degree, appearing to be genuinely interested. Nick found himself enjoying their impromptu visit.

"Well, this is where I turn off." She let go of his arm and moved away from him. "My apartment is up in the next block. I've enjoyed talking with you, Nick."

No way was he going to let Angela walk the rest of the way by herself. He was too much of a gentleman to let that happen—now. At one time, he wouldn't have cared. "I'll walk with you."

A hand went to her hip, and her smile disappeared as she eyed him warily. "There's no reward at the end of the trail, if that's what you're expecting."

It took only a split second for him to get her meaning. "No," he hurried to explain. "It's not what you think. I don't like to see a woman—any woman—walking by herself this time of night. Too many things can happen. I just want to see you home safely, that's all."

The smile returned as she tilted her head and reached out her hand. "Can't blame me for being suspicious. You're right. A girl can't be too careful. I don't want to end up a statistic."

Nick accepted her hand and placed it in the crook of his arm, and they continued their slow walk. "I'm glad you're being careful. Too much orneriness goes on these days. I'd hate to be a woman."

"I love being a woman," Angela confessed, smiling that dazzling smile of hers. "But it does have its disadvantages as well as its advantages."

A lo-rider car drove by slowly, its occupants veiled by darkened windows. Nick felt Angela's grip tighten on his arm, and he was glad he'd insisted on walking her home. The pair watched in silence as the car slowed, came to a stop, and then suddenly took off again, screeching its tires.

"Wonder what would have happened if you hadn't been with me?" Angela asked in a hushed voice. "You'd be surprised at some of the offers I get. None that I'd want!"

Nick shuddered as all sorts of scenarios ran though his mind. "You don't live alone, do you?"

She gave him a puzzled look. "Me? Sure I do. I'd rather live in my one-room walk-up than share a larger apartment with some other woman and her boyfriends. Been there, done that. I could tell you horror stories you wouldn't believe. Nope, I've given up on roomies. I'd rather wing it on my own."

He instantly thought of Buzz and the mess in his half of the dorm room, a half that always seemed to extend itself over onto his side. Not to mention the wastebaskets filled with beer cans the man never thought to empty. "I hear that. I'm looking forward to having my own place someday."

"You got a girlfriend, Nick?"

"Nope. No women in my life," he answered quickly, then wondered if his answer denoted anything but what he intended it should. It wasn't that he was anti-women. Far from it. The sight of a pretty girl turned his head just like it did other men. Someday, he'd like to find the woman God had for him, marry her, and treat her like God's Word says a man should treat his wife. But until he finished college and headed wherever he felt God would have him go, women and dating were off-limits. What woman would want a man who could only leave a seven-cent tip, anyway?

"Nick! I asked you a question."

Angela's words brought him back to reality. "What? Sorry, guess my mind wandered."

"I asked you why there were no women in your life. You're a handsome hunk. I'd think you'd have a string of college girls chasing after you."

"Uh-huh, sure." He shrugged with a laugh. "No time. I'm too busy with schoolwork and my weekend job, and I sure can't afford to wine and dine them."

"Not much I can afford, either. But someday, I'd like to have a little house of my own. A husband and a couple of kids, too."

He caught a glimpse of her beautiful face as a car turned into a driveway, shining its lights across them as they walked.

"Maybe even a dog," she added with a good-natured laugh. "I might even add a white picket fence."

He thought he detected a bit of melancholy in her voice. "That shouldn't be too difficult for a pretty girl like you to achieve. I'll bet you have plenty of guys after you."

"Yeah, I do. But none I'd care to spend any time with, let alone the rest of my life. You don't know what it's like out there for a woman. Most guys have only one thing on their mind, and it ain't marriage. I refuse to be anyone's evening entertainment."

Nick considered her words. She didn't sound at all like the airhead he'd expected. Perhaps she wasn't a party girl after all. Had he misjudged her? A wave of guilt swept through him. How many times had people misjudged him? He well remembered that pain. Although she appeared tough and capable of taking care of herself in any situation, he found a certain softness and vulnerability under that hardened shell she'd created for herself. A softness she apparently wanted to hide.

"What do you want out of life, Nick?"

Her personal question drew him back from his thoughts and gave him pause. What he really wanted out of life—the thing he'd vowed to do above all else—was not something he was ready to share. With her or anyone.

"It's kinda hard to put in words," he offered feebly, not ready to bare his soul.

"Try." She leaned into him as they walked, matching him stride for stride, despite their difference in height.

"Well, I want to be the best engineer I can be, for starters."

"Anyplace in particular?"

He pursed his lips and crooked a brow thoughtfully, wondering if she'd laugh at his answer. "Anywhere God wants me."

Her pace instantly slowed. Even in the darkness, he could feel Angela's stare.

"Are you for real, Nick? Do you really mean that? About God?"

Did her tone hold a bit of ridicule? Or was he imagining it because he expected a ridiculing response from her? "Yes, Angela, I do mean it. Because of Jacob Austin, a wonderful, caring man I met, I dedicated my life to the Lord four years ago. God's will for me is the most important thing in my life."

They took the few remaining yards to her place in silence. "You're really serious, aren't you?" she asked finally as she stepped onto the bottom step of the long flight of stairs leading up to her apartment and turned back to face him.

"Totally serious." In the light of the inadequate string of bulbs hanging along the first-floor landing, he could see her better now. The expression on her face held none of the ridiculing signs he'd expected. "I'm a changed man because of Jacob."

She tilted her head and eyed him for some time, her black lashes nearly shuttering her dark eyes into oblivion. "You're not one of those crazies who chant and wave your hands in the air, are you? Like the ones I see on TV sometimes?"

Nick cupped her hands in his, a big grin stretching across his face. "Not exactly, but I have been known to lift my hands toward heaven in grateful thanks and praise for God's goodness to me."

She swallowed at a giggle. "But you don't roll in the aisles or let snakes wrap themselves around you, right?"

Her naïveté almost amused him. "No, I don't do either of those things."

She leaned against the banister and crossed her arms. "That stuff may be okay for you, Nick, but God never done nothin' for me. I begged Him to make my drunken stepdad stop beating me and my mom, but He never did it."

"Oh, Angela, I'm so sorry." At her words, memories of his own life rushed at him like a runaway truck on a downhill grade. His own childhood had been miserable. His father had beaten both him and his mother mercilessly.

She let out a big sigh. "I'm sure he's still beating on my mom. I've tried to get her to leave him and move here to Dallas with me, but she won't do it. It's a way of life with her now. She doesn't know any different."

"Unfortunately, that's the way it is with many women."

As if eager to get away from the subject, with a playful smile, Angela gave his arm a nudge. "Who is this Jacob guy you keep talking about? One of your fancy professors?"

Nick hesitated, then pulled himself up to his full six-foot-three.

"He's my parole officer."

Chapter 2

Your parole officer?" The words nearly burst from Angela's lips.

Nick nodded. "I haven't been completely honest with you, Angela."

"Jacob is actually your parole officer?"

Even in the dim light, he could tell his statement had shocked her. Was that fear he read on her face? "Yes, but—"

"I—I'd better get on up to my apartment." Grasping the handrail, she quickly moved up a couple of steps, then called back over her shoulder, "Thanks for walking me home," before racing up the stairs and disappearing.

Nick knew what he'd seen on her face had been fear, and he was almost sorry he'd told her about Jacob. Well, not sorry exactly, but he wished he hadn't blurted it out so suddenly. Of course, she was frightened. She'd met him less than an hour ago, and here she was, alone with a stranger in a semidarkened area after midnight. What he wanted to do was rush up the stairs after her and assure her he was not the same man he used to be, but that would only frighten her even more. No, it'd be better to let her go. As often as he went into Al's Diner, he was sure to run into her again. Maybe at that time he could explain.

Buzz was sound asleep with the remote control still in his hand, the TV blaring full blast. Nick rushed to the set and hit the power button. Except for the loud snores coming from his roommate, the room instantly went silent. He picked up a couple of empty beer cans from the middle of the floor, where Buzz probably tossed them when he was through with them, and dropped them into the trash. The man spent more for beer in a week than Nick was able to spend on food.

Nick studied until he finished his assignment, then glanced at his watch. Seeing how late it was, he decided to forgo his shower until morning. He picked up his Bible and tried to read from it, but his thoughts kept drifting back to the cute little waitress and her winning smile.

He had just stepped out of the shower the next morning when he heard a groan and a moan, and Buzz's lined face appeared in the bathroom doorway.

"Hey, man, how come you didn't wake me up? You knew I had that thing to do in class this morning."

"Me wake you up? What happened to your alarm clock?"

Buzz leaned his bulky body against the doorjamb and rubbed one hand briskly over his shaved head and his wrinkled face. "Forgot to set it."

Nick pulled his disposable razor from the medicine cabinet and waved it toward his roommate. "Buzz, are you ever going to grow up and quit depending on other people? You knew what you had to do this morning. Do you even know what the word *responsibility* means?"

Buzz seemed too sleepy to be offended by his words and just gave him a blank stare. "Probably just as well. I wasn't ready for it anyhow."

Softening his tone a bit, Nick clamped a hand on the man's shoulder. "You're gonna fail. Is that really what you want, Buzz?"

Buzz gave a big yawn before answering. "I dunno. Guess it don't make no difference whether I graduate or not. When I'm twenty-two, I can start drawing out of the trust fund my granddad left me. I won't need to work, so why bother myself with good grades?"

Why, Lord? Why do some people have things dropped in their lap, while others, like me, have to work for every little thing? He'd no more than had that thought when another replaced it, one he knew came as an answer from God. *All things work together for good to those who love God.*

"But wouldn't you like to accomplish something on your own? Something you could be proud of, like graduating from college with at least mediocre grades?"

Buzz shrugged. "Why?"

Nick shook his head sadly as he rinsed the razor and placed it back on the shelf. He actually felt sorry for the man, despite his wealth.

"Hey, Nick, old buddy, suppose I could get you to do a favor for me? I'll pay you for it."

He eyed him suspiciously. "What kind of favor?"

"When I was over at the sports bar the other night, me and another guy made a bet as to which of us could drink the most beer."

Nick moved into their room, with Buzz at his heels, and started pulling on the clean clothes he'd laid out after he'd made his bed and straightened his side of the dorm room. "What's that got to do with me?"

"The guy that lost was supposed to wash the other guy's car—by hand. I thought sure I could win, but I lost, and I don't wanna have to wash a car by hand. That's hard work, and I got better things to do with my time."

Nick considered it. The money would come in handy.

"Come on, Nick. Help a guy out. I'll pay you twenty bucks."

"Why don't you just take it to a car wash?"

Buzz sat down on the side of his bed. "Can't. Part of the deal was it had to be done by hand, but we didn't say whose hand. So you can do it for me!"

"Well, I guess maybe—"

"Okay," Buzz interjected quickly, "twenty-five. It'd be worth it to me, and knowing you, you'll do a good job. Please?"

Twenty-five bucks? I'd do it for ten! "Okay, you got a deal."

❖   ❖   ❖

By eleven-thirty that night, Al's Diner was nearly empty. Angela busied herself loading the sugar and creamer packets into the little ceramic holders on each table, filling the catsup and mustard containers, and adding more napkins to the chrome dispensers. Her feet were killing her, despite the white, heavily cushioned sneakers she always wore, but her apron pocket was heavy with the evening's tips. It'd been a good night. She made a final round of her tables, making sure each one and its accompanying chairs were spotless, then lowered herself onto one of the stools at the counter with an outward sigh.

"Busy night, huh?" Al asked, filling his coffee cup and settling down beside her.

She wiggled her toes inside her shoes, hoping the sharp pain she felt wasn't a new blister. "Yeah, but my tips were pretty good. I can sure use the extra money."

"I wish I could pay you more, Angela, you know that, but my wife says we can't do it."

She gave his arm a gentle pat. She liked Al. He'd been good to her right from the start. So had his wife. "I know, Al. I'm not complaining. By the way, thanks for helping me out with those guys who hit on me tonight."

"No problem. I don't like to see anybody hitting on you." He picked up his cup and headed for the kitchen. "Look, it's nearly midnight. Why don't you go on home? I can handle things here. Go on now. I mean it. You've had a rough night."

"Thanks, Al." Angela gave him a weak smile. She was almost too tired to get up off the stool and head out the door.

She grabbed her purse from behind the counter and gave him a wave, then moved through the door and walked slowly across the parking lot. Her breath caught as someone moved in the shadows. She stood motionless, poised to run back in the diner at the slightest provocation, as the figure headed toward her.

"Hi, Angela."

She recognized the voice immediately. It was Nick. She didn't know whether to be thankful it was him or afraid. "Nick? What are you doing here?"

He moved slowly toward her, as if giving her plenty of time to retreat if she decided to run away from him again. "I need to talk to you. To explain about Jacob."

"I. . .ah. . .I. . ." She backed up a step, still not sure if she should make a hasty retreat.

"Would you at least hear me out? Please?"

If he'd meant her any harm, he had certainly had the opportunity to do it the night before when they'd been walking up the dark, tree-lined street toward her home, but he hadn't, and she did like him. He was not only nice, but he acted and spoke like a true gentleman. "I–I guess so."

He extended a hand. "Can I walk you home?"

She gazed at his face and found nothing there but gentleness, and for some reason, her fears of the night before all but vanished. "I–I guess so." She ignored his hand but began to walk in the direction of her apartment.

"I shouldn't have answered your question quite so bluntly when you asked me about Jacob. I realized that later, and I apologize."

She turned her head slightly toward him as they moved onto the sidewalk. "But he is your parole officer, right?"

"*Was* my parole officer. That was several years ago. Now, he's my best friend."

She frowned and shook her head. "Isn't that a little strange?"

"You wouldn't think so if you knew Jacob. If it wasn't for him and his influence on my life, who knows where I would've ended up?" Nick hung his head, as if some memory was all too fresh in his mind. "I was in some pretty deep trouble when that man was assigned to my case. Probably would've ended up in prison like my dad. I was walking right in his footsteps."

Angela drew in a quick breath. "Is your dad still there?" She could see the pain on his face as he shook his head.

"He died in a fight with another inmate a few years ago, before I turned my life over to God." Nick swallowed hard. "I never had a chance to tell him about it."

"And your mom?"

"She's gone, too. Last year. But praise God, my mom became a Christian before it was too late. Once Jacob read to her from his Bible and explained what God said—"

"And because of that, you think she might be in heaven?"

"I know she is. God's Word tells me—"

Angela quit walking as one hand went to her hip. "You know, you seem like an alright guy, but this God-stuff of yours makes no sense to me at all. How can a grown man with a college education believe that just because someone tells God she's sorry for some stuff she's done in her life, she's gonna end up in heaven? Seems more like a fairy tale to me. Something some little kid who didn't know better would believe."

Nick took her hand in his. "That's exactly the way I felt, Angela, before I met Jacob. After explaining God's Word to me and the things God has laid out in the Bible for us to do if we want to spend eternity with Him, Jacob put it this way. Just suppose it is true. Do you want to take that chance and deny it?"

She'd never thought of it that way before. What if the Bible *was* true?

They walked along in silence until they reached the next streetlight. Finally, Nick spoke. "I didn't mean to offend you, Angela, but if you would've known me before God sent Jacob into my life and the way I've changed since that time, you'd believe in miracles. I've done a complete turnaround. Not because of the fear of going to prison or the mumbo-jumbo of the judge's words, but because of the change in my heart brought about by God. Even if I'd gone to prison, I would have been a free man. I no longer want to do any of those things I used to do; I want to do God's will whether He calls me to work and witness right here in Dallas or go to some faraway mission field. I'm His now, Angela, and I love being His."

Angela shrugged. "I guess I'm dense. I just don't get it, but if you want to believe those things, who am I to argue? At least, it's turned you into something better than you were before. I guess that's a good thing."

"I—I'd like to get to know you better."

The shyness in his voice was refreshing. No one had ever said that to her before. Most guys came on like a speeding freight train, barging into her life whether she wanted them to or not. "I—I think I'd like that, too, Nick," she told him, hoping this wasn't some new approach he'd thought up.

When they reached the stairs leading up to her apartment,

she stood for a long moment on the second step gazing down at him, not sure what to do or say next. "I'd invite you up; but—"

He pulled her hand into his again and smiled at her. For some reason, that smile made her insides tingle.

"No, thanks. Some other time maybe. When you get to know me better."

"When will I see you again, Nick?"

"You're off tomorrow night, aren't you? Do you have any plans?"

There was that tingle again. "No, I don't have any plans."

"Good. I'll pick you up about six. Maybe we can take in a movie or something."

Angela said yes so quickly she surprised herself. She stood watching as a smile played at his lips. Finally, ever so slowly, he moved toward her and his lips slightly brushed hers. It was only a hint of a kiss, the sweetest kiss any man had ever given her.

"See you tomorrow night," she said, afraid she must look dreamy-eyed.

Nick gave her a boyish grin. "See you at six, and thanks, Angela, for saying yes."

When she reached the landing, she turned to say good night one final time, but Nick was gone—disappeared into the shadows. *I have a date. An actual date, and with a man I think I can trust!*

Chapter 3

Angela stood at the foot of the stairs when Nick roared into her parking lot a few minutes before six. Ever since he'd asked her out, he'd been questioning his wisdom. Hadn't Jacob told him to be careful about dating girls who didn't share his faith? But how could he witness to someone if he didn't spend time with her? At least, that's the logic he'd used to explain the way he was drawn to Angela. He shut down the engine and pulled off his helmet.

Angela stood gaping at him. "That's a motorcycle!"

He had to laugh at the surprised look on her face. "Good observation."

She moved slowly toward him, her gaze flitting from his smiling face to the old Harley and back again. "I—I thought you had a car."

He threw one leg over the seat and dismounted. "That'd be nice, but I can't afford one. I wouldn't have this if one of the rich college students hadn't decided to trash it when its engine went out. As cheap as he sold it to me, I knew I could fix it and make money on it if I ever decided to sell it." He circled the cycle and eyed the short shorts and halter top she was wearing. "Maybe we'd better walk. That outfit isn't exactly motorcycle garb. Not that I plan to have a wreck, but—"

She lowered her head and stared at her outfit. "Do you have time for me to change?"

Relieved, Nick nodded. "Sure. How about a pair of jeans and a long-sleeved shirt?" Not only was her outfit unsafe to be riding on a motorcycle, it was downright revealing. Even though he would be proud to be seen with Angela, he wouldn't want anyone to see him on a date with someone dressed that scantily. "For safety's sake," he added quickly as she headed back up the stairs.

Angela came back in no time, dressed in jeans as he'd requested. Jeans that looked as though she'd been born with them on, and she'd grown up but they hadn't, and they were low-cut. Really low-cut. Nick stared at her. The short shorts might've been less revealing, but she'd done as he'd asked, without complaining or questioning. He could be grateful for that. Her long-sleeved shirt wasn't much better. It was made of some sheer flimsy fabric, with the tails tied securely in a knot inches over her exposed belly button. *God, keep my mind pure.*

He helped her strap on her helmet, mounted his cycle, then motioned her on behind him. With the twenty-five dollars folded securely in his pocket, he took off out the driveway and onto the narrow street. He hadn't asked her where she wanted to go, but he knew where he wanted to take her.

It felt good with Angela's arms wrapped around him as they rode through the streets of Dallas and turned onto the freeway. The evening was beautiful, perfect for a motorcycle ride. He hoped Angela was enjoying it as much as he was. He peeled off when they came to the proper exit, then drove the two blocks to their first stop. His favorite place for tacos. Mama Guadalupe's Taco Palace.

He grinned over his shoulder as he turned the key in the ignition, knowing from experience there wasn't one thing on the menu over six ninety-five. Even with drinks, his twenty-five dollars would be enough to cover it and still make the tip.

Angela slid off the cycle, quickly removed her helmet, and grinned at him. "How'd you know I like Mexican food?"

"Lucky guess. Mama Guadalupe makes terrific burritos. I come here when I have—when I can."

They stood at the counter perusing the large menu that'd been painted in sprawling turquoise letters on the bright, rose-colored walls.

"What's good?" Angela asked as she stood next to him, one hand on her hip, the index finger of her other hand lightly touching her chin.

He slipped an arm about her waist and pointed to the sign. "The beef burritos. They're my favorite."

She nodded. "Then that's what I'll have—and a fresh limeade."

Nick released his hold on her and moved up to the counter. "Two beef burritos with extra sauce, and two fresh limeades." He turned to give his date a shy grin. "Nachos?"

She nodded and grinned back. "Sure."

By the time their order number was called, they were deep in conversation at a corner table for two. Nick picked up their tray and distributed their food before settling back down, placing their empty tray on a nearby rack. He felt awkward doing it, but he had to ask. " Angela, do you mind if I thank God for our food?"

She gave him a playful frown. "Why should you? You paid for it. He didn't." Then she let out a merry laugh as her hand covered his. "Go ahead. I'm kidding."

He prayed, selecting his words carefully because not only was God listening, but so was Angela. When he said, "Amen," he found her staring at him.

"You really were praying, weren't you?"

Her question surprised him, yet he was pleased by the seriousness with which she'd asked it. It wasn't in a haughty, derisive tone; it was a sincere question, and he was delighted to answer it. "Sure, I was really praying. I told you God has changed my life, Angela. I don't pray because I feel like I have to; I pray because I want to. Everything I have, including each breath I take, is from Him. Sadly, most folks don't want to acknowledge that."

She gave him another one of those smiles that made his heart do funny things, then picked up her burrito and bit into it. Some of the sauce trickled onto her chin. Nick quickly grabbed up his paper napkin and touched it to her face as they both giggled. They enjoyed their burritos and limeades, and even finished off the huge plate of nachos while they talked about some of Angela's experiences work-ing at Al's.

"Where do we go from here?" Angela asked when she came back from the ladies' room, her freshly applied lipstick a vivid red on her full mouth.

Nick couldn't help wondering what she'd look like with-out all that heavy eye makeup and her voluminous hair, which the helmet had flattened down considerably. "You'll see."

They climbed back onto his old Harley and once again Angela locked her arms about his waist. He still had a little over five dollars in his pocket, but the place he planned to take her wasn't going to cost him a dime.

About a mile later, they pulled into a church parking lot loaded with cars. Nick circled the lot several times, finally spotting an empty place at the far end. He maneuvered into it and turned off the engine. Angela's grip on his waist didn't let up.

"You're taking me to church?" she asked over his shoul-der. "I haven't been to church in years, and I'm sure not dressed for it. Why didn't you warn me, Nick?"

"You'll like this, and don't worry about the way you're dressed. Most of the people will be in jeans or slacks. The members of this church don't judge people by the way they dress."

Though she seemed reluctant, Angela finally loosened her grip and slid off the cycle. "Maybe you'd better take me on home, and then you can come back if you want to."

Nick climbed off, took both their helmets, and locked

them behind the tall seat back. "I will, if you want me to," he told her, placing his hands on her shoulders, "but I'd much rather you come in with me. If, once we get inside, you don't want to stay, I promise we'll leave immediately. Deal?"

She gave him a look of skepticism. "You mean that?"

He nodded and reached out his hand. She stared at it for a second, then took it and moved up to walk beside him.

A large crowd filled the church, and they ended up having to sit in the last row. "Why are all these people here?" Angela asked him, whispering.

Nick laughed. "You don't have to whisper. The service hasn't even started yet." But before he could answer her question, a man dressed in jeans and a black T-shirt printed with huge overlapping circles of fluorescent reds, greens, blues, and yellows crossed the platform and yanked a mike off its stand. "Are you ready for some great music?" he shouted at the crowd as he lifted a Bible in the air.

It seemed all those gathered shouted a thunderous, "Yes!" The curtains parted, exposing a band of men and women playing guitars, drums, trumpets, an electronic keyboard, and several other instruments. At the director's signal, the music started.

Nick watched Angela's face, hoping she'd like the Christian band his church was sponsoring as a free-to-the-public concert. He had to smile to himself as her expression changed from one of suspicion, to one of surprise, to one of enjoyment. Her foot began to tap, and her hands began to clap along with the rest of the audience.

"Great music," Angela said as she leaned toward him, a smile on her face when the first set ended. "I like it!"

He gave her a teasing nudge. "Still want to leave?"

"No way. This is great!"

The concert went on for nearly two more hours, with quick inserts of testimony by each of the band's members. Though Nick listened to the music, he constantly prayed. *God, please reach Angela and soften her heart. She needs You.*

At the conclusion of the concert, the leader extended an invitation to those who wanted to know more about being a Christian, asking them to come forward and meet with the band members. Nick waited, his heart pounding as he watched Angela, hoping and praying she'd want to go down to the front, but instead, she turned to him and asked, "Are you ready to leave?" Though his heart did a nosedive, he thanked God that Angela had come with him.

On the way home, they stopped for an ice cream cone at the Big Dipper, giggling like two grade-schoolers as the warm evening melted the ice cream and they had to keep licking the outer edge of their cones. Nick loved Angela's laugh. It was like a melody to his receptive ears. A melody he knew would play over and over in his mind long after he'd left her.

Is it my imagination, or is Angela's grip around my waist even tighter now? he wondered as they rode the short distance to her apartment.

"Wanna come up?" she asked as she handed her helmet to him. "I could fix us some iced tea or a soft drink."

He wanted desperately to say yes, but being in Angela's

apartment, alone with her, might not be a good idea at this stage of their relationship. He grinned to himself. *What relationship?* "Naw, it's late. I'd better get back to the dorm and let you get some sleep."

Angela walked to the stairway and stepped onto the first step, making her nearly equal to his height. "I had a great time tonight, Nick. Honest." She slipped her arms over his shoulders and locked her hands at the nape of his neck. "The concert was great. I'd never heard music like that before, and at church!"

Nick stared into her lovely face, focusing on those big blue eyes framed by too much mascara. She smelled good. Like peaches and cream. "I had a great time, too, Angela. Thanks for being such a good sport. You know, riding on my motorcycle and all."

She leaned her forehead against his and smiled into his face. "And thank you for asking me."

His heart pounded in his chest. She stood so close. So appealing. His lips crossed the no-fly zone and caressed hers before he could stop them. Despite the red flag that waved frantically in his brain, he wrapped his arms about her and kissed her again, this time, lingering even longer.

He felt Angela draw in a deep breath when their lips parted. "Oh, Nick," she said in a feathery voice. "No man has ever made me feel the way you do."

He swallowed hard. Had his desire to witness to her turned into something else? Earthly desires? "I–I like you, too," he finally managed to say. "Ca–can I walk you home after you get off work tomorrow night?"

"I'd love it." She leaned forward, kissing him again.

His head reeled. No woman—and in his teenage years there had been many women—had ever made him feel the way he did with her, either. He wanted to wrap her in his arms and never let her go. Despite his reserves, his lips found hers once again. "See. . .see you tomorrow night," he finally managed to say.

She cupped his cheek and, with her lips brushing his, whispered, "I'll be watching for you."

Finally finding the strength to leave her, he walked slowly toward his cycle. With a final wave, he crawled on the bike and headed for his dorm.

Long after he'd gone to bed, Nick found himself fighting an inner battle. He'd gone and gotten himself tangled up with a woman who not only didn't share his faith, but laughed at it as well. Yet what was so bad about that? Hadn't he done much worse than laugh before he'd gotten himself right with God? He'd actually scoffed and dared God to strike him dead if He was real. He'd been downright anti-anything that even smacked of any sort of religion. Angela wasn't like that. She was more like a child just coming to grips with a world she didn't understand.

◆ ◆ ◆

Early the next morning, Jacob called to say Nick had been on his mind and he'd like the two of them to have supper together, his treat. He suggested Al's Diner, the place he always liked to eat when they were together. He got there before Nick and was already in conversation with Angela when he arrived. "Hey, I see you two have already met."

His friend greeted him with a hearty handshake. "Hey, Nick. I was just telling this pretty young lady how hungry I am. I've already told her what I want. What'll you have?"

Nick nearly wilted at the sweet smile Angela flashed his way as he slid into the booth and grinned back. "Make mine the meatloaf special. Pepper gravy."

The two men settled into a pleasant conversation as Angela scurried off to the kitchen with their order.

"So, what's going on in your life? You seem happier than usual. The last time we talked, you were worn to a frazzle and worried about your grades." Jacob picked up his coffee cup and steadily gazed over its rim as he took a few sips. "You haven't finally found yourself a girlfriend, have you?"

Nick felt as if he were blushing. "Ah, sorta, but not really."

Jacob gave him a mocking grin. "Now, that's a statement if I ever heard one. Care to explain?"

"Well, I have met a girl I really like, but—"

His friend leaned quickly toward him across the table. "She does share your faith, doesn't she?"

"Not exactly. Not yet, anyway." Why did he feel like a naughty child sitting across the desk from the school principal?

Jacob leaned against the booth's upholstered back with a long, deep sigh. "Oh, Nick. You know what problems that can lead to. It's tough enough for two people to get along for a lifetime when they agree, but when they don't share each other's faith, their lives can be miserable."

"You'll like her," Nick said, finding no way to dispute Jacob's reasoning. "She's beautiful. She's nice. She's—" He stopped midsentence when he looked up. Angela stood by him with a full pot of coffee in her hand. Figuring it was as good a time as any, he reached out and took her free hand in his and announced, "Jacob, this is Angela. The girl I've been telling you about."

Jacob nearly choked on his coffee. "Ah—nice to meet you officially, Angela."

Angela stuck out her hand and gave him a friendly smile. "It's nice to meet you, too, Jacob. Nick talks about you all the time." After a few more pleasantries, she returned to the kitchen to pick up the orders Al had called out were ready.

"She's really terrific," Nick said, feeling the need to defend her against the thoughts he was sure were running through Jacob's mind. "You'll like her once you get to know her."

Jacob studied Nick for a long time before he spoke. "Nick, you're important to me. You're like the son I never had. But you're a grown man now, nearly ready to graduate college. You have to make your own decisions. Just promise me you'll keep your eyes on God and listen to His Word, okay?"

Nick nodded, relieved Jacob wasn't going to lecture him. The restaurant soon filled to capacity, keeping Angela busy the entire time they were there. Other than a hasty good-bye, she and Jacob never had another chance to talk.

Later, as Nick walked Angela home, she asked him to tell her about Jacob and explain how Nick and he had become so close, considering he was Nick's parole officer.

"Sure you want to hear this? It's a pretty ugly tale. Looking back on it, I can hardly believe I was once so hardened." He let out a nervous snicker. "And stupid!"

Angela nodded as she slipped her arm into his.

"Well," he began, "you already know I was raised on the streets of New York. I was the leader of a gang called the Invincibles." He reached into the neckline of his shirt and pulled out a large cross suspended from a gold chain. "This was our symbol, only at that time I had no idea of the empty cross's real significance." He studied the cross for long moments before continuing, asking for God to give him the right words.

"By the time I was fifteen, I'd been a regular visitor in the juvenile court system." He ducked his head shyly. "By sixteen, I was caught burglarizing a couple of houses, and that put me into the reformatory until I turned seventeen. I was so mad at being locked away, I vowed I'd get even with the man who saw me leaving with a VCR in my arms and turned me in. One of my gang members recognized him as the pastor of the Bronx Community Church, one of the local churches. I got my guys together late one night—"

He paused and rubbed at his eyes, the memory still fresh and agonizing. "We broke into the church office and took the money that'd been collected that morning, but that wasn't enough to satisfy my need for revenge. Though the church was old and pretty rundown, behind the altar it had a beautiful, huge, stained-glass window of Christ standing at the door, knocking."

Angela gasped as her hands covered her mouth. "You didn't—"

"Yes, and I did a lot of other damage to the church, too. I don't even want to tell you how much," he admitted, hating himself all over again. "We picked up one of the smaller pews from the platform and hurled it through that window. If that wasn't enough, my gang and I, mostly me, pelted the hymnals at what was left of the window, breaking out almost all of it. I'm sure nothing could be salvaged and reused. Some of the guys thought we ought to set the church on fire, but I figured we'd done enough damage to teach that pastor a lesson."

Angela lifted watery eyes. "And you got caught, didn't you? Oh, Nick, I can't believe you would do such a thing."

He rubbed at his eyes with the back of his hand. "Neither can I. Anyway, when I turned eighteen and I got out of reformatory, I was filled with even more rage. How dare anyone lock me up? Me! Nick Bartelli! The old gang was still around, though most of them had been in and out of reformatory several times, too. I called them all together, and we decided to hit a convenience store that night. I had it all planned out real good. But God had other plans."

Her eyes rounded. "What happened?"

"One of the customers just happened to be none other than Jacob Austin. We thought the store was empty since he was in the rest room at the time. He heard what was going on, called the police on his cell phone, pulled out his gun, and walked right out and held us at gunpoint until backup arrived. From the look in his eye, I knew he wouldn't hesitate to shoot if we didn't do what he said. I found out later he'd been a Green Beret. He probably could've taken us with his bare hands. I ended up in jail that time, with the prospect of going to prison."

Angela didn't speak, just shook her head and stared at him. Her expression broke his heart. She had every right to hate him for what he'd done. "So how did you and Jacob—"

"Only by the grace of God, Angela. For some reason, the man saw some good in me. He came to visit me a couple of times before my hearing came up and actually treated me like I was human. Something my own parents seldom did. When it came time for my sentencing, he asked the judge if he could speak. That's when I learned he was a parole officer. He begged the judge to let me off and offered to be my parole officer under certain conditions. I thought his requests were going to be pretty awful to live with, but I sure didn't want to go to prison."

"What did he want?"

Nick gently took Angela's hand in his. "He wanted me to live with him full-time so he could keep a constant eye on me. He even offered to help me find a job, saying he would provide for my needs himself until I got one. There were a couple other things he wanted, but they were minor. I couldn't believe it when the judge granted his request."

"Did you two get along okay?"

Nick smiled as he remembered their first few weeks together and how rough they'd been. "Not at first. Remember, that guy had been a Green Beret. He ran his home like we were in the military. Up at five in the morning, bed made just right, shoes polished, clothes hung in the closet in order, the whole nine yards. We even did calisthenics every morning before breakfast."

Angela frowned. "You didn't rebel?"

Nick gave a snort. "I learned real fast you don't rebel against Jacob Austin. He pinned me to the wall and set me straight real quick. Either I did what he said, or I was off to prison. Didn't give me much of a choice. That man stuck to me like Crazy Glue. He monitored my phone calls, wouldn't let me see any of my old gang, even took me to and from work when I got a job. I never knew when he was going to show up to check on me. But. . ." He gave Angela a smile. "Somehow I knew right from the start, I was important to him. He didn't have to do all that for me, and at his own expense. One word from him, and that judge would've shipped me off to prison. The thing I hated most that he made me do was listen to him as he read from his Bible and a daily devotional book each morning. He explained he didn't expect me to pray because God didn't want to hear from me until I confessed my sins to Him and asked His forgiveness."

He gave her a sideways smile. "I figured, if there *was* a God, He was just sitting up there in the heavens waiting for a word from old Nick!"

Angela let out a gasp. "Nick! What a thing to say!"

"Jacob corrected me on that one, real fast. He said God wasn't the least bit interested in what I had to say, at least not until I said the right thing. I wouldn't admit it at first, but his words kinda shook me up. You know, it wasn't long before I had more respect for that man than any man I'd met or ever heard of. One time, when he came out of the shower wearing only a towel, I saw this big tattoo on his chest. The tattoo didn't surprise me—a lot of military men have tattoos—it was what it was that intrigued me: an empty cross, very much like this one." He pulled the cross from beneath his shirt and held it out for her to see again.

"He stood right there, wrapped in that towel, and told me how that cross was empty because God had sent His only Son to take on my sins. Then He was crucified and left until they were sure He was dead. They buried Him in an empty tomb, but He didn't stay there. After appearing to some of His friends, He ascended into heaven, where He's sitting, even now, at God's right hand, interceding for me. Although I'd heard Jacob say nearly those same words dozens of times, it didn't make any sense to me until I saw that empty cross tattoo. I fell on my knees that day and asked God to forgive my sins and take charge of my life."

He slipped his arm about Angela and pulled her close. "I haven't been the same since. I don't have any desire to go back to being the old Nick. The one who got into one scrape after another. All because one man looked beneath the surface and saw some good in a troubled teen."

Angela snuggled in close to his side and leaned her head on his shoulder. "Oh, Nick, that's a wonderful story. No wonder you and Jacob are so close. But how did you both end up in Dallas?"

"I'd always been fascinated by the way things worked, and after checking out all sorts of colleges, Jacob suggested I attend Dallas Tech. He had no real strong ties to the Bronx, and he thought it would be best for me if we put some miles between me and the old gang. So we checked into it, and Jacob got a parole officer job down here, put up the money for my first semester, and we moved to Dallas. He thought it would be easier for me to study by living on campus, and even though I objected to the extra money it was going to cost him, he stood his ground, and I ended up living in the dorm while he lived in the cheapest apartment he could find."

Angela stared off in space, thinking about Jacob's tremendous sacrifice. "Amazing. What a man."

"Thanks to Jacob, I'd been able to get my GED and then get into college. He still helps me with my tuition and some of my dorm costs. I hate for him to have to do it, but I'd never be able to stay in school without him. Thanks to him and his unselfishness, I'll graduate this spring, maybe not with honors, but I'll be right up there in that top ten percent."

Angela lifted her face to his. "And you can get a good job with a great income. Just think, Nick, you'll be able to have a nice apartment, a new car, and—"

Nick turned quickly to face her. "No, Angela. I'm not working this hard at school to fill my life with fancy things."

She gave him a puzzled look. "Why then?"

"God has called me to the mission field."

Angela pulled away and stared at him. "Surely you're kidding!"

"Kidding? No! I've pledged my life to God, to serve Him wherever He wants me."

Angela couldn't believe her ears. "Nick, I know this religious thing is important to you, but isn't this carrying it a little too far? Whose idea was this? Yours or Jacob's?"

"Mine, Angela! Jacob had nothing to do with my decision. This was strictly between me and God. Not only that, but I vowed someday I'd replace that stained-glass window and make things right with that church."

She placed her hand on her hip. "Nick! Do you have any idea what that window would cost? Probably thousands of dollars! How are you going to do that with what they'll pay you to be a missionary?"

With a slight chuckle, Nick put a consoling hand on her arm. "They don't pay you for being a missionary. You have to raise your own support!"

Angela's jaw dropped. "You're joking!"

"Nope, dead serious."

"Well, then," Angela said, cupping his hand with hers and giving it a squeeze, "I guess that means you'll be around Dallas long after you graduate, having to raise all that money by yourself."

He grinned that boyish grin that brought out his sweet side. "We'll see. At least I'll have you to keep me company. Maybe I can get Al to put up a jar in the diner. *Help a poor boy get to the mission field.* How much you think that would raise?"

Angela leaned into him again. "With me there to tell them

how wonderful you are, you might be surprised how much money you'd find in that jar. I'm sure Al would help, too."

They bantered back and forth, joking about placing jars all over town, in all the restaurants and coffee shops. Finally, after they'd had their fun, Nick became serious. "I'm not worried about raising the funds, Angela. If God wants me to go to the mission field, He'll supply my needs. Meantime, I'll wait on Him to show me His will for my life." He kissed her good night, waited until she climbed the stairs, then waved a good-bye.

Angela watched from the railing outside her door until he disappeared into the shadows. *I'm going to marry you, Nick Bartelli, but I refuse to go to the mission field with you.*

The next few weeks were the happiest Angela and Nick had ever spent as Angela moved to the day shift at the diner so she could spend evenings with Nick. She finally talked him into bringing his books to her apartment, where he'd have peace and quiet and not have to put up with Buzz and his rowdy friends. She loved watching him while he labored over his books. She made sure she had plenty of good hot coffee on hand; sometimes she cooked a meal for him; and she moved about the apartment quietly, not wanting to disturb him. But when he closed his books for the night, he always took her in his arms and kissed her, and it made all her efforts worthwhile.

◆ ◆ ◆

After spending many evenings with Angela, Nick finally confessed to himself that he had fallen deeply in love with her, even though as yet she had not accepted his God into her life. Somehow, Angela, who considered herself a good person, could not believe God would be cruel enough to turn good people like her away on the Judgment Day. In fact, she still wasn't convinced there even was a God. Though Nick had tried to talk to her about it dozens of times, she still didn't want to have any part of his faith, and that knowledge ripped at his heart. He knew he should break things off with her, but he loved her and couldn't do it. His love for her had grown too strong and too deep.

The night before graduation, Nick and Jacob headed for the church to hear a team from Builders for Christ, a group of men who traveled the world helping with various building projects needed by missionaries. They'd advertised that they were going to speak about their work and show slides. Nick had wanted Angela to come with them, but one of Al's evening shift waitresses had been in a one-car accident and been hospitalized, so Angela had agreed to work a double shift that day.

"You and Angela still together?" Jacob asked as he turned the car into the church's parking lot.

"I love her, Jacob. I've asked God to take that love out of my heart if Angela and I aren't supposed to be together, but instead, it seems my love grows stronger for her each day."

Jacob put a reassuring hand on his shoulder. "I can see why you love her. Being around Angela these past few months, I've learned to love her, too." He gave Nick's shoulder a squeeze and a quick grin. "Not in the same way. Don't get jealous. She has such a sweet innocence about her, despite the heavy makeup and her short skirts. But Nick, I'm worried about you. You've come so far, and you've felt God's calling on your life. Since Angela seems to want no part of that, are you sure your love for her isn't going to keep you from doing God's will?"

Nick stared at the floor. He'd been so sure he'd be able to win Angela over to the Lord by now, and it hadn't panned out. How could he be sure of anything? "I'm still planning on doing God's will, but I want Angela by my side. Surely He'll work that out if He wants me to go to the mission field like I'd promised." As Jacob shut down the engine, Nick put his hand on Jacob's shoulder. "Pray for me, Jacob. I want to do the right thing. Honest I do."

The two men entered the sanctuary and were ushered to two seats near the front. Nick listened with rapt attention. It seemed all the things the team mentioned they were doing were the very things he'd learned in his engineering classes in college. He became increasingly excited as they showed slides of the work they were accomplishing in the various countries. Was this what God was calling him to do? The desire to join them in their ministry became even greater with each slide.

Finally, the main speaker summed the work up at the conclusion of the service. "We can always use dedicated, trained people on the field, but right now, we are in desperate need for a young man with structural engineering training to help us with a much-needed building project in Quito, Ecuador. This is a rush job. A storm destroyed their hangar and part of their landing strip a few weeks ago, and we need to get that airfield back up and running as quickly as possible. Many missionaries in that area depend upon those planes for their supplies. We hope you'll join us in praying for this need. Maybe one of you out there in the audience has such skills or training or you know of someone who does who might be willing to serve God in this way."

Nick felt a sudden jab in his ribs as Jacob leaned toward him. "That could be you, Nick."

The excitement that flowed through him was surreal. He'd never had such a feeling and was sure he was being touched by God Himself. The minute the service ended, Nick bolted to the front, with Jacob at his heels, to speak with the team leader. When the man saw him coming, he broke away from those with whom he was speaking and met Nick in the aisle.

"I–I think I'm your man," Nick blurted out. "I've got the training you've asked for, and I've dedicated my life to God, to serve wherever He wants me. Even Ecuador."

The man quickly rounded up the other members of his team and led them, along with Nick and Jacob, into a side room where they could talk. After asking Nick a multitude of questions, both about his qualifications and his relationship with God, with Jacob's high recommendation and all of them kneeling together asking God for His Will, they agreed Nick was the perfect candidate for the engineering job.

"We're only asking for a one-year commitment. If you want to stay longer than that, we'd definitely want you, but as a first-time missionary, we only ask a year of you."

"Only a year?"

"Yes. How soon can you go?" the leader asked.

"I–I can go most any time. I graduate tomorrow," Nick answered, adrenalin pumping through his body. "I have no idea how long it'll take to raise my support. I've never done anything like that before."

Jacob stepped in with a proud smile. "I can help with some of it. How much do you think it'll take?"

The leader placed his big hands on Nick's shoulder. "Don't worry about support. Getting that hangar and airfield back in operation is so important that the mission board has decided they will provide food and housing to whoever will take the job. All you'll need is money enough for your personal needs."

He gestured toward Jacob. "We'll work on getting you a visa, Nick. And of course, you'll have to have a passport, but according to Jacob, you got one last year when there was a possibility you might be able to take a short-term mission trip. The sooner we can get you there and you can get to work, the better. If we can get things worked out, can you be ready to fly out by a week from today?"

Without hesitation, Nick stuck out his hand to the man. "Yes, Sir. I'll be ready."

They spent the next three hours going over their plans and facts about the mission, the country, and the work Nick would be doing. By the time he and Jacob climbed back in the car, Nick was so filled with anticipation, he hardly heard what Jacob was saying until the man asked one question: "What are you going to do about Angela?"

Chapter 4

Nick rehearsed his speech a hundred times in his head. He had to make her understand that although he loved her, his first calling came from his God.

"You *what?*" Angela screamed at him when he told her what had happened and how he'd agreed to go to Ecuador. "Are you out of your mind? That's half a world away. What about us, Nick? Did you even think about me when you made up your mind?"

He tried to pull her to him, but she backed away. "Of course I thought about you, but you knew I'd committed my life to serve God. They said my first commitment was only for a year, Angela. Twelve months. That's not so long."

She began to cry. The sound tore at his heart and blanketed out some of his happiness.

"I—I thought you lo—loved me. How can you le—leave me like this? A ye—year is an eternity!"

Despite her attempts to pull away from him, he gathered her in his arms and planted soft kisses on her wet cheeks. "I do love you, Angela, but I love God, too, and I feel He wants me to do this. Don't you understand? This is what I've been training for—for four years. I could never be happy knowing I'd turned my back on Him when He gave me a job to do."

"But you co–could turn your ba–back on me?"

"I'm not turning my back on you. I love you."

She jerked away and rushed up the stairs. "Go to Ecuador for your God, but don't expect me to be here waiting at the end of the year, Nick Bartelli. There are plenty of men out there besides you. Maybe I can find one who won't say they love me and then desert me like you are." When she reached the landing, she leaned over the railing, pointing an accusing finger at him. "Just forget you ever met Angela Enrico, 'cause Angela Enrico is gonna forget all about you!"

Nick shuddered when he heard her door slam. Giving Angela up was the hardest thing he'd ever have to do, but if God wanted him to go, Nick was sure He'd put a peace in his heart about it.

When Angela didn't show up at his graduation, he went in search of her, but she wasn't at home or wouldn't answer the door.

He tried all week to reach Angela, to explain again why he was leaving, but she wouldn't take his phone calls, and when he showed up at the restaurant, she made sure one of the other girls waited on him. He even tried to see her at shift change, but she'd taken up with some new guy and always exited the restaurant with him. In desperation, after bidding a final farewell to Buzz, Nick wrote her a good-bye letter, asking Al to give it to her when he was gone.

◆　◆　◆

Nick stared out the window as the plane touched down in Ecuador. It'd been a long flight, and although he was filled with anticipation and gratitude to God for giving him this chance to serve Him and put four years of training into good use, a part of Nick was still back in Dallas with Angela.

Two of the Builders for Christ staff members were waiting for him when his plane landed. They whisked him off to the little apartment he would be calling home for at least the next year of his life. He tried to phone Angela, to let her know he'd arrived safely, but as usual, her answering machine picked up. He left a message, trying once again to explain how God had called him to Ecuador and leaving the phone number and mailing address where he could be reached, though, as upset as she'd been that'd he'd left her so quickly, he doubted she'd contact him.

The next few weeks were busy, filled with twelve- to fourteen-hour days, as he settled into the job God had sent him to do. It seemed everything he'd learned at Dallas Tech was exactly what he needed to know to get the Ecuador project up and running. He liked his coworkers and had made many new friends among the nationals.

He wrote at least three letters to Angela each week, giving her a rundown of his work and telling her how much he missed her. He always signed them, "With love, Nick." He longed to hold her in his arms and kiss her sweet face, but deep within his heart he had to wonder if this was God's way of putting some distance between him and the woman he loved, who still did not share his faith.

◆ ◆ ◆

Tears ran down Angela's cheeks as she listened to Nick's latest phone message. She'd hoped, once he was out of her life, she'd forget about him. But she hadn't. Each letter and phone message declared his love for her, and she had to admit she still loved him. Though he always started out his letters telling her how much he loved her, his love for what he was doing in Ecuador came through loud and clear. Nick had no doubt God had led him there to do a job for Him— a job Nick had consented to do willingly.

She stared at the answering machine long after his message had ended, then picked up the phone and dialed the number he put at the bottom of every letter. He'd mentioned the time was the same in Quito as Dallas, so hopefully, he'd be in his little apartment by now. He answered on the first ring. What should she say? By the time he'd said hello twice, she knew she'd better say something quick or he might hang up. "Hi, Nick. It's me."

"Oh, Angela, I can't believe it. You have no idea how much I've wanted to hear your voice. I—"

"I'm sorry, Nick," she blurted out, her tears now flowing freely. "I—I love you. I'm sorry for being so stubborn those last few days before you left. I'm surprised you don't hate me."

"How could I hate you, Angela? I love you. I wish you could be here to see what we're doing. I have no doubt God sent me here. How. . .how are things going for you?"

"Fine, I guess. Still working for Al. I am going to school three nights a week now to learn computer. I figured it was about time I began thinking about my own future. I actually bought a computer."

"A computer? Good! If you get on the Internet, we can e-mail back and forth!"

Angela brightened as she brushed away a tear. "I just signed up for the Internet this morning, but I haven't learned how to do it yet. My teacher is going to show me after class tonight."

"As soon as you get an E-mail address, Angela, e-mail it to me, and I'll send you some pictures of our work here."

She frowned. This was all so new to her. "You can send me pictures on my E-mail?"

He went on to briefly explain the workings of the Internet and E-mail. The rest of their conversation was mainly one-sided as he described Quito and the surrounding area. He told her about the people and the small church he attended with some of the staff. "God is so good, Angela. I'm amazed daily by the miracles we see here." After an interminable pause, he added, "I love you, Angela, but God and His will have to come first in my life."

She swallowed and blinked hard before answering. "I–I don't understand how you can waste your four hard years of college by going to some far-off country to work for nothing more than food and a roof over your head, when you could be making a terrific salary here in the States. It just doesn't make any sense to me."

"That's because you don't know my God, Angela."

Realizing it would do no good to argue with him, she quickly changed the subject, telling him all about her classes. Their conversation ended with Angela promising to send him her E-mail address as soon as she got it. Though they'd had a wonderful conversation, nothing had really changed between them. She still just didn't get it!

◆ ◆ ◆

When the phone rang a second time, Nick snatched it up, thinking perhaps it was Angela again, but it was Jacob, calling from New York City to check on the airfield project's progression. With Nick no longer living in Dallas, Jacob had decided to move back to New York and the city he loved. Nick told him about Angela's call, and as he'd expected, his friend again cautioned him about his association with a woman who didn't share his faith and his beliefs. Nick knew his friend was right.

The next evening as he checked the computer in the field office, Nick found an E-mail addressed to him by someone with the nickname *Nicksgirl*. His heart soared as he clicked on the name. Sure enough, it was from Angela. Those nightly E-mails became one of the highlights of his day. He could come in from the field dead-tired, but one look at the word *Nicksgirl* on the computer screen, and he would be refreshed and excited.

Her E-mails were always newsy, filled with stories of the younger students he'd gone to school with who were regular patrons of the diner, comments about Al and his wife, the things she was learning in her class, and complaints about her inability to type accurately. Each E-mail brought smiles to his face as he visualized Angela struggling over every word, trying to type it perfectly. In turn, he responded by giving her a rundown of his day, including little tidbits about the people he worked with. He always ended his messages with a Bible verse, hoping she'd be encouraged to pick up the Bible he'd left with her and read it for herself.

By the end of his sixth month in Ecuador, Nick was in the full swing of things. The airfield project was ahead of schedule. The superstructure of the huge hangar, which was his main responsibility, was up, and they were starting to put the roof on. Each day on the mission field confirmed God's calling on his life. He loved his work, which was still something Angela had trouble understanding, but she no longer argued with him about it. She'd told him her computer classes were going well. She'd learned how to work with documents, set up spreadsheets, use her paint program, and surf the Net. She and Nick had even been able to set up voice-to-voice communications, using the computer instead of making those expensive, long-distance phone calls.

When one of the workers came running across the field, yelling Nick had an emergency phone call, he hurriedly crawled down from the roof, rushed into the little makeshift office, and grabbed the receiver.

"Nick Bartelli."

"I'm sorry to have to phone you like this, Mr. Bartelli, but a friend of yours has been rushed to the hospital. He asked me to call—"

"Who?" Nick shouted into the phone, his heart nearly leaping from his chest, both from anxiety and from his sudden sprint across the field.

"Jacob Austin. He's had a heart attack. That's about all I can tell you right now. I'm a friend of his. I was with him when it happened and called the ambulance."

Nick frantically clutched the phone. Not Jacob! Not the man who had done so much for him. Jacob had become more important to Nick than his own father. "Where? What hospital?" He scribbled the information on a pad and thanked the man. Next, he dialed the hospital.

"Are you a relative?" the woman asked when the switchboard had finally sent his call to the right place.

"No, but he's like a father to me. Please, I'm calling from Ecuador, I have to know how he is."

The woman paused. "Well, all I can say, since you are not a relative, is that he is getting the best care possible. I can't really give you his condition at this point."

Nick hung up the phone and paced about the little room, combing his fingers through his hair with frustration, begging God to spare Jacob's life. He had to go to him! After arranging with the team leaders for an emergency leave of absence, he called the airlines and made a reservation on the next plane out of Ecuador. Next, checking his watch, he called Angela.

He broke down and wept when she answered the phone,

but finally he was able to blurt out, "Jacob has had a heart attack. I've got to go to him. I'm leaving Quito in two hours and will be arriving in New York City first thing in the morning."

"Oh, Nick, not Jacob!" He could hear her weeping through the receiver. "I–I love him, too. You know that. What can I do?"

Without thinking about it, he shot back, "Meet me in New York. If. . .if anything happens to him, I'm going to need you, Angela. I don't think I could go through that alone."

"Of course, I'll meet you, Nick. Give me the time your plane arrives and the name of the hospital. If I'm not at the airport to meet your plane, I'll take a taxi directly to the hospital. I want to be there for him, too. He's been so kind to me."

He gave her the necessary information, tossed a few things in a small bag, and headed for the airport, feeling somewhat better knowing Angela would be with him to face whatever lay ahead of them.

◆　◆　◆

Nick was frantic when his plane landed over an hour late at LaGuardia. He pushed himself through the deplaning passengers without taking time to explain his rudeness. Thankfully, Angela was waiting just beyond the security doors and hurried toward him, her arms outstretched. He dropped his bag and snatched her up and held her close. How he'd missed her.

"Oh, Nick, I'm so sorry about Jacob," Angela said, looking up at him. "I called the hospital as soon as I landed, but they wouldn't give me any information except that he was still in intensive care."

He picked up his bag and, with one arm still wrapped around Angela, headed for the exit. Thirty minutes later, they entered the Montefiore-Einstein Heart Center on Bainbridge Avenue in the Bronx. Once Nick told the nurse on duty he had come all the way from Ecuador to see Jacob, she allowed him to go in for a few minutes. He hated to leave Angela in the waiting room, but the doctor had left word Jacob was to have no more than one visitor at a time. Nick forced himself to hold back a gasp as he looked at his friend and the machines beeping around him. The man was as white as a brand new T-shirt, his lips were blue, and he lay as still as death.

"Jacob," he whispered softly near the man's ear as he bent low. "It's me. Nick. I'm here." To his surprise, Jacob opened his eyes.

"Nick," he said in a halting whisper. "Ha–have to tell you something."

Nick shook his head. "Not now. You need to rest."

"In closet. In bedroom. Metal box. Note inside."

"Jacob, rest. Please. You need to get well." He gave his friend a smile. "Angela's here. She wanted to be with you, too."

The man took several laborious breaths, then blinked his eyes as if to say he understood. "Ne–need to see her."

"You can see her later. She and I are both going to stick around until you're better."

"Now."

Confused, Nick frowned. "Okay. You're the boss. I'll get her."

"Why would he want to see me?" Angela asked when, with tear-filled eyes, he explained about Jacob's request. "He's barely had time with you."

Nick began to cry openly. "I–I don't know. I saw his doctor on the way back out here, and the news isn't good." He swallowed hard at the lump that had risen in his throat. "He. . .he says Jacob won't make it. This isn't his first heart attack. He's amazed he's lived as long as he has with such a bad heart. He said it'd be okay for both of us to go in, that if we wanted to see him and spend time with him. . ." Nick gulped hard. "He said we'd better do it now. He was surprised Jacob had the strength to speak. He's barely said three words all morning."

◆　◆　◆

Angela had never been in a cardiac care unit before. She glanced nervously from side to side with misty eyes as they walked toward the curtained-off area where Jacob lay. "Hi, Jacob," she said softly, bending to kiss his forehead while trying to hold back the multitude of tears seeking full release.

"Sit," he said so softly she wasn't even sure *sit* was what he'd said. But smiling all the while, she pulled the lone chair up close to the bed and carefully wrapped her fingers over his.

"You know Nick and I both love you, don't you?"

"Got to. . .accept God." He took a couple slow breaths and continued, even though Nick discouraged him from talking. "Died on cross. . .your sins, An–ge–la."

Angela stared at him, not sure what to say.

"Con—fess. Tell. . .God. . .sorry." After pausing, he added, "God loves you. Need to o—open heart. . .before. . ."

Nick gently patted Jacob's shoulder, then pulled the sheet up to cover it, his own pain etched across his weary face. "Don't talk more, Jacob, please. Save your strength to get well."

Angela stood transfixed, her gaze fastened on Jacob's pleading eyes. This man was dying, yet he was using his last breaths to express his concern for her and her relationship with his God. Her heart was so deeply touched, she couldn't speak.

Jacob inhaled another breath, closed his eyes, and slowly turned his head to the side.

Angela shot a quick look at Nick and found him staring at Jacob. "Is he. . . ?"

◆　◆　◆

"Someone, help!" Nick screamed out as panic seized him. "Don't let him die, please!"

The head nurse rushed in, shooing them away from the bed. They stood huddled together just outside the curtained-off area as Nick held Angela in his arms, audibly praying for God to spare Jacob's life, but in his heart he knew it was too late. Minutes later, the nurse confirmed his greatest fear. Jacob Austin had gone home to be with his Lord.

They stayed around the hospital, filling out the necessary paperwork and taking care of arrangements.

"You're fortunate, given you're not a relative," the woman at the desk told Nick. "Your friend took care of all the details and the legalities before his death. Otherwise, we wouldn't be able to give you his belongings."

Just before Nick and Angela left, the woman gave them a big black plastic sack containing the clothing Jacob had been wearing, his wristwatch and rings, a set of keys, and a sealable plastic bag containing other personal items they'd pulled from his pockets. Angela was still crying. Nick wasn't much better off. His eyes were swollen, and the tremendous loss he felt ripped at his heart.

They decided that Angela would stay in Jacob's apartment for the night and Nick would try to find a room nearby. Neither felt like eating, so they went directly to the apartment, where Nick phoned the mortuary to set up a time for Jacob's graveside service. He had no idea how to reach Jacob's friends and hoped they'd either call to check on him or read the obituary in the newspaper.

About seven, he followed Angela into the little kitchen. She opened the cabinets and found a can of chicken noodle soup, which she heated in the microwave. Though neither of them was hungry enough to eat it, they went through the motions while sitting at the kitchen table reminiscing about the wonderful times they'd had with Jacob.

Well after ten, Angela reached across the table and wrapped her hands around Nick's. "Come back home, Nick. You don't have to stay in Ecuador. If you feel you have to work for God, you can do it in Dallas. You could get a good-paying job as a structural engineer at some big company, go to church on Sundays, maybe teach a Sunday school class or something, and we could be together. I love you, Nick. Every minute without you since you've been in Ecuador has been agony for me. I need to be with you, Sweetheart. We belong together. Can't you see that?"

Nick lowered his head momentarily to avoid her pleading eyes. Just the sight of her beautiful face made him wish he could do what she asked, but he couldn't. God had called him to serve full-time—he was sure of that—and He'd called him to Ecuador. Yet how could he explain Angela's appearance in his life just months before he graduated and the overwhelming love he had for her?

"I–I can't, Angela. Can't you see that? Haven't you known me well enough to realize I have to do God's will? I'm His. I've committed my life to Him, to serve Him wherever He leads me." He lifted her hands to his face and kissed her fingertips. "I have no other choice." The tears that trickled down her cheeks broke his heart.

Angela stared into his face, meeting and holding his gaze, then started to speak, gave her head a hopeless shake, and pulled away from him. "I–I knew that's what you'd say."

Tearfully they kissed each other good night as Nick held her close. It felt so good to have her in his arms again, despite the sorrow he felt in his heart at the unexpected loss of his friend. Leaving her a second time was going to be even harder than the first time. Just before he fell asleep in the room he'd found two blocks from Jacob's apartment, Nick prayed, *Father God, You know how much I love Angela, but I can't let that love keep me from doing Your will. Speak to her heart, Lord, please. I know Jacob's words touched her today. I could see it in her eyes. I need her in my life.*

❖   ❖   ❖

Angela was already up, dressed, and preparing breakfast when Nick got back to Jacob's apartment early the next morning. The smell of bacon frying in Jacob's big iron skillet immediately awakened his taste buds. Other than the half bowl of soup, neither of them had eaten anything in the past twenty-four hours.

"I'm so sorry about Jacob," Angela told him as they did the dishes together. "I know how much you loved him. I loved him, too."

Nick held his breath as he watched Angela's eyes fill with tears, afraid he, too, would break down again. He leaned over and kissed her cheek. "I know you did, Honey."

They finished the dishes in silence, both of them jumping when the phone rang. It was the mortuary asking Nick to bring over the clothes he wanted Jacob to be buried in.

"Do you want me to get them?" Angela asked as he hung up the receiver.

Nick shook his head with a heavy sigh. "No, I'll do it, but I'd appreciate it if you'd pick out his tie." He took her hand in his and led her into Jacob's bedroom. "He always liked his dark brown sport coat with the leather patches on the elbows. Think that'd be okay?"

Angela nodded as she moved to the little rotating tie rack mounted on the closet door. "He looked good in that jacket."

Nick pulled the jacket from the closet, then searched out a pair of dark brown trousers while Angela continued to peruse the ties. "The man on the phone asked me if Jacob had ever mentioned what kind of service he'd want for his funeral. I thought that was a strange question, but he said many people have their funeral all planned out, especially if they have a severe health problem, so they can save their loved ones the pain of having to do it." He stood staring at the closet.

Angela turned to him with a frown. "What are you looking at? Don't you like the brown jacket?"

Nick continued to stare. "No, I think that one will be fine. I was just thinking of something Jacob told me at the hospital. Something about a metal box in his closet. He was sure he was dying, and it seemed important to him that I find it and open it. I wonder if maybe he put his funeral plans in there."

Angela gave him a teary smile. "Knowing how organized Jacob was, it wouldn't surprise me one bit."

Nick quickly placed the brown trousers on the bed and made his way back to the closet, stooping to search through the shoes, boots, and other things Jacob had stored neatly on the floor. Finally, way at the back, under a pile of old blankets, Nick found the box Jacob had used some of his dying breaths to tell him about. He tugged it out and placed it on the bed.

Angela sat down beside it, her eyes rounded with curiosity. "What kind of a box is that?"

"I'd say, considering its camouflage coloring, it's from his

Green Beret days." He stared at the heavy padlock on the box. "I wonder if the key to this might be one of those keys on his key ring."

Angela hurried into the living room and retrieved the keys, handing them to him.

He knelt beside the bed and inserted them one by one. Finally, the lock opened. Just inside the lid was the note Jacob had told him about. He carefully unfolded it and read it silently, not sure if Jacob's words were intended to be heard by anyone but him. Halfway through, he stopped reading and looked up at Angela, his jaw dropping. "He. . .he says I'm the son he never had." He went on, barely able to believe what he was reading. "He's leaving everything he owned to me, Angela."

She cupped his cheek with her hand. "I'm not surprised. He loved you, Nick."

Nick swallowed hard as he continued to read. "He says although he didn't own much in the way of worldly goods, he does have some money in the bank and a few certificates of deposit, and he has—"

Nick paused and stared at the note. "And he has a fifty-thousand-dollar life insurance policy, with me as his beneficiary! I can't believe he did this. He's already done so much for me. If it weren't for him and the way he took me in—"

Angela wrapped her arms about his shoulders. "He was a good man. I'm so glad I got to know him."

Nick wiped at his eyes with his sleeve and read on, a sudden frown denting his forehead.

"What's wrong, Nick?"

"I—I don't understand this last part. He says that what's in the box will help me make things right with that church I vandalized. What could be in the box that would do that? This insurance policy wouldn't begin to repay the costs of what we stole from the office, the horrible things we did to the church's interior, and that stained-glass window."

He laid the note to one side and looked into the box. Whatever was inside was wrapped in a couple of Jacob's old khaki T-shirts, ones he'd no doubt worn as a Green Beret. He lifted the object out and carefully pulled the shirts away. He'd never seen anything like it: a book of some sort and very old. The writing on the brown leather cover was in a foreign language.

Angela leaned closer for a better look. "What is it?"

Nick shrugged. "I don't know."

Her brows lifted in question, nearly disappearing beneath the dark ringlets covering her forehead. "His letter didn't say what it was?"

Quickly, he picked up the note and read aloud the last few lines.

"I love you, Nick. Someday, we'll meet in heaven. Being around you and watching the change in you, knowing I had a small part in it, made my last years worthwhile. Continue to serve the Lord, Nick, and never give up on Angela."

"That's it."

He turned back to the oversized book, carefully lifting its fragile cover, and tucked inside found another note. This one much smaller. His heart filled with both gratefulness and anticipation as he picked it up and read the words aloud. They, too, were in Jacob's handwriting.

"Nick, be careful with this. It's worth millions of dollars. It's a volume from one of the original Gutenberg Bibles and contains the Old Testament from the Book of Proverbs on through the New Testament. My father said it had been handed down through the generations of my family since 1715. No one knows I've had it, or it might have been stolen from me years ago. Sell it, Nick. Use the money it brings to repair or rebuild that aging, dilapidated church and replace that stained-glass window. Make things right, Son, and clear your conscience. It's time you go forth with your life without carrying that burden of guilt.

Live for God,
Nick"

Nick trembled as he stared at the Bible, its edges showing signs of being lovingly handled. He could almost hear Jacob's voice saying, *Make things right, Son, and clear your conscience.* Oh, how he'd longed to do that very thing, but he'd never been able to begin to imagine how he'd do it. Carefully, he folded the note and—

"Oh, Nick! Help me!"

He turned quickly to find Angela on her knees at his side, weeping hysterically.

"What's wrong?"

"I can't fight it any longer. I *am* a sinner, just like you and Jacob said. Just like the Bible says. I need God, Nick, oh, how I need Him! Help me find Him. Show me the way. I don't know what to say to Him!"

Her pleading eyes and the look of panic on her face almost frightened him, yet he was overjoyed by her words of surrender. He'd never seen her like that. It was as if she were hanging onto life by a thread that she feared was about to unravel and break. "Oh, Angela, you know I'll help you. I've waited for nearly a year to hear those words."

His heart filled with joy, Nick shared God's words with her, much like Jacob, his mentor and friend, had shared them with him when he was teenager.

When they finally rose to their feet, they placed their hands on God's Word and pledged to live for Him and always give Him first place in their lives.

After blotting away Angela's tears of repentance with his handkerchief and wrapping her in his arms, Nick kissed her, a new sense of peace filling his very soul. Angela, his Angela, had finally accepted his Lord. The wall that separated them had at last been torn down.

Touching a finger to her chin and tilting her face to his, he asked, "Angela, my dear one, my sweet one. The one I've loved since the first day I met you. Will you marry me?"

Epilogue

The Bronx, three years later

Colorful shafts of light in varying shades of reds, blues, yellows, and greens fell across the highly polished pews in the newly restored Bronx Community Church as Mr. and Mrs. Nick Bartelli sat on the front row, holding hands.

"This church is wonderful, Nick," his wife of nearly three years told him. "I loved our wedding, but I wish we could've been married right here, in front of this stained-glass window of Christ knocking at the door."

With a playful nudge, he gave her a sideways grin. "I could never have waited that long to make you my bride."

"I–I couldn't have waited, either," she answered quickly as she gave him a coy smile. "I loved you too much to wait."

He could see the same adoring love in her eyes that he felt in his heart for her. Unable to resist, he leaned toward her and kissed her cheek.

"It's the most beautiful window I've ever seen," she told him as her gaze shifted away from him and back toward the front of the sanctuary. "I love reading that story in Revelations chapter three, verse twenty about Christ at the door. I'm so glad you took pictures of the window so we can remember every little detail. The artist who made that window has depicted the scene just like I'd visualized it."

As Nick watched Angela's eyes fill with tears, he knew they were tears of joy, and he rejoiced right along with her. No one but Angela could know the satisfaction and relief he felt seeing that glorious window restored.

She brushed a tear from her cheek and continued. "God knocked at the door of my heart so many times, but I kept Him shut out of my life. Once I opened the door, He came in and took up residence, and I haven't been the same since. I'll never be the same again."

He gazed fondly at Angela, his beautiful wife. "And now because of that decision, we're serving God together as missionaries in Ecuador. What a blessing."

"I'm not only serving because I'm your wife, my darling, and I love you, but because I felt God's call upon my heart, too." Her hand cupped his cheek. "There's no place I'd rather be than at your side, my love, wherever God calls us."

Nick gave her a squeeze and smiled at her, then leaned back and spread his long arms across the back of the pew as he gazed at the front of the sanctuary, taking in the wonderful old oak lectern, one of the few original pieces that had been spared by him and the members of his gang. He fought back tears of regret as his thoughts went back to that dreadful night: thoughts of a very foolish young man filled with rage and anger at the life of poverty and abuse to which he'd been born. He shook his head sadly. "How could I have done such a thing, Angela? I deserved to be put in prison for what I did and would have been if it hadn't been for Jacob."

"I'm still amazed at the way God worked things out," Angela confessed as her gaze flitted with admiration from the window to the choir loft, to the organ, then to the beautifully carpeted platform. "To think Jacob kept that valuable Bible hidden away all these years and never sold it is truly a miracle, though I'm sure he could've used the money."

Nick nodded with a smile of agreement. "He must've known that one day God would have a great use for it. It's hard to believe that old Gutenberg Bible would bring more than enough money to do all of this."

"Only you, Nick Bartelli, would take the lesser offer."

"Well, I much preferred selling it to the Ravenhurst Museum rather than to the others who wanted it, even though their offers were much higher. If one of the other parties had gotten it, no telling where that precious Bible would've ended up. Probably in some rich man's private collection, hidden away from the world. This way, it will be on display for anyone who wants to see it."

Nick blinked hard, still feeling deeply the loss of his friend and mentor. "I'm glad that old Ravenhurst Castle has been turned into a museum. It's the perfect home for the Gutenberg Bible. That had to have been God's doing, too."

Angela leaned closer to him. "Who would've ever thought that Gutenberg Bible would find its way back home to Germany after all these years? Everything about this is a miracle."

He bent and kissed Angela, the only woman he'd ever loved, the woman God had given him to be his wife and helpmeet in his ministry with Builders for Christ. "Though it's been a long way, Angela, and it's taken many, many years, the Gutenberg Bible is finally back home, and this church and its stained-glass window have been restored. All because of Jacob and his unselfishness and his love for God."

"And his love for you, Nick," she said tenderly as she gazed at him through misty eyes. "He knew the terrible burden you were carrying."

"I know he did," he murmured, his heart so filled with gratitude to both God and Jacob he could barely speak the words.

Angela smiled up at him. "And now you're free."

"Free? Yes, the burden of restitution has been lifted now that the church and the window have been restored, but to my dying day, I'll bear the memory of what I did all those years ago. God promised us forgiveness of our sins, but He never said He'd make us forget."

"But look at what God was able to do through all of this, Nick."

He nodded with a slight smile. "I know you're right, but it makes me—"

She put a finger to his lips to silence him. "Don't say it, Sweetheart. Don't you see? You, Jacob, me—we were all a part of God's plan."

"I know. But why would He use me? A troubled kid

about ready to go to prison?"

"I–I guess we'll never know the answer to that, or why He'd use an ex-Green Beret parole officer to lead you to Him, or why He'd send you to Dallas. Or why I'd go to work at Al's Diner. But because of you and your witness to me, and because of Jacob's concern for me on his deathbed, I committed my life to God, too."

"Our Lord has been good to us, hasn't He, Angela?"

She leaned against him. "Yes, He has."

"Now, if only Buzz would turn to God."

"Were you able to reach him?"

Nick smiled victoriously. "Yes, we made arrangements to meet in Dallas next week while we're there for the mission conference. I had to see him before we head back to Ecuador."

"Oh, I'm so glad you were able to set up a time. You know I'll be praying for you. You've had a burden for Buzz ever since you two roomed together at college."

"Thanks, Sweetheart. I have a good feeling about our meeting. I know God is going to work in his life." Attempting to hold back the emotions of love and thankfulness that were about to overwhelm him, Nick took Angela's hand and rose slowly. Together, they walked up the steps of the choir loft to the magnificently crafted stained-glass window and stood before it, their arms wrapped about each other, their hearts filled with thoughts and memories of Jacob.

As Angela listened, Nick read aloud the words engraved on the brass plaque mounted just below the window's base: "In loving memory of Jacob Austin, who heard his Lord knocking and opened the door."

JOYCE LIVINGSTON

Joyce is a real Kansas "lady" who lives in a little cabin that her husband built overlooking a lake. She is a proud grandmother who retired from television broadcasting and now keeps very busy writing stories of love and laughter. She is also a part-time tour escort, which takes her to all kinds of fantastic places. She has had books and articles published on a number of subjects. In 2000, she was voted **Heartsong Presents'** favorite new author. Two of her **Heartsong Presents** books were named favorite contemporary book of the year, in 2000 and 2002. In the 2003 **Heartsong Presents** Readers Poll, she was named author of the year and her first historical novel was voted #2 historical of the year. Her books are consistently in the top ten. She feels her writing is a ministry and a calling from God and hopes readers will be touched and uplifted by what she writes. Joyce loves to hear from her readers and invites you to email her at: joyce@joycelivingston.com, or you may visit her on the Internet at: www.joycelivingston.com

A Letter to Our Readers

Dear Readers:

In order that we might better contribute to your reading enjoyment, we would appreciate your taking a few minutes to respond to the following questions. When completed, please return to the following: Fiction Editor, Barbour Publishing, Inc., P.O. Box 719, Uhrichsville, OH 44683.

1. Did you enjoy reading *Bound with Love?*
   □ Very much—I would like to see more books like this.
   □ Moderately—I would have enjoyed it more if _____
   _____
   _____

2. What influenced your decision to purchase this book?
   (Check those that apply.)
   □ Cover   □ Back cover copy   □ Title   □ Price
   □ Friends   □ Publicity   □ Other

3. Which story was your favorite?
   □ *Right from the Start*   □ *Of Immeasurable Worth*
   □ *A Treasure Worth Keeping*   □ *The Long Road Home*

4. Please check your age range:
   □ Under 18   □ 18–24   □ 25–34
   □ 35–45   □ 46–55   □ Over 55

5. How many hours per week do you read? _____

Name _____

Occupation _____

Address _____

City _____ State _____ Zip _____

E-mail _____